About the Author

Now retired and living in Spain, Frank Aulton is an ex-coal miner and a qualified dog trainer. He is the founder of Aldridge Dog Training Club, which is still going strong after 42 years. He was told when he was at mining college that one day he would write a book. (He is a late starter!)

Frank Aulton

Man of the Mountains

Austin Macauley
PUBLISHERS LTD.

Copyright © Frank Aulton (2016)

The right of Frank Aulton to be identified as author of this work has been asserted by him in accordance with section 77 and 78 of the Copyright, Designs and Patents Act 1988.

All rights reserved. No part of this publication may be reproduced, stored in a retrieval system, or transmitted in any form or by any means, electronic, mechanical, photocopying, recording, or otherwise, without the prior permission of the publishers.

Any person who commits any unauthorized act in relation to this publication may be liable to criminal prosecution and civil claims for damages.

A CIP catalogue record for this title is available from the British Library.

ISBN 9781785549793 (Paperback)
ISBN 9781785549809 (Hardback)
ISBN 9781785549816 (E-Book)

www.austinmacauley.com

First Published (2016)
Austin Macauley Publishers Ltd.
25 Canada Square
Canary Wharf
London
E14 5LQ

Romulus and Remus

Part 1

Introduction

Paris 1945

Franz strode briskly across the square. There had been a light shower during the night which the early morning spring sunshine was doing its best to dry up. There was also a cold breeze sweeping across the open space. Pulling his collar up his eyes searched for the small bookshop on the opposite side that stood on the side of the square, and waited for the early morning traffic to clear before he could cross the street. Looking back he could see the University de Paris looming in the distance. He was staying there for two nights as a guest speaker to promote his book. Professor Zachary had invited him to and after some gentle persuasion Franz had agreed.

He looked across the street and once the traffic cleared he crossed over. It was true what the professor had told him, the shelves in the window were piled high with his book. A large poster had also been displayed in the windows "Man of The Mountains by Franz Aulton". He gave a shiver as the sun disappeared behind a cloud and his attention was drawn to the rich aroma of coffee from the café, but something else had attracted his attention. The solitary figure of a woman sitting at a table outside the café staring into a cup she held in her hands. He looked away not wanting to be seen staring at her. He caught her reflection in the shop window but it was obscure. A sense of familiarity swept over him as his brain tried to deal with the flashes from the past charging through his mind. "No it couldn't be" he found himself saying. He reached for the book in his pocket and opened it pretending to read but once more he took a sideward glance at the woman sitting twenty yards away still gazing into the cup.

The sunshine glistened on her hair as Franz turned and started walking towards the café still holding the open book and still pretending to read. He drew closer to her still casting furtive glances in her direction. He couldn't forget the first time they had met, her blonde hair had covered her face but when she looked up it revealed a beautiful face but deeply etched by sadness and this was the same face he was looking at now.

Franz decided that a direct approach would be the best way to find out but he was struggling to put a name to the face. He stopped outside the café still pretending to read his book suddenly he started flipping over the pages frantically searching for a name. Of course her husband was Professor Anderson and hers was Margaret and her daughter was Joanna. He closed the book and strode over to where she was sitting still gazing into the cup.

"Excuse me," he said politely, "is your name Margaret Anderson?" She was startled by the sound of his voice, obviously she had been deep in thought and oblivious of what was going on around her. Placing the cup on the table she slowly raised her head.

"Why do you want to know my name? I don't know you," she replied eyeing him up and down. She looked sad; there was no warmth in her cold blue eyes as they stared at each other, Franz was now so sure of himself.

"Do you not remember our journey through the mountains when the Gestapo were after you and your daughter?" She stared in total amazement, her mouth dropped open as she tried to speak. Suddenly Franz realised how different he looked. His long hair had been cut short and his bearded face was now clean shaven, how could she recognise him, the face from the past. He placed the book on the table with the rear cover facing up. The photograph showed him as he really was, long hair and flowing beard with his fur hat perched on his head.

"Franz, is it really you?" She gasped as she tried to get up. Her eyes glued onto the photo and a total look of surprise and then a faint smile. "I would never have recognised you," she blurted out. "What a coincidence after all this time, it's a good job you recognised me or else this would never have happened."

He reached out to help her up off the chair. A cool wind was blowing across the square as they stood there looking at each other. Franz put his arms around her shoulders and gave her a hug. "We've so much to talk about, let's go into the café where it is nice and warm and a nice cup of coffee wouldn't go amiss."

Franz guided her to a table close to the fire crackling in the grate. "It's cold out there," he said, nodding towards the window. The waiter came over and Franz ordered two coffees. "I haven't even had breakfast yet," he said, "what about you?"

She shook her head, looking down at the cup of hot coffee. "I can't afford such luxuries these days," she answered.

"Okay, then it's breakfast for two," said Franz beckoning the waiter. "We have a lot to talk about, may I call you Margaret?"

She looked up and gave a weak smile "why not."

The waiter brought the food to the table and said something. "I don't know what he said," replied Franz, "I can't speak or understand French."

He just said, "Enjoy your meal," a faint smile creased her lips. They tucked into the breakfast casting fleeting glances at each other across the table.

"Tell me what happened to you when those resistance fellows took you away?" Franz asked, sipping at his coffee, "and how is your daughter?"

The waiter cleared the table and Franz ordered two fresh coffees. There was a silence as they waited for him to return. She had taken a handkerchief from her handbag and dabbed her eyes. "Must go to the ladies," she got up and left the table. It was still drizzling with rain outside when she returned. Franz noticed that she had applied fresh makeup and combed her hair. She looked refreshed but still a sad look appeared in her eyes despite her effort to smile. "My daughter is fine now," she began, "and now she is in England."

"So please tell me what happened to you when you left with the resistance?"

"It's a long story, Franz, are you sure you want to hear it?" Fiddling with her handkerchief she looked out of the window.

"Yes, I do, Margaret, most definitely," insisted Franz.

"Well first of all let me thank you for rescuing us from the Gestapo. Before we left I came back into the house after helping Joanna into the car. I don't know how much you remember because you were in a bit of a bad state yourself. When we arrived at the farm, Ingerborg and Hans were horrified, especially when they saw Joanna's face. Immediately Hans disappeared outside only to return ten minutes later with the doctor. You had practically collapsed on the sofa, you were losing a lot of blood. The doctor looked at your wound and gave you an injection. He then began to examine Joanna. When he removed the bandages you had put on he was shocked at what he saw. Joanna's face was black and blue and such a horrible sight he began to cuss profoundly.

"Who did this to you, how did this happen?' He began to examine her face very gently. I told him it was the Gestapo. Once more he began to cuss profoundly, 'They should be hanged, you poor child what animals they are.' After a thorough examination he turned to me and said, 'She needs to be in a special hospital where they can reconstruct her face, I can only ease the pain for her.' He gave her injections into her neck and arms. 'There is a hospital but it is 200 kilometres from here. It is a convent hospital which is run by nuns. It is the only place I can send you to where you will be safe.' Two men appeared, they had been waiting for us. He turned to the resistance and spoke to them in French. They looked very nervous but appeared to agree with the doctor. He then applied fresh bandages carefully covering the damaged eye socket and covering her broken nose and her broken jaw. He gave me a bottle of tablets that he said were painkillers and then he wrote a letter for me to hand in at the convent. 'You must only feed her liquid food through a straw, I'm sorry I cannot do more for her.'

"The resistance men beckoned for us to follow them to the car. Ingerborg had filled a small holdall with things she said would be useful. I thanked her and followed the men to the car. Joanna was half sedated so she was more or less moving in a trance. I made her comfortable on the back seat which was quite roomy inside and covered her with a blanket. As an afterthought I ran back into the house where the doctor had just removed the bullet from your shoulder. He wiped it clean and offered it to me 'a souvenir,' he said quietly. I had just come to say thank you but you were unconscious. I turned to Hans and Ingerborg and embraced them. 'Please say thank you to him.' I ran outside and got into the car. The driver said something and beckoned me to hurry. We drove off at high speed, both men seemed very nervous. At times they would drive off the road and wait to see if we were being followed. As it got darker they seemed more relaxed and chatted cheerfully.

I must have dozed off and Joanna was in a deep sleep. We were driving through some woods and it was very dark. Every now and then we would stop and the men would get out and stretch their legs then change over; they took it in turns to drive. During the daylight hours they would find some secluded spot in the forest and park up. We were allowed to get out and stretch our legs but the men would always be watchful. They also carried handguns. We continued our journey as soon as it started to get dark. We ate biscuits and cakes and drank water. Joanna managed with a straw. Ingerborg had been very thoughtful. We both seemed to drop off to sleep lulled by the purring of the car engine.

"I awoke with a start as we pulled off the road onto a bumpy forest track. It was pitch black except for an occasional break in the clouds allowing the moon to shine through. We followed the track until we came to some high iron gates. They were open so we passed through and drove another half mile or so until we came to another set of gates which were closed. The driver's companion got out and opened them trying not to make any noise but they did squeak a bit and that seemed to echo through the forest. As we passed through I could just make out a sign on the gate 'Convent Hospital'. Closing the gate we drove slowly towards what looked like an old castle which I found out later was a 16th century monastery which had been donated to 'The Sisters of Mercy' to turn into a hospital. All was in darkness as we drove around to the back of the building. They pulled up to a door and one of the men got out. The driver switched off the lights but kept the engine running. The other man knocked on the door and tried to open it but it was locked. He knocked several times before it was eventually opened by a nun holding a lantern. She beckoned us into the building indicating that we must be very quiet closing the door behind us then led us along a corridor and down some steps which led into a small dormitory. She lit another lamp and put it onto a table. There were two single beds, a table and two chairs in the room. She indicated one for me and one for Joanna. She then signalled to the two men to follow her and they left the room."

Franz listened intently without any interruption. "You won't mind if I smoke?" she asked, opening her handbag and pulling out a packet of French cigarettes. "This is my only luxury these days." She searched in her bag and retrieved a small object. "Here is my souvenir," she said holding out the bullet, "do you want it back?"

Franz looked at it. "Such a small object can hurt so much, no, Margaret, that's yours to keep forever."

It was still drizzling outside and people outside looked into the café as they passed by, the morning traffic had increased as the work force made their way to their employment. "So what happened next?" asked Franz anxious to hear more.

"Well, we were preparing for bed when there was a knock on the door. It opened and a nun dressed all in white entered. She was carrying a tray with some food and drink on it, another nun dressed in black followed her in with a lamp. She put the tray on the table and introduced herself as Mother Superior. She then went over to Joanna and looked at her face. 'The doctor will be down shortly, but we must be very quiet and very careful, there are Gestapo officers being treated here at the moment they take advantage of our being a neutral country and send us casualties frequently.'

"She spoke very quietly and perfect English. She said that we would have to confine ourselves to the dormitory for the moment and keep the doors locked at all times. The nuns would always knock quietly when they wanted to come in. She apologised for the lack of electricity and hoped we could manage with the oil lamps. There was a knock on the door and a man entered followed by another nun. It was the doctor. Mother Superior introduced him as Doctor Karl Muller. 'The doctor wishes to examine your daughter's face, he will be very gentle, he must remove the bandages first.'

"He spoke very quietly to Joanna as he carefully removed the dressing. After a careful examination of her bruised and battered face he turned to me and asked what had happened to her. I handed over the letter and he read it. I told him about the Gestapo. He said something in

German I did not understand. He then spoke in perfect English with hardly any trace of an accent. He explained that it would be necessary to take Joanne up into the hospital for X-rays. That would be arranged later when all was quiet. There were German military personnel being treated at the hospital, taking advantage of the country's neutrality. He spoke French to Mother Superior who passed him his small bag. Another injection was given 'to reduce the swelling,' said the doctor.

"Mother Superior said they would come for Joanna as soon as it was safe to do so. She told us to relax and not for Joanna to move about too much or try to talk, just try to take food through the straw. When they left I looked at Joanna who was very tearful. I knew she was in great pain and gently hugged her.

"It was the next evening they came for Joanna, put her in a wheelchair and took her away. I waited patiently for her return. It was well over an hour before they brought her back. She was much sedated so they carefully placed her on the bed. The young nun who was with Mother Superior wasn't much older than Joanna she carefully lay Joanna down and covered her up. She seemed very friendly and talked softly to her. I think she was speaking in English but she talked so quietly I couldn't hear her. Mother Superior sat next to me on the bed, 'There has been a lot of damage done and the doctor and his team are planning how to reconstruct her face, but we will have to wait, maybe tomorrow we will know more, but it has to be done urgently or her face will be paralysed for ever.'

"When they left I lay beside my daughter on the bed and wept quietly, my beautiful child had had her face caved in by a maniac called Gruber – a name I shall never forget.

"Over the next few days she was taken backwards and forwards several times up to the hospital wing, always at night to avoid anyone seeing her. They were apparently making a frame to fit around her face which would slowly be adjusted to pull everything back into line. It was going to be a long slow progress and painful for Joanna."

Franz looked at Margaret across the table; she was reaching for her packet of cigarettes. It was still raining lightly outside and few more people had come into the café for an early morning coffee or breakfast probably on their way to work. The waiter came over and asked if we wanted anything else. Franz ordered two fresh coffees; Margaret had been talking a long time so he guessed she would be thirsty. She blew the cigarette smoke into the air. "Do you want me to go on?" she asked.

"Oh yes, please do," replied Franz he was very anxious to hear everything although he was wishing to himself that he had known all this before he had written his book. This would have filled a few more chapters and answered questions he had asked himself over the years. Again the handkerchief appeared and she wiped away a tear. We stayed at the convent hospital for what seemed to be an eternity. On some more occasions we were allowed to wander through the grounds but always in the company of one of the nuns who kept a sharp lookout. Eventually after the frame had been adjusted several times Joanna was taken for another X-ray and finally the frame was removed. According to Doctor Muller everything had been pulled back into line and was settling down and now a light plaster cast was applied just to support the reconstruction for a short while.

He visited one evening and sat down on the bed. He said everything would be fine and in time Joanna's face would be as beautiful as it was before. But now he had some bad news. The war in Europe had escalated and France was fully occupied by the Germans. More casualties were being brought to the hospital. It had been decided we would be safer if we were moved on. News had reached the convent that the Gestapo were still hunting us. Apparently one of the Gestapo officers and some of his men had disappeared − believed murdered by the resistance.

"We were told that a hospital vehicle would be used to transport us back into Paris. All borders were so heavily guarded by the Germans it would be impossible to escape back to England. The idea was that Joanna would be heavily bandaged and that I would be dressed as a nun also heavily bandaged after a throat operation. Neither of us would be able to talk due to our operations. The doctor explained that our papers were being arranged and would soon be ready. He also said that he had written a letter to a colleague at the hospital in Paris and he would be contacting us when we were housed safely. I asked, 'Why Paris?' The doctor smiled and said the resistance had agreed that we would be safer hiding under the noses of the enemy and to put our trust in them as they knew what they were doing. He stood up and shook my hand and wished us both a safe journey. Once more I began to feel scared."

Margaret had smoked three cigarettes so far whilst she had been talking. Franz thought to himself how stressed out she must be. No wonder after what she had been through. While she had been talking all sorts of things had been racing through his mind. This woman needed help and he was about to offer it.

"Margaret, I want to help you, before you say anymore will you listen to what I have to say?"

She nodded, looking away as if embarrassed. "You have already helped me once, how can I ever repay you for what you did?"

Franz reached over the table and touched her hand. "Well at least the mayor kept his promise and supplied me with a generator, now I have electricity at the monastery."

She smiled weakly. "I'm glad."

Franz looked at his watch they had been in the café for an hour and a half. "The reason I am here is to promote this book I have written. Thanks to all people concerned it has proved to be a winner. Professor Zachory contacted me and asked if I would accept an invitation to the university and give a talk on my success. I accepted, it was quite a surprise.

"They have accommodated me in a two bedroom flat at the university and tonight I will be giving that talk. It's about my journey into the mountains and my achievement with the monastery. Margaret, would you be willing to come as my guest and repeat all that you have told me in front of the audience?"

She shook her head. "No, I could not do that, I am not a speaker and my French isn't that good."

Franz reached across the table and put his hands on hers. He could see the misapprehension in her eyes. "I would be at your side all of the time and we would only be speaking in English."

Again she shook her head, "You don't understand, Franz, I have to find a job and somewhere to live, at this moment I am homeless, unemployed and broke so you can see I have enough to contend with, I'm sorry."

It had stopped raining and a warm ray of sunshine lit up the pavement outside. "Will you walk with me a while, Margaret, I have more to say?"

"I really must go, Franz, I have to get a job today and find somewhere to live or else I will be sleeping rough tonight."

"Please, Margaret, just hear what I have to say first. I want to help you, it won't take long." Franz took her arm and led her across the road. "Just a walk around the square?"

"I have been thinking what I could do and I have come up with an idea but I don't know what your reaction would be."

She looked at him suspiciously. "You have done enough already," she replied, "and I can never repay you for saving our lives."

"Margaret, your journey through the mountains is mentioned in my book and I'm sure the audience will love to hear what happened to you when you left, it's all part of the story and besides, I am going to give you a percentage of the royalties it produces." Franz paused. "I would also like you to come back with me to the monastery for a long rest and for you to get well, and when you have rested I promise I will see that you get back to England in time for Joanne's wedding."

Again, the handkerchief appeared to wipe away the tears. Franz led her to one of the wooden benches dotted around the square. He wiped away the few droplets of rain and beckoned Margaret to sit down. "I've never met anyone as kind as you, Franz," she whispered. "Why are you being so kind to me?"

"Well, it's about time someone showed you a little kindness — you have been through enough," said Franz. "Please let me help you." There was a silence which lasted two or three minutes. Franz knew that she would be running through her mind what he had proposed. "I did once give a talk on dressmaking," she blurted out, "but only to about twenty women."

"That's more than I have ever done," said Franz.

"Well, it's going to be something new for both of us," she said hesitantly.

Franz looked at her, a broad grin creased his weather-beaten face. "Does that mean you will do it, Margaret, it will make me so happy and I promise I will look after you."

She seemed to be more relaxed and an occasional smile passed her lips. She said she would have to collect her belongings from where she had been living and pay the landlady what she owed her. She questioned again the offer to stay the night at the university. Franz assured her that the professor had told him that the apartment was totally at his disposal. Franz stood up. "Okay, Margaret, let's take a taxi and do that first." A tingle of excitement ran through his body, now he was looking forward to this evening with renewed vigour.

They collected her belongings and paid what she owed and said their goodbyes as Franz led Margaret down the stairs to where the taxi was waiting. As it sped through the narrow streets she vowed that one day she would pay him back for all his kindness. He assured her that her appearance with him this evening would more than compensate that.

The professor stood open-mouthed as Franz introduced his guest and shook her hand vigorously saying how fortunate it was and how much more interesting the evening was going to be. He told Franz that as far as he knew the auditorium was going to be a full house. He also added that the university restaurant was at their disposal free of charge.

Chapter 1

Margaret looked around the apartment, it was basically furnished but it was a palace compared to what she had been living in for the past few years. She looked disapprovingly in the mirror. "I look like some tired old bag lady, my hairs a mess."

Franz was making coffee but he caught what she had said to herself. He looked at his watch, it was only 11am. "Let's have a drink and then we will do something about that. By the way I never did know what brought you and Joanna to France in the first place and how did the Gestapo get hold of you?"

She sat down and lit a cigarette. "My husband was a scientist and he was working on a new type of explosive. The company he worked for had a parent company in Paris. He was always travelling backwards and forwards between the two companies and then one time he never came back from France. We made intensive inquiries but the company were very vague with their answers. We decided to go to France and find out what was happening. I wanted to find my husband. We were advised not to go by the passport people and by the company but they would not give us any information. We were determined to find out for ourselves." She puffed on her cigarette and took a sip of coffee. "Of course it was a bad time for travelling, things were happening in Europe but we thought we would be safe in France.

"Of course when we were being chased by the Gestapo we never did find the time to tell you anything, we were in such a bad state, frightened and very tired. Joanna was in such pain, there just wasn't time for explanations.

"Anyway, when we finally managed to get to Paris and found the company's headquarters everything had been shut down. Totally deserted except for some old security guard who told us that the company had moved to somewhere in the mountains but he didn't know where."

Another puff on the cigarette and a sip of coffee, she was getting some colour into her cheeks and Franz noticed that she was becoming more relaxed. He listened intently as she unravelled her story.

"When I told the security guard the purpose of our visit he suddenly remembered that a man living not far from the company premises who used to drive the company bus and used to ferry workers backwards and forwards to the test site in the mountains and maybe he could help them. Struggling with his pigeon English he told us the man's name, Pierre Bleriue and he could be found in a certain bar around the corner. We thanked him and gave him some francs complimenting him on his good English.

"It was almost lunchtime so when we located the bar we ordered soft drinks and a sandwich. While he was serving us I asked the barman if he knew Pierre Bleriue. Whether he understood my poor French I do now know. He walked away and began talking to a group of men at the other end of the bar. A few minutes later a man sauntered over and looked at us suspiciously.

'My name is Pierre Bleriue, what you want?' he said in good English. I told him who I was and what I had come for.

'Ah! The Englishman. Oui, I used to take him to the railway station every month when he went back to England, always a good tip. Yes I remember him very well. But now they have all moved into the mountains and I no longer work there. It has been three months since any of them have been seen. No one seems to know what is happening up there.'

I asked if he would be willing to take us up there.

'But I do not have any transport now,' he replied.

'Could we hire a car?' I asked.

'Oui, madame, if you have money.'

"I told him I had money and would pay him also, he seemed very pleased and suggested that we meet at the bar the following morning at 9am. We had found a cheap hotel to stay in for a few days and nights so we rested feeling very satisfied that we had found someone to help us. The next morning after a quick breakfast we made our way back to the bar. Pierre was already there so we followed him through a couple of narrow streets to a small garage. The car was already waiting for us. We paid over the money Pierre asked for and got into the back seat. It was one of those old Citroens with the big headlights. I had always liked the look of them."

Franz watched the smoke curl upwards towards the ceiling as she lit up another cigarette. It reminded him of the times his dad would relax in the tin bath and light up.

Franz got up and searched for his pipe, not that he was a heavy smoked but on the odd occasion when his mind was concentrating on something he would smoke a pipe full of tobacco. He offered a coffee refill that was eagerly accepted.

"Go on, Margaret," he said quietly.

"We drove out of the city into the surrounding countryside, Pierre making occasional polite conversation. He said that he felt that a terrible time was coming, especially as things in Europe were hotting up. He suggested that we should get back to England as soon as we could. We drove for about 30kms before turning into a side road which seemed to be heading into the mountains. Pierre said that a new test site had been found away from the city to accommodate the scientists and the new explosions. We drove a further 3kms when suddenly as we drove around a bend in the road we were stopped by a makeshift barriers across the road. A group of men were gathered there wearing dark uniforms and carrying guns. Pierre said he didn't know who they were, probably security guards he suggested.

"Two of the guards walked over to the car as Pierre pulled up to the barrier and wound down the window. The guards poked their guns through the window and said something.

'They want your papers,' said Pierre, 'have you got your passport with you?'

"I detected a nervous tone in his voice as we handed over our passports to the not so friendly guards. They still pointed their guns at Pierre and indicated that Joanna and I get out of the car. They walked us past the barrier to where a big black car was parked. The window opened and our passports were handed to a stern-looking man all dressed in black. Some conversation was taking place which I could not follow, it was in another language which I had never heard before. I noticed that Pierre had quietly started to turn the car around. One of the guards had also noticed and started to run back to the barrier but Pierre had already completed the turn and was speeding away down the road. The guard raised his gun as if he was going to shoot but a voice from inside the car shouted "Nein, Nein." We were bundled into the backseat of this car and the doors slammed shut. There was another man sitting in the front seat also dressed in a black suit and wearing trilby hat to match. The driver kept looking in the mirror at Joanna and said something to his companion. Both laughed and the other man turned in his seat and looked at us both but focused his attention on Joanna.

"In the distance I could see buildings and more vehicles with a lot more uniformed men milling around all carrying guns. I spoke to Joanna but the man in the front shouted at me and not in a friendly tone. I eventually found out that these evil men were 'the Gestapo'.

"We were taken to a building and roughly pushed inside. The door was slammed shut and we were left alone. It was damp and cold inside and more like a building site hut. A dim light flickered on the wall illuminating our new abode. Two single beds with straw filled mattresses and a dirty washbasin accompanied by a stinking toilet that smelled of urine. We looked at each other both of us terrified. What had we let ourselves in for? I was wondering if Pierre had led us into this, but dismissed it from my mind, he had been too nice a guy and they probably would have shot him.

"We held onto each other all sorts of things were running through my mind. I tried my best to comfort Joanna. I told her that they were just security police who were always bullying people. We sat on one of the beds trying not to give away our fears. About an hour passed before the door was opened and two of the guards entered. They grabbed Joanna and pushed her towards the door. I tried to intervene but one of the guards pushed me away and pointed his gun at my head. My heart sank as they took my daughter away. What took place I can only imagine? Joanna would never reveal at the time what I had already imagined but when I saw her torn clothes and battered body I knew. They had kept her for two hours, the door was opened and they just threw her inside. I screamed at the guards but they just laughed in my face and pointed their guns at me. I knelt down on the floor and tried to pick her up in my arms. She screamed out in pain as I tried to help her to the bed. Her lovely blonde hair was matted with blood and what I saw next horrified me. Her face was completely disfigured. I tried to pull her hair away from her face but she cried out in pain at the slightest touch of my hand. All I had was a handkerchief in my bag. I ran some cold water from the tap then tried to bathe her face, but she cried out in pain. I cried with her. I suddenly remembered that I was wearing a cotton underslip which I quickly removed and tore into strips, it was the nearest thing to a bandage. Soaking it in cold water I began to cover her face leaving her mouth and left eye uncovered. It was all I could do to help Joanna. She eventually cried herself to sleep in my arms. My whole body ached as I tried not to move and disturb her. The hours ticked by and I must have nodded off. Suddenly there was some shooting going on in the distance and then voices which seemed to get closer. More shooting, then suddenly the door burst open. One of the guards was pushed in with his hands raised above his head followed by two more men with guns raised. Their faces were concealed by black balaclavas. They hit the guard on the head bringing him to his knees. They quickly looked around and came over to us. The one removed his balaclava and spoke to us."

"'It is me Pierre, please hurry there isn't much time.' I grabbed Joanna and tried to lift her. Pierre lifted her body and carried her outside. I grabbed our handbags and followed. There was that lovely Citroen again waiting outside. Pierre helped us in to the backseat then ran back into the hut. There was a shot and Pierre came running out carrying the heavy overcoat that the German guard had been wearing.

'She needs a hospital,' said Pierre, 'but that's impossible at the moment, we must get you away from here right now, there are more Germans on the way and we have to try and blow up this place.'

"I asked Pierre about my husband but he just shook his head.

'I don't know madam,' was all he said. 'This is all I can do.' He wrapped the overcoat over Joanna. 'Now please go with my men, and good luck to you.'

Chapter 2

"It was dark and it had started to snow. The car swerved several times as the snow began to stick on the roads. We could feel the temperature drop as we climbed through forests and mountains. It was obvious we were sticking to side roads. The two men in front only spoke French so there was no conversation between us they also seemed very nervous. If they saw any lights approaching they would pull off the road somewhere and hide the car. The further we went the more vehicles we encountered, many army looking vehicles which bore the German insignia.

"As it started to get light they looked at their map and soon we had pulled off the road and driving through a forest. The road was very bumpy and the driver kept apologising. Soon we came to a clearing in the forest. In the half light of the early morning I could make out piles of logs and some kind of machinery. There was a log cabin tucked away in the trees. We drove through the snow and came to a halt. I could just see a faint light in one of the windows. The driver got out and walked towards the cabin. The door opened and a man stood there holding a lantern. We were asked to get out and walk towards the open door. I had to help Joanna she was still half asleep. I caught sight of a woman coming from another room and she beckoned us to follow her. It was lovely and warm and very welcoming. We were led into a larger room. The men were talking amongst themselves probably discussing our journey. It had started to get light, the woman sat us down at a table and soon were given bread and hot soup. She spoke to us but of course we could not understand what she was saying so she spoke to the resistance men. I heard the name Gestapo so I guessed she was asking what had happened. She came closer and looked at Joanna. Immediately she could see her damaged face and opened a draw and gave Joanna a straw to drink the soup and a cup of tea. She shook her head and looked at me pitifully. She broke the bread up into very small pieces for Joanna to swallow. Looking at her I imagined that at some time she had been in the nursing profession. She was very gentle and understanding. After the meal we were led into another room, a bedroom with a large double bed. She pulled down the covers and indicated us. She left the room briefly returning with a bowl of warm water and some cloths. Between us we removed the temporary bandaging and very gently began to clean up Joanna's face. The congealed blood took some removing and caused Joanna to wince and cry out in pain. The woman's name was Gertrude she was very gentle she mentioned hospital. She applied some cream and gave Joanna two tablets which I guessed were painkillers and between us we applied fresh bandages. Soon we were enjoying the best night's sleep I have ever had. Joanna had gone to sleep as soon as her head hit the pillow.

"The night attire Gertrude supplied was very warm and relaxing to our tired bodies. It was light when I woke but it seemed to be getting darker. I looked around the room and noticed a small clock on the dresser, it said 4 o'clock. I realised we must have slept the whole day long. Joanna was sleeping peacefully so I did not disturb her. I quietly splashed my face in the wash basin and quickly got dressed. I opened the door and saw Gertrude laying the table. The smell of cooking coming from the kitchen was aromatic I realised I was very hungry. She looked up and beckoned me into the room. She then led me into another bedroom and opened a large wardrobe full of clothes. She indicated for me to choose some for myself and Joanna whose clothes were in tatters. I could hear men's voices outside and carefully glanced through the window. The resistance men, whose names were Jean-Paul and Gerard were pouring petrol into the tank of the car. I guessed we would be shortly moving on. I awoke Joanna and we sorted some clothes out. I gently helped Joanna, the pain was still etched in her face and the tears began to flow. After a friendly greeting from everyone we sat down and ate a hearty meal. Gertrude helped Joanna, I think she must have worked in a hospital at some time she was so gentle and talked very softly all the time.

"The men were talking to Gertrude's husband and I heard Switzerland mentioned but that was all I could understand. I cursed myself for not learning other languages but we English people are like that, we don't want to bother. Finally we were asked to get ready to leave; it was dark outside and still snowing. After attempts to show our appreciation we settled for hugs and kissed Gertrude and her husband. Gertrude gave me some tablets for Joanna to take. I thanked her and we got into the car. Once more we headed out into the darkness. I tried looking for place names but it was impossible to see anything. Gerard turned around and said something to me but once again in my ignorance I failed to understand. He pointed to a place on the map but I couldn't make out any names just a load of squiggles and lines. We passed several convoys of lorries which we did our best to avoid again travelling through the night watching the snowflakes falling. Joanna snuggled up to me covered by the heavy overcoat Pierre had taken off the German guard. I couldn't understand why such importance was being given to our escape. It was very good of the resistance to go to all the trouble and we certainly appreciated being rescued, but I thought it would have been easier to dump us back in Paris. All of this just because I wanted to find my husband, later when it was all over we found out why."

Franz interrupted, looking at his watch. "Okay, Margaret, you can tell me more later; let's go and see what the food is like in the restaurant downstairs."

She looked in the mirror and combed her hair, "Will I do?" she asked.

In the restaurant a young man led them to a table, he spoke French but with an English accent, Franz asked him his name. "My name is Peter," he said. "Oh you are English, that's fine, it makes it easier for me."

"Oh! You must be the man from the mountains. The professor told me to look out for you – I shall be coming this evening to listen to your life story. I am looking forward to it. I have already purchased a copy of your book."

Franz smiled at him. "Thank you, Peter."

They finished their meal and Franz again consulted his watch, it was 1:30. "Right, Margaret, let's go and do some shopping and get your hair done ready for this evening."

Again she thanked him for his generosity promising to pay back every penny. They proceeded out onto the streets of Paris looking for clothes boutiques and hairdressing salons. Franz looked at Margaret.

"I'm leaving you to choose whatever you want," he said with a smile, "no expense spared I'm just going to follow you."

The weather was warming up so they walked slowly along the streets looking in shop windows occasionally venturing inside and looking around. Margaret complained about the prices and how the war had affected everything. She looked at a two-piece costume and asked Franz his opinion. "Green suits you," he said sheepishly, "but I'm no expert on such matters – you choose for yourself and remember the price does not matter on this occasion and you will also need a new handbag to go with that and also new shoes and other things, please be my guest."

Whilst she was in the hairdressers Franz sauntered down to the railway station to cancel his return ticket and to enquire about train times for the following day. Finding one at a suitable time he purchased two one-way tickets to Zurich.

He could not help notice how good she looked when she walked up to where he was waiting. The sunlight on her blonde hair seemed to bring her alive. She gave him a smile and said, "That's better, that's the first time I've been to a hairdressing salon for years. Thank you, Franz."

He showed her the tickets. "Tomorrow at 3 o'clock we depart for home."

The rest of the afternoon was spent planning the evening's event. Franz assured her that he would be at her side at all times. "Just repeat what you have told me."

"There's not much more to tell. After another long journey through the night we eventually ended up in that small village on the German/Swiss border. The resistance men were nervous. Being in a German village with two Gestapo prisoners had really unnerved them and they seemed desperate to get rid of us. There was a lot of angry shouting going on between Gerard and a man from the village. Apparently the Gestapo were hot on our heels. The resistance wanted the Mayor to hide us whilst the resistance led a false trail for the Gestapo to follow, but the Mayor wasn't that keen on the idea. He wanted to remain neutral and to keep his village out of the war, Gerard was pleading with him. Finally we were taken to a farm at the end of the road where once again arguments took place. The Mayor was pleading with the farmer to do something. We didn't know what was going on. The farmer's wife took us inside and we were shown into a bedroom. We were given food and drink. She seemed very worried but did her best to make us comfortable. The rest you know. We woke up to hear you shouting. We were very worried and frightened I can tell you and even more when we saw you I thought you were some big hairy monster."

Franz smiled. "I want you to tell all this to the audience this evening, Margaret, exactly as you have told me. I wish I could have put all this into my book but at least some people will know what you and Joanna went through during those horrible times.

Part 2

Franz walked up to the podium and shook hands with the professor who had just made the introduction and he was now sitting next to Margaret, Franz waved to the audience in response to their loud applause. He felt very nervous in front of so many people. The auditorium was filled to capacity all seats were taken and even people standing up at the back. As the applause died down Franz cleared his throat. "Thank you for such a warm welcome. When I first started to write this book never in the world could I have imagined standing here in front of such a vast audience? My thanks go out to Professor Zachary for contacting me and arranging all this, I promise you an interesting evening. I haven't always lived in the mountains I picked up the title when I moved to Switzerland what seems to be a long time ago. The local people started calling me that when they found out what I was doing.

"I was born into a coalmining family on the English/Welsh border during the First World War. My father worked down a small privately owned coal mine which was run by a manager. He was a good man as manager's go and my mother used to work for his wife keeping house and cooking. His wife was a frail woman and could hardly do anything for herself. All in all it was a good setup. We lived in one of the cottages belonging to the mine owner and Mum's wage paid the rent so we had Dad's wages to spend on our home and a few luxuries. Dad didn't have to go to war as the coal miners were needed to fuel the foundries and other industries needed to make armaments.

"From the age of two I can remember Mum carrying or walking me to the front gate and waiting for Pa to come walking up the hill with his friends when they had finished work. They would wave and call out when they saw us. Dad would always kiss mum on the cheek and then rub his black hands over my face. 'Now you look like a miner's son,' he would say and laugh. The wash house was attached to the side of the cottage it was where the boiler was where Mum did her washing and where we would have a bath. Mom would always have Dad's bath ready for him and he would go straight in there and strip off, his dirty clothes and then he would lower himself into the long bath in front of the fire. Mum would scoop up his clothes and take them outside and shake all the dust off them before she put them in the boiler. Dad would give a moan of ecstasy as he lowered himself in the warm water; it brought great relief to his aching body. There was always a mug of tea on a stool at the side of the bath with an ashtray and a cigarette. I would watch as Dad enjoyed them. Mum would tell me to leave Dad to enjoy his bath and we would go into the cottage and start peeling the veggies for our tea.

"When Dad had finished his bath and had fresh clothes on he would come into the cottage and pick me up and play with me for a while before he lay down on the sofa for a sleep. I would lie with him and we would nap for a couple of hours. Mum would be washing Dad's clothes and putting them through the mangle that sat outside the wash house. She would then hang them on the clothes line to dry. Mum always insisted that Dad went to work every day in clean clothes. If it was raining she would put a clothes horse up in front of the boiler fire and spread them over. They would be ready for Dad next morning.

"When Dad had slept for an hour or so he would wake up and start tickling me. We had a bit of fun and then went down the garden to see what's what. He showed me which were weeds and which were crops. I would of course make the occasional mistake and pull up a half green carrot. It was my job to carry the weeds to the compost heap and Dad eventually got around to making me a small wheelbarrow. We would spend an hour gardening and then go and sit on a wooden bench Dad had made. He would have another cigarette and Mum would bring us a drink. Dad always had a little penknife in his pocket and he always brought home from the pit what he called kindling, odd pieces of wood which he would chop up for Mum to light the fire with, but he always kept a piece back for his whittling as he called it. He would hold the wood up in his left hand and shape it using his pen knife with his right hand. He showed me how to hold the knife pointing away from him to void accidents he'd say. I'd watch as he carefully carved away. Another propeller he'd say holding up the finished article. We would fasten it somewhere down the garden where the wind would spin it round, keeps the birds off the garden he would say.

"At 4 ½ years old I was ready for school. Mum took me and sorted all the details out. I was taken to a classroom with the other children who had just started. When Mum said it was time for her to go I became a bit upset so did the others but the teacher told us that our mums would be coming back for us later. We settled down in our desks and were given a slate, a piece of chalk and a rubber. The lad sitting next to me saw my new rubber, leaned over and stole it leaving me with his tatty old one. I gave him a stern look but he put up his fist at me so I let it go. His name was Leather Barrow he had difficulty pronouncing his words, I called him

Dickie Dub Dub but later I nicknamed him Wheelie and so did everybody else. I had another brush with Wheelie later on, he was a bully but he only picked on smaller kids.

"My mother had knitted me a woollen scarf, which I was wearing as I walked home from school, Dickie Dub Dub came up to me and grabbed both ends of the scarf and pulled them tightly around my neck. I was gasping for breath as he pulled tighter and tighter. If it hadn't been for a woman passing by he would have strangled me.

"I didn't enjoy sporting activities at school. The cricket ball hurt when it hit you and when playing football I was always getting my ankles kicked. My only interest was woodwork and was I glad when I was twelve years old that's when were given woodworking lessons. We were taught how to plane, how to saw and various other useful tasks, that's when I excelled at school; I liked doing joints especially dovetail joints I think they are so neat and tidy. First thing I made was a tray for my mum. I spent a lot of time on the joints and the teacher said they were perfect. When I had finished staining and varnishing Mum's tray the teacher exhibited around the class. 'A true work of art,' he said. My mum was delighted and Dad said it was perfect. My next project was a wooden pencil case for myself. There was a lot of chiselling to be done and the teacher showed me how to keep the chisel sharpened which was very important. I liked making things for people and I made Dad a few things. I decided to make Mum a new clothes horse as the one in the wash house had collapsed. There was a lot of planing to be done and the joints were different. Mortice and Tenon but I put my heart and soul into it I wanted it finished for Christmas.

"We were all nearing the age of fourteen in our class and there was a lot of talk about what we were going to do when we left school. A lot said there was only the pit locally and that seemed to be where most of us would end up. I asked Dad about it. He looked at me and shook his head 'One idiot in the family is enough, son, I'll find something for you.'

"I thought no more about it I put my trust in my dad. A few weeks before August in my fourteenth year Dad sat with me down the garden on the bench. 'Frank, I want you to come with me to the pit on Saturday morning, you've got an appointment with the manager and bring some of those bit and bobs you've made.'

"Saturday morning came along and Mum sorted out my smart clothes. I was done up like a dog's dinner but Mum insisted on me making an impression. Dad ran his eye over me, 'Did you collect some of those bits and bobs, Frank?' I showed him a bag with my selection, especially the horses heads I had carved; when the pit ponies came up at holiday times I had spent hours drawing their heads and more hours carving them out of some oak pieces I had collected, now they were stained and varnished they were perfect.

"We knocked on the manager's door and waited. I was nervous, Dad hadn't told me anything. 'A surprise,' he said. As we stood there waiting I had visions of walking up the hill with Dad and his mates after a hard day down the pit.

"'Come in,' said a stern voice, dad opened the door and took his cap off. We closed the door behind us and stood in front of a large desk. The manager looked up and greeted us in a pleasant manner, and told us to sit down. 'So this is Frank, eh! Jack, well, Frank, your dad has been telling me something about you. You have a gift for woodwork, is that right?' Dad told me to show the manager what I had in the bag. I carefully laid them out on his desk he leaned forward and carefully picked up each item. I placed the horse's heads last. The manager looked at them and picked each one up individually. 'My god, lad, these are brilliant I could name each one as I see them this is Punch, this is Robin, this Ernie and this is Jolly. Frank, they are perfect.' He looked at Dad and nodded. 'Now, Frank, do you want to come and work for me as a carpenter?'

"'Yes, sir, please,' I replied, and so that's how I got my job as a junior working in the carpenter's shop at the pit. Bill the foreman would give me jobs to do, like sweeping up and bagging sawdust. I was also the new tea boy and also the fetcher and carrier.

"I settled in well with the other carpenters although I was not allowed around the machinery if it was running. Circular saws looked awfully dangerous. Bill took me down the timber yard where all the timber stocks were kept and introduced me to the different woods. He wrote the names on them so that if I was sent to get any I would know what to look for. After a while I got used to the different smells and could tell just by a sniff which was which. Two years passed by quickly and I was enjoying being a worker. I gave Mum all my money and she would give me pocket money, but even at half a crown I still managed to save some of it and had my own Post Office savings book.

"During the summer months occasionally dad would hire a horse and carriage for a day and we would pack up a picnic basket and head off somewhere for the day, how I loved doing that. I never really mixed with the other lads in the village all they seemed to want to do was chase girls and drink whatever they could get. Beer always seemed to be their priority.

"When I turned seventeen, Bill said the manager wanted to see me. I was a bit apprehensive and wondered if I had done anything wrong. My fears were allayed when the manager called me into his office. He rambled on about the good report that Bill had given me and asked if I was happy at the job. When I said I was he leaned back in his chair, 'Well, Frank I'm going to give you an apprenticeship, would you want that?' he asked. I admitted that I wasn't sure what was involved but when he explained what it entailed I became very interested.

"My apprenticeship was to last four years and I was also to attend a college one day a week during that time. I was to learn all aspects of woodwork, joinery, drawing and planning. It was a good education and not a chance to be missed.

"I was eighteen and at college on the day I first saw her. I used to take my lunch and go and sit on a bench in the church gardens, especially on a sunny day. I was nibbling on a sandwich and reading a magazine when I first became aware of someone looking at me. I gazed over the top of the magazine and saw this dark-haired girl looking at the bench. 'Do you mind if I sit here?' she said, in good English but with an accent. I picked up my sandwiches and shuffled along to make room. 'No not at all,' I stammered, 'Gracias – thank you.' She sat down and proceeded to read a book which I noticed was titled "How to speak English."

"'You are not from around here I take it,' was my next attempt at conversation. She gave me a broad smile revealing a beautiful set of teeth enhanced by a lovely tan. She waved the book, 'Is it that obvious?' We both gave a little laugh.

"'No, I am here to attend the college to make my English better, my home is in Spain.'

"I finished my lunch and looked at my watch. 'I am at the college also studying woodwork and joinery and it is time to get back.' She looked at her watch. 'Si, it is also time for me to get there also.' We walked across the road together, said our goodbyes and made our way back to the college.

"That was how I met Carmen who was to have a great influence on me. We would meet every college day and either sit on a bench and talk or walk around the shops. This went on for a few weeks until I managed to pluck up enough courage to ask her for a date. She smiled and said 'gracias' but it was not possible as her parents had laid down rules about only going out if chaperoned and her Aunt Rosa who she was staying with whilst in England was also very strict.

"I suggested we could go to the local cinema on a Saturday night and take Aunt Rosa with us. Carmen laughed and said she would ask Aunt Rosa and let me know next Friday at college.

"I helped Dad with his garden as he was having trouble with his chest. The doctor told him he had a touch of bronchitis. I suggested he stopped smoking as that didn't help. Poor Dad – I watched him going downhill, but still he would sit on the garden bench and whittle away at a piece of wood, somehow it seemed to relax him and now I understand why I felt the same.

"Carmen greeted me with a big smile Aunt Rosa had said yes. We held hands and walked around to the cinema to see what was on *The Wizard of Oz* Carmen said her Aunt Rosa would love to see that. I wasn't so sure myself but anything to be with Carmen.

"Mum asked me where I was going as she watched me getting spruced up. She seemed to be dropping hints about girlfriends. I gave her a hug and told her she could be right as I was taking two ladies to the pictures that night to see The Wizard of Oz. She laughed she thought I was pulling her leg.

"I caught the bus into town and made my way to the picture house where we had arranged to meet. I was a bit nervous about meeting Aunt Rosa but when we were introduced she put me at my ease by saying how ridiculous their Spanish customs were, but she had promised Carmen's father she would chaperone his daughter whilst she was in England. The ice had been broken and I found Aunt Rosa easy to get on with, but she still acted as chaperone on other occasions when we went out together, although sometimes she would drift off on her own and look around the shops leaving Carmen and myself to a little privacy.

"The days rolled by and the months passed I was twenty and had one more year of my apprenticeship. Carmen said that she had almost finished her English course and would be returning to Spain at the end of summer. We were beginning to feel a bit downhearted at the thought of parting. I said I would take a holiday in Spain the following year and Carmen said she would ask her father if she could visit Aunt Rosa for a couple of weeks before the grapes were due to be picked, but we both knew that we were in a precarious position. We arranged to go to the cinema with Aunt Rosa again but this time I was going to invite my mum also. I told her it was about time she met my two women. Mum was delighted and so it was arranged for the following Saturday. As we waited outside the cinema Mum would keep looking at the young girls passing by and kept saying 'is this them?' Was she surprised when Aunt Rosa walked up and held out her hand, Carmen had a huge smile on her face as I made the introduction. Of course Mum was surprised but during the evening she got used to it and she and Aunt Rosa chatted away like two old friends.

"On the day Carmen was due to leave I took a day off work and caught the early bus into town. I knew what time the train was so I waited at the station. Her sad face turned into a happy smile when she saw me and Aunt Rosa shook her head in disbelief. We again said our goodbyes and Aunt Rosa slipped out of sight when I kissed Carmen. It was a tearful farewell but as the days and weeks passed by and we wrote to each other twice a week we fell into a routine. I would visit Aunt Rosa and sometimes Mum and I would meet her in town for a meal and a chat. They were becoming good friends which pleased Carmen and me. Aunt Rosa didn't think Carmen's father would let her come to England again so soon. They were working hard at the vineyard and the bottling plant was just starting to pick up. She gave me a wicked grin. 'But I am thinking of visiting Spain for a holiday, what about you?'

"Well that was that, I found out when the pit holidays were and left it all to Aunt Rosa. I wrote to Carmen and told her I would be seeing her soon; I couldn't contain my excitement. I told the manager and he laughed. 'Well that's more than I can manage. Two weeks in Brighton is all I can look forward to.'

"Mum was pleased as I would be home for my 21st Birthday, so was I. I would not have missed my coming of age at home with Mum and Dad. We planned a small party in the garden with some family friends. Aunt Rosa was invited but wouldn't be able to make it. I brought some new clothes for my holiday I wanted to make a good impression on Carmen's father and mother. Aunt Rosa made all the travelling arrangements she said she had years of practise. Her husband never came he said it was too hot.

"I slept at Aunt Rosa's the night before our departure it was an early start and the train to London was always on time. I paid Aunt Rosa for my ticket and asked about currency conversion. 'Leave that to me, Franco,' she said smiling, 'in Spain they will call you Franco, so get used to it.'

"I had never left home before so it was a new experience for me I followed Aunt Rosa like a puppy dog she was a very seasoned traveller and pointed out lots of useful things to me. The ferry was a new experience to me but I managed to avoid throwing up over the side. I hadn't realised how big the world was until we had travelled through France and then Spain. How small England was in comparison. I also noticed how warm it was getting. We both nodded off from time to time as the journey seemed to go on forever. At last, when Aunt Rosa started to powder her nose and check her make-up I realised we must be getting near our destination. Barcelona, that's what the ticket collector was shouting as he passed through the carriages. During the journey Aunt Rosa and I had some interesting conversations from bull fighting to religion. Aunt Rosa knew everything; she made it quite clear that Carmen was Roman Catholic and if we ever intended marriage one of us would have to change their religious beliefs. I had always been Church of England but I was never a religious person. Church going was never at the top of my list only on special occasions. I said I had no problem with changing religion. Aunt Rosa said I would have to attend classes in religious instruction to adopt the Catholic Church. I told her it was not a problem for me.

"At the station I handled the luggage whilst Aunt Rosa searched for whoever was meeting us. I spotted Carmen amongst the host of waiting faces. Our eyes met and my heart leapt into overdrive. She was more beautiful than I could ever remember. We hugged and kissed oblivious to whoever was around us. It was when I noticed a stern-looking man talking to Aunt Rosa that I realised Carmen's father was watching our performance. We were quickly introduced to her mother and father. Her mother bore a great resemblance to Aunt Rosa, sisters I imagined. Her father had a firm handshake and said something in Spanish which Carmen interpreted into 'Nice to meet you, welcome to Spain.' We made it out of the station amongst a throng of other enthusiastic visitors. Outside the sun shone very brightly and I noticed at once how hot it was. It was midday and the hottest part of the day. We were led to where horses and carriages were tethered. Not many motorised vehicles in sight. Carmen's father took the luggage and stashed it on the front seat and then backed the horse and carriage out. Aunt Rosa and her sister sat on one side and Carmen and me on the other side. Her father sat up front as he was driving.

"We soon left the city limits and heading off into the countryside I held Carmen's hand but was aware that we were being observed closely by the women. I gathered that at times we were being talked about. Carmen would smile and squeeze my hand and say 'yes that's true.'

"We followed a long road and I couldn't help notice that in almost every field there were lines of grapevines. Carmen pointed out a building in the distance that was 'My Casa'. Turning off the road we followed a wide track that eventually led to My Casa. I could understand how much work there was involved, there were fields of vines as far as the eye could see and there were people picking grapes. It was hot making it a very uncomfortable job. The fellow driving the tractor which was pulling a trailer waved to us. Carmen said it was Carlos her brother.

"We reached the Casa which was a lot bigger than it looked, a rambling sort of place that spelt many years of existence. Apart from the house there were other buildings. A large one that Carmen said was the winery or wine producing plant. A couple of dogs bounded up to greet us and Aunt Rosa made a fuss of them like old friends. The luggage was unloaded and the horse and carriage taken away. Carmen held my hand and led me inside My Casa. It was old but with a touch of class and everywhere and everything seemed to echo 'class'. It was two hundred years old said Aunt Rosa waving her hand around. 'We were born here.'

"I couldn't see anything modern in the place. The furniture dark carved wood and the ornate grandfather clock ticking away in a recess. I loved it. My suitcase was taken upstairs by Carmen's father and Aunt Rosa pointed out that I would be sharing a bedroom with Carlos. Actually Carlos who was about a year older than me was a nice guy with a sense of humour. He spoke pigeon English so some of the time I could understand what he was saying. We got on well together.

"We gathered on the back porch which was well shaded and as the afternoon sun sank in the west it became a little cooler which suited everyone. Drinks were brought to us and Carmen held a glass of wine, 'Here, Franco, taste our wine.' I'm not a drinker and have hardly drank any beer let alone wine. I did not know what to expect. My first sip brought laughter to the family as they watched the funny face I pulled. I have always had a sweet tooth and the wine wasn't sweet. I grimaced and then took another sip. This time I didn't pull a face I merely nodded in appreciation. I still didn't like it but I tried not to let it show. Aunt Rosa made her excuses and went upstairs. 'I'm tired,' she said. Carmen asked if I was and if I was hungry. I answered yes to both questions.

"We sat down to our main meal at eight o'clock of the evening. The table was laid out on the porch where it was still warm but with a welcome breeze. I admired the lovely sunset and commented on it.

"I am usually an early riser but on this occasion I was still fast asleep when Carmen knocked on the door, she entered the room and laughingly jumped on the bed and started tickling me. It was 9 o'clock and everybody was up and working. I never heard Carlos get up. Carmen said my breakfast was on the table waiting for me. She kissed me and was gone.

"The coffee was still hot and the buttered toast still warm. It was quiet in the house the only live thing around was a cat and a friendly dog who sat there waiting for me to hand out the toast. I ate my fill and went looking to see where the action was. All I had to do was follow the dog. Carmen, her mother and Aunt Rosa were in the winery, washing and cleaning the stainless steel containers ready for the next load of grapes to be pressed. Carlos was on top of the press scraping out the previous load and washing out the huge container. Carmen said this had to be done first thing in the morning and everybody gets up at six o'clock to get it done. Her father had loaded all the empty baskets and was distributing them around the fields ready for the pickers. All of this was done before breakfast. At 10 o'clock all was done and they went to the casa where a light breakfast had been set out on the rear porch. I asked if I could do anything. Aunt Rosa laughed. 'Si, you can wash the dishes and feed the cat and dog.' Everybody burst out laughing. 'Manana, six in the morning I knock on your door, and wake you up.' Once breakfast was over the first crates were brought in. I helped unload them and the ladies put them into the washer and so the process began. Carlos loaded the empty crates back onto the tractor and took them round the fields.

"Carmen's father Senor Martinez, said he would show me something. I followed him to the very end of the building where the large barrels stood on their racks. He pointed to the different dates written on them. We stopped at one that was two years old and then pointed to a car that had just pulled up. A well-dressed man got out and entered the building shaking hands with both of us. Apparently this was the chief taster for the Bodega and it was not until he gave the say so could the wine be bottled. We followed him around and watched as he checked the dates with his own information. It then came to tasting. I watched as he tapped the barrel and then took a sample which he tasted and then spit out into a bucket. He waited a few minutes and then took another sample which he sniffed and sipped and rolled around in his mouth. He said something to Senor Martinez and drew another sample which he gave him to taste. After a minute of talking both men smiled and nodded their heads in agreement. A certificate was handed to Senor Martinez and the two men shook hands and parted. This meant bottling could commence. It was like being on a production line. Grapes coming in washed, squashed and barrelled. I enjoyed what little time I spent there.

"I had to get Carmen's father alone so that I could get his permission to court his daughter. I waited for the right moment. I saw him going into the Casa so I followed discretely. He was sorting some paperwork out when I entered. He looked up and smiled. 'Senor Martinez, I would like to speak with you,' I said. He was still smiling as he invited me to sit down and take a glass of wine with him. 'I would like your permission to court your daughter.' The words came out somewhat rushed but at least I said it.

"'Of course, Franco, and I respect you for coming to me, the women folk have been talking about it for days. I know how fond you are of each other and I am pleased to see my daughter so happy. Aunt Rosa speaks highly of you and that is a good recommendation. My only concern, Franco, is that you are going to take her away from her family.' I listened to every word he said, his command of the English language surprised me greatly. 'We Spanish are very family orientated and as you can see we are running a family business of which Carmen is an important member and also a shareholder. What happens if you take my daughter away from us? We lose and important part of the work force, an important part of our family and I lose my daughter. I had always wished for Carmen to meet a good, honest Spaniard who would blend in rather than break up the family.

"'Franco, I speak to you honestly as a father. I believe you to be a good, honest, hardworking man with a good trade to your hands, I have no doubt Carmen would be safe in your hands but I want you to know my thoughts as a father. If only you had been a Spaniard; not that I have anything against the English. Aunt Rosa seems happy enough but at the end of the day it will be yours and Carmen's decision.'

"That evening Carmen and I get down to some serious discussions. First I asked her to marry me. She said yes so then we tried to decide when. It had to be a year hence to allow for us to make more decisions. It was difficult for us both. One of us was going to leave the family nest. Carmen had everything going for her as regards prospects. What would she be able to do in England and where would we live, in a miner's cottage when one became available? If she wanted to work what were the job prospects. Aunt Rosa had to find a job cleaning to start off with and then managed to get a job in a shop. On the other hand Carmen was already a share holder in the family business and stood to inherit 50% of it eventually. In Spain when people build their houses they always leave it open for extension for family additions. It had already been extended when Carmen and Carlos came along but still there was room for more. Carmen felt that her father would extend further as a wedding present to them. I would also share in the family business when we were married. Moving to Spain was the best option for me although leaving Mum and Dad tore at my heart strings. We agreed to postpone our final decision on where we would live until I had a chance to talk it over with my parents.

"Whilst I was there the telephone company were putting up telephone poles to the area where the vineyard was. Senor Martinez said they would soon be connected to the outside world by telephone. This was good news and Aunt Rosa said she would also have a phone installed at home. The two weeks seemed to fly by. I had my first try at picking grapes which was backbreaking. I loaded baskets on the trailer and watched as Aunt Rosa and Carmen washed the grapes and prepared them for the crusher or press as they called it. Senora and senor Martinez started the bottling of the wine passed by the inspector. The whole procedure was a united effort and I could see what would happen if a link in the chain was missing. That evening Carmen and I were enjoying a glass of wine on the porch or 'naya' as they called it. We had agreed that I should return home and discuss our future with my parents. It was in the back of my mind to stay in England until after my 21st Birthday and possibly Christmas, after that I would if everything went according to plan leave for Spain the beginning of the New Year. We said our goodbyes and Aunt Rosa and I boarded the Train. Carmen was in tears, I held her in my arms and told her that the time would soon pass. The journey home seemed endless. Aunt Rosa chatted away freely but my thoughts were of the future. Mum and Dad greeted me warmly, it was the first time I had left home for such a long time. That evening I talked over what I had planned with them. They were pleased for me and glad I would still be at home for my 21st Birthday in a month's time and also that we would be celebrating Christmas together just one more time. I collected my certificates from college and went up to see the manager in his office. 'Frank, you have done us proud,' he said shaking my hand. 'So how was your holiday?' I told him that it had been an experience of a lifetime. I then went on to tell him of my plans to live in Spain and get married to Carmen. 'So we will be losing you after Christmas, Frank?' I said, I had appreciated everything he had done for me and it had been a reluctant decision. He was very understanding and wished me well. 'There will always be a job here for you, Frank, if ever things don't work out.' He shook my hand and wished me well.

"My 21st Birthday came along and we had a good party at the cottage with many friends and neighbours joining in the celebrations. Dad bought me a gold ring with my initials engraved on it. Mum a leather wallet with my initials on the front and a lovely gold plated watch. Aunt Rosa sent her apologies and sent me a nice book on learning Spanish which I treasure. Carmen sent me a lovely card with a lovely letter inside. I also received a parcel from Spain, six bottles of their own wine delivered by a parcel delivery company. We made a fuss of that at my party.

"Christmas was always a family affair and we enjoyed a nice quiet one. I had been sorting through my belongings trying to decide what I was taking to Spain. Mum and Dad had bought me a brand new suitcase. We met up with Aunt Rosa and her husband and we all went for a meal. Dad got on well with them and Mum and Aunt Rosa were like old bosom pals. Dad asked how they had met. Aunt Rosa laughed. 'In France, both working for the same company.' She had written a list for me: instructions on what trains to catch and where to get the best exchange rate for my money. I said I wished she was coming with me as I would probably get lost and end up in Australia.

"Saying goodbye to my parents was heartbreaking. I promised to write often and let them know how I was doing and promised I would visit them whenever I could.

"I had to catch an early train so I stayed the night at Aunt Rosa's and she made sure I did. Saying goodbye at the station didn't seem half as bad as I knew we would be meeting again in the not too distant future, after all, I was going to be part of the family.

"The journey to Spain seemed to take forever, having to find my own way harder than when you're just following someone, but I followed Aunt Rosa's instructions and got on the right ferry and the right train and got to Paris without a hitch and finally after changing my currency found the right train to Barcelona.

"Carlos and Carmen were there to meet me and made a great fuss. It was nice, and I was glad to see them. Carmen never stopped talking as Carlos drove the carriage home. The weather was cooler and much more comfortable. Senor and Senora Martinez were waiting at the casa and greeted me warmly. I looked around and thought to myself, *this is your new home and it's a long way away from the pit*.

"Carlos took my luggage and I was led into the Naya where a meal had been prepared. Wine was served and Senor Martinez gave a toast to a new life. He also asked me what I thought of the wine. I raised my glass and said 'Muy bien'. He was pleased.

"Carmen's father had already had some work done on the extension of the house. It was to be a two bedroom and a bathroom/toilet upstairs with a kitchen and dining room/lounge with a naya overlooking the fields. We would see some spectacular sunsets; there would also be a downstairs toilet. What a wedding present. I asked Senor Martinez if I could do some of the woodwork to save some expense but he said I wouldn't have the time to spare as he already had a job for me. He wanted wine racks along the length of the walls of the winery as high as could reach. He planned to bottle some wines and then put them in racks. He explained that the bottles had to be turned a fraction every week and that was going to be one of my jobs. There was also the pruning of the vines and cultivation of the soil. It did sound as if I was going to be busy. Carlos said he had purchased a secondhand carriage or float as we called it. He was going to get someone to overhaul it and spruce it up and a pony to pull it and that was to be our wedding present from him and if I wanted to I could do the work on it myself. I could if I had the time.

"I asked Senor Martinez if Carmen and I could get engaged he said it was okay.

"As the spring approached work started to increase. Carlos drove the tractor and cultivated the ground around the vines. Senor Martinez showed me how to prune the vines and the spraying. Carmen and her mother were busy in the winery preparing labels and sorting out the bottling. The builders had started the extension. By the end of the day everyone was exhausted. We started at seven o'clock in the morning, had breakfast at ten o'clock. Started work again after half an hour and worked until one o'clock. Lunch would be served, basically a salad or cheese and ham rolls. We would rest for a couple of hours and then work until about seven o'clock. We would have a cooked meal at eight o'clock and that would be our day. If the weather was unsuitable we would work inside on various jobs. I asked Senor Martinez if he would order the wood for the wine racks so that I could make a start. He gave me a drawing of what he wanted and said Carlos would bring the tractor and trailer and he would take me to the timber yard which was about three kilometres away and I could select what I wanted, so now I was being given responsibility.

"Carmen and I talked about our wedding plans. I had already been enrolled for Roman Catholic indoctrination and attended church on Sundays with the family. I also received tuition one evening a week at the church, Carmen would come with me to explain what was what. Religion has never played a big part in my life so I just went along with what they were teaching me. Carlos had brought the float home and shown it to me so now I had something to play with. We planned to get married after the grapes had been picked and the work had eased off a bit. I had already asked Senor Martinez if I could marry Carmen and he had given us his blessing so we could make our plans. Each evening Carmen and I would sit out in the naya and make lists. Senora Martinez also went looking for smart clothes we also enjoyed a few glasses of wine whilst we were doing it. Senor Martinez said it would help with our concentration.

"The extension on the casa was almost finished and Carmen and I went shopping every opportunity we had. The furniture was delivered and Carmen and her mother enjoyed looking around for curtains and other things. I had spent some time refurbishing the float Carlos had brought and he and I went looking for a suitable pony to pull it. We settled for a white mare called Maria, she was a beautiful white three-year-old which we all fell in love with.

"Everything had been planned for a first weekend in October for the wedding. A small community hall had been booked for the reception and Carmen and I booked an Alpine Chalet at the foot of the Pyrenees for our honeymoon."

Franz paused and took a drink of water the memories came flooding back which brought a tear to his eyes. The eyes of the audience in the auditorium were on him.

"Our wedding was a lovely occasion which will always be remembered as the happiest days of my life. Mum and Aunt Rosa came to the wedding. When we returned from our honeymoon we enjoyed moving into our casa which was a momentous and heartwarming experience. I felt like I was the luckiest man alive. Even during the winter months there was always plenty to do. Casks had to be cleaned and all the other equipment to be checked and maintained if a certain wine had been passed by the inspector that had to be bottled. I was busy building the wine racks and other maintenance work was always there. The vines had to be checked and sprayed, but it wasn't as demanding as when the grapes were harvested. Senor Martinez or Papa as I now addressed the family, informed us that the yearly harvest had been a good one and that we had made some money. Carmen's mother suggested we go out to a restaurant and celebrate.

When spring came it started to warm up. Even in Spain it can be cold at night and it's nice to sit in front of a log fire. We saved most of what we earned, we would all eat as a family in the naya and then after a long chat we would disperse to our own private places. Carmen and I would enjoy the evening in our own casa. As the summer approached the work intensified. The vines had to be checked regularly for parasites and the new supply of bottles labelled and sterilised. I had completed the wine racks along one wall of the winery and asked Papa if he wanted another row on the other wall. He said he didn't mind when I had the time.

It was approaching my 22nd Birthday when the picking started and it was really warming up. Carlos and I alternated the heavy work between ourselves leaving Carmen and her mother to handle the bottling plant. Pappa would organise the pickers and generally supervise us all, but he too worked hard.

I woke early one morning to find Carmen fast asleep which was unusual. She said she didn't feel too good so I suggested she take a day off as we could always get more help for her mother. She began to pick up later in the day and joined them in the winery. Two days later she felt ill again. On this occasion, Momma decided a visit to the doctors would be a good idea. She harnessed up Maria and the float and off they went. I waited for them to come back anxious to find out if Carmen was alright. Both women confirmed as everything was going to be fine, no major concern, Carmen just needed to rest and to take things easy.

A week before my birthday Carmen and her mother went shopping. Carlos and I relaxed on the porch playing cards. The women finally returned laden with bags and boxes and in good spirits. Carmen insisted on a little privacy that evening so that she could wrap up my presents. I went down to the winery and looked at what timber was left for me to make more racks Carlos joined me and we chatted away. I asked him if he had a girlfriend yet. He replied that he was interested in one young senorita but she was playing hard to get.

When I returned to our casa Carmen had already gone to bed. I guess the shopping had tired her out.

When my birthday arrived it was on a Saturday which was a day off for us. Carmen got up and fetched my presents and laid them on the bed. I opened the first parcel and was surprised to find a fluffy teddy bear. I laughed hysterically as I opened the next one: another fluffy toy. Carmen was bursting with laughter I opened another and found what looked like baby clothes. I was mystified, she was still laughing when she placed my hands on her tummy and said I would have to wait a while for my big birthday present. I was absolutely flabbergasted, I hugged and kissed her and we cuddled passionately. I couldn't wait to break the news to the family but of course they already knew.

Of course we were all over the moon with excitement and I started looking for wood to start making a crib. Carmen looked beautiful as she began to develop a tummy. She had a lot of the morning sickness and many times she had to miss working in the bottling plant.

Christmas was a family affair with an extra guest, Carlos had eventually won over his girlfriend and borrowed the pony and trap to do his courting. I said I would buy him one for a wedding present. I had started on the crib and had painstakingly carved a pretty pattern on the headboard which I had hung up in the winery for all to see. The New Year came and Carmen started to look tired, she was getting bigger and needed to rest a lot. Carlos's girlfriend Rosita took over helping with the bottling plant and fitted in well, she got along well with everybody. Carmen and her mother visited the doctors and clinics frequently to make sure everything was going on alright. In the seventh month of the pregnancy alarm bells started to ring Carmen was having a lot of pain and dizziness. Frequent visits to the doctors and then hospital visits. We were all getting a little concerned. The hospital doctor Dr. Santchez suggested Carmen stays in hospital for exploratory examination. When we visited Carmen, Dr. Sanchez took us to one side and said there were complications, apparently the foetus had suffered heart failure and died inside. Carmen had not yet been told as she was also very ill. An operation was necessary to remove the foetus and I would have to sign a consent form. I asked if Carmen was going to be alright to which the doctor said that when the foetus had been removed Carmen would grow stronger.

They prepared her for the operation and it was decided to operate that evening. We stayed until the operation was completed. We were told everything had gone alright but Carmen had lost a lot of blood and maybe she needed a blood transfusion they would watch her progress during the night. We went home and went to bed.

Momma said she was going to phone Aunt Rosa before she went to bed. At five-thirty the following morning the phone rang. It was the hospital we were asked to get to the hospital as soon as possible. No one spoke as we made the short journey but I knew something was wrong. The doctor was waiting for us and the look on his face confirmed our worst fears. Carmen had a heart attack despite the transfusion everything had been too much for her. We were ushered into the room where she lay. I broke down as soon as I saw her. Momma collapsed and had to be sat in a chair. Pappa held Carmen's hand and broke into a flood of tears – I stood on the other side of the bed, Carlos stood beside me and held onto my arm. The tears came fast and furious as I looked down on Carmen's face. I was paralysed with fear how could my lovely wife be lying there lifeless, was this a bad dream a nightmare from which I would suddenly waken up from. I had never known grief before and I know now that I couldn't handle it. My whole body was shaking and I was sobbing loudly and so was everybody also. I knelt down beside the bed and leaned over and kissed my lovely wife as I had done so many times before expecting her to spring to life with a lovely smile on her face. This did not happen and I kissed her again. I touched her hand and felt the coldness of death. Once more a flood of tears erupted Carlos was kneeling also and I felt this strong arm around my shoulders together we cried. I gathered my strength from him he was a stalwart. The priest stood at the foot of the bed saying prayers. He asked us to join in; we did but the prayers had done nothing for Carmen and now my faith in the heavenly father had depleted rapidly.

After a short while a nurse came in and asked us to say our goodbyes as Carmen's body would have to be taken into the mortuary and prepared for burial. Again a flood of tears erupted, I kissed her again so did the family. We were escorted into an office where the priest was and also the doctor. Forms had to be signed and the doctor tried to explain they had decided to give Carmen a blood transfusion during the night because she was failing fast. At first things seemed to go well and then her heart started to reject the new blood causing her to have a massive heart attack from which she died.

The funeral was arranged for two days according to Spanish law. We would be notified by the hospital and the priest would contact us regarding times etc.

We drove home in silence; everybody wrapped in their own thoughts. I was like a zombie – my mind was in overdrive and my heart ready to burst. I had never in my whole life experienced the pain I was feeling at that time and that pain is still with me today, it never goes away, time has not erased it.

The funeral was arranged for two days. Carlos went out early on the second day with the pony and float only to return an hour later with Aunt Rosa and Mum. I ran to greet her and immediately broke down into a flood of tears. Mum put her arms around me and just held me for a while. She said, 'Frank, none of us are ever prepared for such times as these we can only endure the pain and gather strength from each other. Your Pa sends his condolences and says be strong.'

We went to the chapel of rest at the hospital where we paid our last goodbyes to Carmen who lay in her coffin. I placed a red rose in her hand and bent over and kissed her she looked so beautiful how could God have done this to me after all the prayers I had said asking him for help.

We made our way to the church for the service. We were greeted by the vicar or priest as they call them in Spain. His words of condolences and the mysterious workings of God fell on deaf ears as far as I was concerned there was no God. The hearse arrived and the coffin carried into the church and placed in front of the altar. The priest started the service and one or two hymns were sung. I was just a zombie looking on; I gazed at the coffin and could only picture one thing my beautiful Carmen lying dead inside. She had looked so beautiful we had agreed to lay her to rest dressed in her wedding gown and that is the picture of her that is locked forever in my heart and mind.

Mum and Aunt Rosa were to return to England early next morning so after the funeral and a light wake we made our way back home. Carlos unharnessed the carriage whilst the rest of us went inside the Casa. Papa disappeared whilst Momma and Aunt Rosa prepared drinks under the Naya. Mum sat by me and took my arm. 'I want you to be strong, Frank, for yourself and for the family, remember it's their loss too, not just yours. I want you to promise me that you will help each other over this – don't just think of yourself. Carmen would want you to help them too.' I made my promise and said I would make a good effort for us all.

The days that followed were very difficult, the weather was hotting up and the work was hard: ploughing in-between the vines and clearing the weeds. Carlos would drive the tractor whilst I used the hoe. Momma and Poppa were busy in the bottling plant with the help of Rosita. I never went back into our casa after the funeral I moved back into the family casa and slept in Carlo's room. He didn't mind. The problem was I couldn't sleep – my mind wouldn't let me. I would get up in the night and sit under the naya with a glass or two of wine reflecting the past. Carmen was never out of my mind: I wished often that I could die and be with her I felt so lonely. In an effort to sleep I took to drinking, first of all wine but that didn't send me into oblivion what I was seeking. One day I decided to take a walk into the village where I browsed around the shops. Whisky held my attention as I looked around the Bodega. I purchased two bottles which I took home and hid in the winery. As the summer grew hotter I became more depressed what it was all for I asked myself. I became more dependent on the whisky to bring me solace and to launch me into oblivion every night that was the only way I could escape the torment which was destroying my mind. I would walk through the vines sometimes very late at night calling for Carmen. I missed her so much but my life was being taken over by demons brought on by the whisky which I thought was helping me. I became a burden to the family I had promised to help. Most days I was in a drunken stupor unable to help anyone. Carlos would wake me up every morning when he got up but most days I would drop off back to sleep and awake another couple of hours later, by then everybody else had had breakfast and would be working.

I was sitting in the naya one morning eating a cold breakfast when momma came in for something. She looked at me in disgust. 'Carlos needs help,' she said sharply, 'when are you going to pull yourself together.' I looked at her with bleary eyes, I felt ashamed but my head just couldn't cope. I got up and walked out. I could see Carlos in the fields with the spraying pack on his back. It was late morning and the sun was getting hot. I walked over to where the equipment was kept and tried to put the other pack on my back but I could hardly manage it. Poppa came over and told me he would do it himself as I was in no condition to help anyone. I felt ashamed.

Three months had passed since Carmen had died. I had not visited her grave or been to church with the rest of the family. I was a drunkard capable only of walking into the village and replenishing my ticket to oblivion. The man in the bodega knew me quite well and would reach for the two bottles of whisky as soon as he saw me. No words were ever spoken I just paid him and left the shop. On one of these frequent occasions I was leaving the bodega when I noticed that a new shop had opened opposite. I walked across the street and looked at the large poster in the window. It showed a large snow covered mountain with trees and valleys. The sun reflected off the whiteness of the snow dazzling me. I could feel the coolness shrouding my body as I gazed at the poster. It was a holiday poster advertising holidays in Switzerland. The new shop was a travel agency. I went in and asked for a brochure and if they had a small poster like the one in the window.

That evening we sat around the table I promised that next day I would be ready for work. I asked Carlos to drag me out of bed if necessary. No one spoke they just looked at me and shook their heads. Momma eventually asked me why I wasn't living in the casa Poppa had had built for us. I just looked at her and got up and left the table. I couldn't tell her that I could never live in there again without Carmen. I would see her everywhere I looked, no, I could never do it.

I tried to pull myself together but without the whisky I could never sleep that was my ticket to oblivion. I gave it my best but the family treated me coldly. I would retreat to the winery where I kept my supply of whisky. I sat on a bail of straw and gazed at the picture of the mountains in Switzerland they seemed to beckon me. I always felt the coolness enshrouding me. One day after a hot day in the vineyards, I picked up the holiday brochure and walked into the village, this time I didn't go into the bodega I went into the travel agency and enquired about Switzerland. That evening as we sat around the table I announced that I would be leaving. It was a surprise to them all. Momma was very hurtful. 'So you are running away, Franco, well we all can't do that some of us have to face the future, I wonder what Carmen would have said.' I told Momma that I had to get away to find myself. The heat was getting to me and it wasn't helping me come to terms with my loss, Poppa said it was their loss too.

I wasn't very popular; Momma and Poppa became distant, only Carlos remained friendly. He said when I was ready to leave he would drive me to the station. I phoned the station to enquire about trains only to find that due to problems arising the services had been disrupted and it would be advisable just to turn up and see what was available. I had given no thought whatsoever to what was happening in Europe, with Hitler invading everywhere. I had been too engrossed with my own problems to take any notice of worldwide actions. It appeared as if Hitler was invading Europe and the threat of war with England was inevitable.

It wasn't my war and I didn't want to get involved. I started packing my suitcase. All I wanted was peace and quiet and to be allowed to fight the war going on inside my head. Momma fetched my clothes from inside our casa and asked what to do with other personal things. I said it would be good if Carlos and Rosita got married and lived in the casa and made use of anything left behind. Momma asked if ever I was coming back. I told her I did not know. We gathered in the naya the night before I was due to leave, I had an early train to catch so it was best to say our goodbyes then. Momma looked at me with tear filled eyes, she said nothing but gave me a big hug. Poppa started talking. 'Franco, you are still our son-in-law and you have a share in this estate, I will still put money into your account, don't forget if ever you need anything. We hope this isn't a final farewell.' He shook hands and embraced me. Momma and Poppa retired for the night leaving Carlos and myself. We looked at each other and reached over to shake hands. Carlos erupted in a floor of tears. 'I'm sorry to see you go, Franco, I have enjoyed having you as my brother-in-law, perhaps when you have had time to adjust you will come back to us amigo.' I told him the pony and float was his and that he and Rosita should get married and take over the casa. Maybe I will come back one day but only for a visit. We shook hands at the station and we embraced. 'Adios me amigo,' he said. I boarded the train which was a straight through one from Barcelona to Zurich I didn't have to wait long and then there were lots of people getting on.

Part 3

I was hoping to get a carriage to myself but I was disappointed when two women with young children entered and put their luggage on the racks. I sat by the window gazing out at the scenery as the train pulled out. The two children also sat opposite me looking at what was going on but after a while they became unsettled and moved restlessly around the compartment. I suddenly felt an irritation in my throat and began to cough. I reached for my handkerchief to cover my mouth. The two women looked at me and said something to the children who immediately moved further away from me. I had purchased a Spanish newspaper, not to read but to cover the English book I was reading. The two women talked between themselves in a language I didn't understand, they were probably Swiss.

The journey seemed endless as the hours ticked by. The children seemed bored and started to play up a bit. Another spasm of coughing and they moved away to the other end of the compartment. After a while the scenery started to change. Mountains and rivers emerged making it more interesting to look at. The ticket collector came along and punched our tickets. 'Zurich one hour,' he said. I immersed into my book gazing out at the mountain range, their high peaks in the distance reflecting the afternoon sun on the snow covered slopes.

As the train pulled into the station I reached for my luggage and stood waiting to set foot in Switzerland. One thing I noticed immediately was the temperature, it was a bit nippy. I made my way to the exit where I had to produce my passport. I was asked where I was going and how long for. I was a bit vague on my duration as I was on my destination. I told the man I was taking a holiday for health reasons and had not decided how long I was staying. I also said I wanted to travel around a bit and take a look at their beautiful country. I was treated suspiciously and suddenly it occurred to me why. Germany was sweeping through Europe and had been threatened by Britain that if it did not stop we could be at war. I had picked up bits of information from the Spanish newspaper but I did not fully understand the situation.

I followed the crowd out of the station into the busy streets looking for some kind of hotel where I could relax for a couple of days until I got my bearings. I didn't want to stay in the city I wanted peace and quiet for a few days whilst I decided what I was going to do. I passed a couple of expensive-looking hotels in the main street I decided to try one of the side streets leading off and was soon rewarded by a sign in the window of bier Keller or gasthouse whatever they were called. I was greeted warmly as I entered the building. The young woman smiled and beckoned me to follow her to the reception. I asked for a single room for three days and enquired about food. She spoke perfect English and asked where I was from. There was a small lift leading to the second floor and a young man helped with my luggage. The room was light and airy and looked out onto a courtyard which had tables and chairs placed around it. Through the trees surrounding the courtyard far away in the distance I saw the snow-capped mountains glistening in the afternoon sunlight. I started to unpack my suitcase. The Spanish newspaper lay on the bed bearing the news about the German invasion of Europe. I glanced at the date of the newspaper and uttered a cry of surprise. It was my birthday and I hadn't even noticed. Suddenly a pang of unhappiness shot through my body as I realised it was just one year ago that Carmen had announced that she was pregnant. I immediately flopped on the bed amidst a flood of tears as the past years events erupted in my mind. The journey had given me a temporary break from the heartache of losing Carmen and my baby. I must have cried myself to sleep helped by a tired body and an aching heart.

"It was early evening when I woke up, the sun had disappeared and an eerie darkness engulfed the bedroom. I rose quickly and switched on the lights. I began to feel hunger pains. I put on my jacket leaving the unpacking for later. Taking the lift I descended to the ground floor and followed the smell of food. The young receptionist saw me and pointed towards a door opening into a small restaurant where a waiter greeted me and showed me to a table overlooking the courtyard. A wine list and menu were handed to me. With the eruption of memories still wracking my brain I asked for a large whisky. I looked at the menu and struggled to make out what was what. The waiter tried to explain some of the delicacies and we finally decided on potatoes, a pork steak and green vegetables. His command of the English language was about as good as mine of the Spanish language but we managed to sort something out and he understood when I asked for another whisky.

After a hearty meal I went back to my room to finish unpacking. The map I had brought from the travel agency lay on the bed. I opened it up and tried to follow roads and railways etc. but unless map reading is your profession it becomes a blur of lines and squiggles. However, I did look at the names of towns and villages which the railway seemed to pass through but again they were just mysterious destinations on a large sheet of paper. Some of the names were that small I could not make them out so I decided that tomorrow I would invest in a magnifying glass.

The meal, especially the two whiskies had me feeling drowsy so I decided on an early night hoping I would sink into oblivion.

I awoke early next morning with the sun streaming through the window. I had forgotten to close the draw over curtains. A quick shower, shave and fresh clothing I was ready for breakfast. I chose sausage, scrambled eggs and tomatoes with two slices of toast. That would set me up nicely for a day's look around. The coffee gave me an extra boost.

The streets were busy even at ten o'clock in the morning. I guess the sunshine brings people out. As I browsed around the shops I couldn't help noticing how calm I felt and very relaxed. I figured it was the cool fresh air blowing in from the mountains a remarkable and welcome change from the hot sun and vineyards that I had left behind. People seemed friendly and would encourage conversation. Changing to speaking English when they realised you were not a local. I found a stationery shop and looked around for a magnifying glass. I chose a big one to explore the small villages on the map. It was fun and relaxing walking along the streets in the lovely autumn sunshine. I went into bookshops and estate agents just looking at places of interest. In one estate agent a young girl asked if I was planning a holiday. I told her that I was looking for a small village which opened up in the mountains where I could walk freely in the cool fresh air. She invited me to sit with her at her desk then ordered me a coffee and then opened up a very large book of maps. She pointed out where we were then asked how I would be travelling. When I said the railway was my only option she began following the tracks with her finger naming several little villages she thought would be appropriate. As we scanned the map she told me how far we had travelled and what interests were available. She was very knowledgeable and knew her job. She also said she lived in a small village an hour's drive away and also liked walking in the mountains. She also went in for rock climbing and skiing. I said that would not be what I was looking for. As I watched her trace her finger along the railway lines on the map I saw lots of names I could not read because of the small print. I leaned over and produced my new magnifying glass. She pushed the map closer and indicated several small villages accessible by rail. She said that most of them were small farming communities and was doubtful if there would be much in the way of entertainment on offer. I told her that I was looking for peace and quiet and seclusion. There was one big town a two-hour train journey which also offered a small shuttle train service around the farming communities. I looked along the rail track to where she had indicated. My attention was drawn to a small village a little further on. I gasped with surprise as I peered through the glass. I pointed to the name 'Carmen', 'What is this?' I asked. She looked. 'Oh that's just a quiet village, a few shops a couple of pubs and a small station where the shuttle train passed through. A farming community that's all nothing really exciting.' I told her I would want to go and visit the village it sounded ideal. She said I would have to book at the railway station their office had nothing on offer there. I asked her to write the name down for me which she did. She also gave me a copy of the map.

I returned to the bier Keller, had a quick lunch and disappeared to my room, my heart was beating like a drum so I had a quick whisky to help me cope. I opened up my large map on the bed and traced the railway track alongside the map the girl had given me. With the aid of my magnifying glass I retraced the railway lines to where the girl had pointed out the small town. From there the shuttle train to Carmen. My heart was pounding, 'I must go there' I said to myself. It was still early in the day so I put on my coat and made for the station, map in hand. The ticket office was still open so I asked when the next train would be leaving for Bern. I was told there would be one in an hour or I could catch one the next day at one o'clock. I booked my ticket for the next day. I also asked about the shuttle train. I was told it ran about every half an hour. I was excited and looking forward to my journey. As I packed my suitcase I kept looking at the map. Suddenly a fear gripped me, what was I doing, I was becoming obsessed, what was I doing in Switzerland when I should be over in Spain helping out in the vineyard supporting Carmen's family, I wondered if I was losing my senses. Grief had really taken over should I seek help before I went too far. I sat on the bed and mulled it over in my mind. I had worked myself up into a frenzy. I finished packing and went downstairs to reception I paid my bill and asked if I could have an early lunch before I caught the train. As I sat down for my meal the waiter asked what I would like to drink. 'Whisky please,' I said anticipating a restless night. If I didn't sink into oblivion when I hit the pillow I would be in for a night of torture as my bitter experiences ran through my mind. Another whisky and I went to my room and got ready for bed. As my head hit the pillow and the room started to spin I sank into a deep sleep.

Again I had forgotten to pull the draw over curtains and the brilliant sunshine lit up the room introducing me to another dawn. Breakfast was simple and I soon found myself walking down the street towards the shops. The travel agency was open and as I peered inside the young girl looked up from her desk and saw me. I stepped into the shop and gave her a big smile. 'I'm booked on the one o'clock train,' I said. She returned the smile. 'I hope it's what you want, if not come back and we will try again.'

I passed the time away just browsing around the shops at 12 o'clock I made my way back to my room and gathered up my belongings and made my way down to the restaurant. It was 12:45 and I was standing on the platform waiting for the train. During my moments of contemplation I had reached a decision. I would find my way to Carmen, stay there a few days just doing what I had planned to walk in the mountains on my own and see if I could find myself. If I did not find peace of mind I would return to Spain and seek help.

The train to Bern took just over an hour. I gazed at the surrounding countryside encased by the high and low peaks of the mountains. It was farming land and some of the fields glistened in the afternoon sunshine enriched by whatever crops had been sown. I could smell the countryside and the freshness of the cool air gave me a lift. I stood on the platform waiting for the shuttle. It was a narrow gauge railway having two carriages, enough for the numbers of passengers who used it. Every little village it passed through apparently held its own market on different days and the locals used the train at different times depending on which market they wanted. I sat by a woman passenger who chatted away freely. She enquired which village I was visiting and said how pretty it was, she was going to the next village for her vegetables and eggs. The train rumbled on at about 15kms an hour my village was the second stop. Soon I was standing on a small platform watching the train slowly puff away. A few yards away the main street into the village opened up. There were a reasonable amount of people walking about doing their shopping or standing in groups talking. No one took any notice as I walked through the village looking for some suitable accommodation. I stopped outside what I took to be a small hotel. There were signs in the window which I could not read but assumed was advertising rooms to let. I opened the door leading into a lobby and was greeted by a pleasant young girl, slightly younger than myself. She said something but I shrugged my shoulders and said English please. She immediately broke into perfect English. I don't know why it is but these foreigners seem to know our language better than we do. I asked for a single room but only booked for one week just in case it wasn't the place for me. I also booked breakfast and evening meals. I was shown to a room on the second floor with views to the mountains it was perfect. Meals were served from six o'clock down stairs unless I wanted to take my meals in my room. I opted to use the diner downstairs.

I unpacked my suitcase and changed out of my travelling clothes before descending down stairs. It was very quiet in the hotel and only a handful of people occupied the diner. The girl once again presented herself with the menu and asked if the room was suitable. I had not been there very long but already I was consumed by the friendliness of the people. Even strangers entering or leaving the diner would smile and greet me as if they had known me forever. The waitress who wore a badge on her lapel bore the name Christina was very friendly asking me if I had been there before. I said that this was my first time to Switzerland and how beautiful it was. I said I was just visiting and taking a short break, I also said I wanted to go for walks in the mountains. She said it was a lovely experience but I would need to get some good walking shoes and warm clothing as it can get quite cold up there.

The following morning brought some lovely sunshine. I ate a hearty breakfast and hit the streets browsing the shops looking for the things I would need. The boots came first a lovely comfortable pair of fur lined leather boots. They weren't cheap but what the hell. Jumpers and trousers followed with warm socks included and a pair of gloves just in case. A fur Russian type hat was offered but I settled for a woolly hat instead.

With my purchases I headed back to the hotel and tried everything on. I felt ready to tackle the mountains. The light waterproof jacket I had brought with me seemed tight on top of everything but I thought it would do. As I made my way downstairs I met Christina on her way up with fresh bedding. She looked me over and gave her approval but suggested I need a warmer jacket if it got any colder. She asked if I was going walking in the mountains. I said I was about to try it. She said I should keep one eye on the weather and one eye where I put my foot. She also suggested not to venture too far for the first time and to keep looking back to where I came from. It was important as I would need to find my way back. She looked at her watch. "You must be back before six or I will have to notify the rescue team." She laughed but I think she meant it.

I walked through the village until I reached the last shop which was an ironmonger. The street turned into a lane just about wide enough for a horse and cart which was about the only kind of traffic passing through the village. Well it made sense really, this was a farming community. The absence of motorised vehicles seemed to make this the perfect place. Occasional wide footpaths would lead off the main street and disappear into narrow country lanes. The name Carmen appeared above a few of the shop windows which brought on a spell of the blues reminding me of my loss and the reason I was here. It was a strange feeling but it was peaceful.

I followed the lane for another two hundred yards until I came to a five barred gate leading into what appeared to be a farm. I stood and looked not knowing if I would be trespassing if I ventured further. The farm house and other buildings lay off to the left and stood back about one hundred and fifty yards away the grassed field contained a few sheep grazing peacefully. I noticed a small gate to the side which appeared to be for walkers to enter the field. I passed through and stood looking at the farm with the smoke curling upwards from the chimney. A man came out of the barn and gazed in my direction he called out and waved. I waved back and started to follow the path up into the woodland. The man started casually towards me and held out his hand in a friendly manner. I shook his hand and bid him "good morning" he reciprocated in a sort of mixed language. I pointed up into the mountains commenting on their beauty and serenity. His wife came out and called his name, he beckoned her over and said something. She held out her hand and introduced themselves as Ingerborg and Hans. I said my name was Franco and I was just going for a walk in the mountains. They both eyed me up and down and remarked on my clothing. "Very good," said Ingerborg. Hans was looking up at the sky and pointed "Not too far today" he managed to say in pigeon English. Ingerberg said the weather changes quickly. "You must not be more than two hours." I thanked them and made my way up the gradual slope. Entering the timberland I looked back. The village looked very picturesque and the smoke curling up through the trees made it look homely.

I turned right as I ventured the wooded area and followed what may have once been a track not used much recently as the vegetation indicated. I had begun climbing gradually although I hadn't noticed. I came to a semi steep bank which I decided to climb, off to the left. It took me away from the woods and I found myself climbing gradually. I could now see over the tops of the trees and had a lovely view of the village and surrounding countryside. In the distance I saw the smoke from the shuttle train making its way into the countryside. Occasionally its whistle would echo and reverberate through the mountains. I climbed higher looking back over my shoulder. I came across a large slab with initials carved into it, evidence that I was not the only visitor to this place. I checked my watch and was surprised to find that the first hour had slipped away very quickly. I sat on the rock and looked round. Eagles riding high on the thermals caught my attention and as I surveyed the area other wild life came into view rabbits, squirrels scampered through the undergrowth. I sat for ten minutes and then started to make my way back I had had my first taste of the mountains. I felt an inner calmness that I had not felt in the vineyards.

Hans was working outside the barn when I emerged from the woodland, he raised his hand and I walked over to see what he was doing. Ingerborg came out and greeted me warmly. They both asked if I had enjoyed my walk to which I replied that I had found it very stimulating.

I asked Hans what he was doing he said the barn door was rotting away and needed replacing. He was trying to manoeuvre it to the ground so that he could measure up for some wood. I helped him move the door into a suitable position so it could be laid flat on the ground. It was almost falling to pieces, a big door and quite heavy. I looked at it and checked the condition. It wanted a couple of replacements. I said to Hans it would be a waste of time and money trying to patch it up. He scratched his head and agreed. He picked up his tape measure and began measuring. I told him I would measure if he wrote everything down. We worked well as a team and Ingerborg kept us supplied with hot coffee. When all was written down I checked the steel hinges. They were quite robust and reusable. Hans thanked me and said he would get the new wood tomorrow. I said I would make the door for him if he could get the wood and had some decent tools. Ingerborg told Hans that we must not put on me as I was on holiday. I assured her that tomorrow was my day off from walking and I would come and gladly help. Hans took me into the barn and opened up a cupboard which housed a complete set of tools, saws, hammers, chisels, the lot and they looked quite new. Ingerborg said it was a present from their children two years ago when Hans was sixty. I checked the list of timber and gave it back to Hans, he said he would be at the timber yard first thing tomorrow.

At the hotel, Christina asked if I had enjoyed my walk. I told her that I had climbed as far as the flat rock where all the initials were she replied that hers was up there somewhere.

I enjoyed my evening meal and then went and sat in the bar and ordered a drink. Half an hour later a well-dressed man in his fifties entered the bar and bought himself a beer. He looked around at the few people in there and then walked over to my table and introduced himself as Dietre the librarian. He had seen me in the village and guessed I was a traveller. I said I was a visitor just finding my way around and how pleasant I had found the village and how friendly everyone had been. He asked if he could sit down and join me. He was just enjoying his one beer of the day before he went home. He asked if I was English or perhaps Spanish. He remarked on my tan and asked if Switzerland was warm enough for me. We sat chatting away simply exchanging polite conversation. I asked why it was that almost everyone I had met could speak English. He laughed; it was our second language and was taught in schools throughout Switzerland. I commented that in England we never had a second language. He also said that many people also spoke German which he thought might be appropriate considering what was happening with the war. I replied I had no idea what was happening in Europe as I did not want to get involved, it wasn't my war, and I did not start it. We changed the subject and he then asked how long I was staying in Carmen. I laughed a little "I like it so much I might stay forever." He finished his beer and got up to leave. "That might be a good idea my friend."

Christina came over and picked up the empty glasses. "I see you have met Dietre, he's a nice man so polite."

The following morning I lay in until nine-thirty. The weather looked grey and miserable it had clouded over and had started to rain. I showered and dressed and laid out the map on the bed. I was looking to see if there were any sort of trails or paths going through the mountains, I couldn't find any. I had breakfast and went back up to my room for my waterproof jacket. As I walked through the gate to the farm I could see Hans was unloading the wood from the cart. He must have harnessed the horse and cart and gone out very early. Ingerberg waved as I approached she was helping to unload. I greeted them both warmly and examined the timber. I suggested to Hans that we should work undercover in the barn in case it rained. We cleared a space on the floor and laid out the timber. Hans asked if I had done anything like this before. I laughed uncontrollably to his and Ingerberg's amusement. I removed my jacket and got stuck in. Hans tried to take charge but I told him to make the coffee. Ingerberg watched as I expertly did what I was trained for. Midday and the frame was half constructed. Hans did whatever I asked him to do and suddenly realised I was the professional. We stopped for lunch and Hans started pumping me for information. I told him I was a qualified carpenter and was enjoying myself. He laughed and asked how long I would be staying.

The afternoon brought a finished door moved outside ready for hanging. The door was quite heavy. Eight foot high and six feet wide and that was just half of the barn door as it happened the other half was okay. Hans was well pleased.

I went back to my hotel and had a shower and changed. There were a few more people in the restaurant probably people passing through or locals treating themselves. After my meal I went into the bar; there was only one man sitting in the corner with his beer. I ordered a beer and was just paying when I felt a hand on my shoulder.

"Good evening, my friend, let me buy that for you," Dietre stood by my side smiling and asked if I had had a good day. He asked me to join him and began to walk over to the man in the corner. They shook hands and Dietre introduced me to his very good friend Heinreiche who kept the ironmongers shop just up the street. "Heinreiche meet my new friend from England his name is Franco but we will call him Franz that's the Swiss version." Heinreiche stood up and held out his hand. He was at least six feet two inches and about nineteen stones he had a very warm smile which put me at ease straight away. His English was pretty good but with a strong accent. Dietre went on to say Heinreiche had moved to Switzerland many years ago and refused to leave he loved it that much. I said I could understand why and said I was very impressed myself. We talked small talk for an hour, I replenished the empty glasses.

Eventually the conversation got around to the German invasion of Europe. Heinreiche asked me how long I was staying. I said I was booked into the hotel for another week. He looked at me serious. "Franz, do not go back to England, your country is now at war with Germany you will be killed. Stay here with my friend you will be safe. Switzerland has declared its neutrality and has refused to take any part or join any side in the ridiculous war." Dietre, agreed it was best not to get involved. Heinreiche seemed rather upset. He said he was a German but had abandoned his country because of the warlike attitude and warned us about this so called Fuehrer who was hell bent on world domination. He called Hitler the Arch Angel an evil man who would lead Germany into destruction "stay, here, Franz, you will be safe here."

As I lay in my bed pondering over the evenings events I really began to think about the possibilities of staying in Switzerland. The following morning brought a ray of sunshine streaming through the window. I dressed for a walk in the mountains. Hans was up the ladder creosoting the new door. He waved I said I was going on a walk about. As I climbed I could feel the air changing. It was getting cooler although the sun lit up the landscape. I got as far as the flat rock and looked around. The left looked a bit easier to walk on so I branched off and made my way along. I was still climbing higher and the village was now in the distance. I studied the way ahead of me and followed an easier way up to another lever. Not forgetting to look back I piled three pieces of rock on top of each other to mark my trail. I looked at my watch two hours had nearly passed by. I made my way down, Hans and Ingerborg were standing outside of the house. They waved as soon as they saw me and I walked over to them. They said they were getting a bit worried about me. Ingerborg invited me in for a coffee I told them that I had ventured a little further and that there was no cause for alarm. Hans asked how many more days were left of my holiday. I said my hotel was booked for another four days. Ingerborg said she would be sorry to see me go, and Hans chipped in that England was ready for war with Germany. I sat drinking my coffee, I said that Heinreiche had mentioned that I should stay here. Hans looked at me surprised. "Yes, that's what you should do, it would be too dangerous to travel, Franz, why don't you?"

Ingerborg chimed in, "You could stay here with us, Franz, we have room for you and you wouldn't have to pay anything, we would be glad to have you, isn't that so, Hans?"

Hans nodded his head, "Yes, Franz, please stay with us and be safe." I sat there pondering it over, maybe they were right. England was in trouble and I wasn't sure about Spain. I was still having bitter memories maybe a little more time was needed. I told them that they had convinced me and that I would move in when I had checked out at the hotel but only on condition I work to pay for my keep.

When I told Dietre and Heinreiche that evening they assured me that I had made a wise decision. Heinreiche asked what job I had been doing, I mentioned working on a vineyard in Spain and that I was a qualified carpenter. He clapped his hand. "That's just what we need in Carmen, a carpenter," he laughed.

Part 4

I moved into the farm, it was early autumn and I could feel it getting colder. Ingerborg had made up a nice room at the back of the farmhouse and Hans had cleared out the small fireplace and had already prepared it for a fire. "I will light it and air the place out a bit," he said.

I settled in and helped Hans around the farm, he taught me to harness the horse and cart and drive around the field distributing feed for the animals. The huge compound at the back of the farm was where he kept the sheep during the winter months.

I didn't venture into the mountains if the weather wasn't right. Hans would say if it was going to be fine. Heinreiche asked me to call into his shop when I had time. It was a rainy day when I got around to calling on him. He asked if I could renew all the shelves and other things that were in need of repair. I said I could and starting taking measurements. Hans said I could borrow the horse and cart and Heinreiche showed me the way to the timber yard. I worked solidly for a week on his shop and he was highly delighted with the finished result. He asked how much he owed me. I said for a friend it was free but he shoved a wad of notes in my hand. I gave half back to him saying I might need a favour off him one day.

Ingerborg or Hans never questioned me about my past but one night as we were preparing for Christmas, putting up the Christmas tree, I had a flashback of Carmen and me doing the same thing. It was a very emotional moment and all of a sudden a flood of tears erupted down my face. Ingerborg thought I was ill and pushed me into my room where I completely broke down. I lay on the bed and let the tears flow. Ingerborg left me alone for a while and then came back with a hot chocolate drink. I don't know what it is but women can sense when there is something hidden away inside. She sat on the bed and asked me to unload my heartache. I poured my heart out to her and she listened without any interruptions. When I reached the part where I had left Spain she put her arms around me and just held me for quite a while. "I knew there was something hidden inside of you causing you pain, you have suffered a terrible and heart wrenching experience, Franz, it is good that you have shared it with me."

I had a good night's sleep, maybe it was a release from all the tension welling up inside me or what but I woke up refreshed and the sun shining in my face. I dressed in my walking gear ready to tackle the mountains. The smell of bacon greeted me as I entered the dining room. Hans was already tucking into a hearty breakfast and Ingerborg filled me a plate of bacon and eggs. Hans greeted me and said it was a good morning for a walk. He finished his breakfast and said he was cleaning out the pigs this morning. Ingerborg smiled at me and came round and gave me a huge hug. She said what you have done was the right decision to get away for a while. She said she admired my courage.

On the high peaks the snow glistened in the morning sun and I watched as the hawks and the eagles searched for their prey. I reached the highest point I had been on the previous visit and scanned the layout before me. I tried different paths searching for an easy accessible route to follow. I sat on a rock and had a sudden idea. I should get a compass and a map and mark out my route. I tried several options before I chose one to follow. I wasn't a nanny goat I needed an easy path to follow if I was to fulfil my dream. That was to find an easy trail into the heart of these mountains. It was very challenging and I looked forward to it every day.

When the snow came everything had to be put on hold, I helped around the farm there was always plenty to do. I found a job inside the farm house, cupboards in need of repair, chairs a bit rickety and I built Ingerborg a new work surface in the kitchen she was delighted. She worked hard too, the eggs had to be collected for her to take to the market every Friday as well as the cakes and pies she baked. Hans had to make sure the cows were milked as well as the goats. These two people would put any English work force to shame. Only after the evening meal would they sit down in front of a lovely log fire and read the newspaper and listen to the radio. There was a nice comfortable settee in front of the fire with an armchair either side one of which was allocated to me.

Hans would during the summer months take the horse up into the woods to the felled trees and drag them down to the farm where I would take my turn cutting them into logs for the fire. Gas was connected throughout the village but you could always see smoke coming out of the chimneys of some of the houses. They had all the services to the village, main sewers, electricity, and running water. It had all the mod cons but it also had all the characteristics of a quaint rural village.

Ingerborg would be up early Friday morning gathering her goods ready for market. She would take heavy baskets into the village and then come back for more. She said she enjoyed it and meeting friends who came from the other villages to shop. Of course there was hours spent on gossip and Ingerborg would also buy goods.

Christmas was a village affair with the town or village hall decorated out for the festivities, music and dancing and at some time during the day everybody in the village would make an appearance and have fun. Evening time everybody would drift off to their own homes where they would enjoy their own private activities. As we walked back to the farm through the few inches of snow, they both agreed that they always enjoyed Christmas. So did I. I had danced with Christina from the bierkella and also Olga from the travel agents. Not once did I hear any referral to the war but if people met in small groups in the restaurant or bierkellers they would talk in hushed whispers. My best information was from Heinreiche who seemed to know everything.

The Germans were rampaging through Europe causing havoc and destruction they had been supported by the Italians. Heinreiche was very bitter about his countrymen and their leader.

Spring came as the winter eased and the heavy snows began to disperse. A bit of spring sunshine lightened everybody's heart. The snowdrops and crocuses began to appear in the gardens bringing a splash of colour to the village. I looked longingly up into the mountains itching to get up there. Hans warned me not to be too anxious as melting snow sent lots of water cascading through the many gullies running through them and could be very dangerous. I waited patiently for the weather conditions to improve. I told myself there was no rush, the mountains weren't going to disappear.

Heinreiche greeted me as I walked into his shop. I browsed around not quite sure what I was looking for. I had had an idea that was circulating through my mind to camp out in the mountains and instead of returning home every day I could stay and then move on a bit further each day this would save a lot of time. I would of course have to return at times to replenish food supplies and fresh clothes. Heinreiche showed me some small one man bivouacs which the skiing fraternity used when they went on skiing trips. They were very light and came all packed up in a little bundle. Sleeping bags, oil lamps small stoves he had everything I needed in his shop. He told me to be careful not to overload myself. He reached a frame backpack off the shelf and fitted it to my back. Then the bivouac was placed on it and then the sleeping bag, lamp and stove were added with spare canisters of gas, then my cooking tins and plate.

He asked if it was getting heavy. I said it was comfortable. He said it would get heavier the higher I climbed and the longer I walked carrying it. I saw his point. I told him I was planning to make a trail through the mountains that would be easily accessible and that I planned to do it in easy stages. I would make camp after travelling for two hours and establish camps along the trail. I would return every two days to replenish my stocks. He said I was mad but I wasn't hurting anyone so why not, but I must be careful if I got hurt or anything nobody would know where I was. I told him about my little pile of rocks I used as my guide. I asked him how he knew so much. He laughed at me. "When I was your age I was in the German army and was on ski patrol in the mountains and if he had been younger he would have come with me." He said he was jealous. I took my goods and went back to the farm. Ingerborg and Hans asked what I was planning to do. I told them what I had planned but would wait another couple of weeks for the weather to settle.

Ingerborg asked why I was doing it and I replied, "I don't know, I just feel as I have to do it."

She looked at me and said, "There's something calling you, Franz, but be careful."

I reached my first base camp within the predicted two hours and set about establishing my camp. I found a nice flat spot sheltered from the wind and erected my bivvy. The ground was safe so I rolled out my sleeping bag and tried it for comfort. There was still plenty of daylight left so I went walkabout looking for my next trail. I tried different routes it was important not to have to climb up rock faces it had to be relatively easygoing.

That first night was nice, I had used my little stove to cook a meal, beans and sausage, and they went down well. My lanterns provided both warmth and light so that I could mark my map. Heinreiche had shown me how to use the compass and to plot my course on the map. The tent flapped about a bit during the night but apart from that all was quiet. I was awakened early by the screeching of birds I climbed out of my sleeping bag and went to investigate. A flock of birds were attacking an eagle who was poaching on their territory, it was interesting to watch as they saw the eagle off. I made my breakfast, coffee and homemade cakes that Ingerborg had made for me. Heinreiche had told me that I should find plenty of pools of water amongst the rocks which I did and enjoyed a nice freshwater wash.

I now felt it was time to proceed further and establish camp two. I would go back to the farm and purchase another bivvy and sleeping bag I didn't want to move camp in case I had an off day and wanted to rest.

I was greeted enthusiastically by Ingerborg and Hans they always treated me like a long lost son. I told them that I would be off again in a couple of days and they accepted that. Heinreiche was always pleased to see me, he was a good friend and soon fixed me up with things I wanted. He asked me to join him in the beirkeller that evening for a drink he said Dietre had been asking about me. I went back to the farm and asked if anything important needed doing. Ingerborg said we should start stocking up with logs for the winter, although it wasn't even summer yet. I harnessed up the horse and went into the woodland where Hans had already been felling trees. He was in the field checking the sheep and lambs − some of which were sold for slaughter. He waved as he saw me leading the horse towards the woodland. After several journeys dragging the cut trees down to the farm, I unharnessed the horse and prepared the trees for sawing. They would dry out in the sun and when I came down from the mountains next time I would cut them up into logs. We ate our evening meal and chatted away like any normal family. Hans had sorted some lambs and couple of sheep out ready to be collected by the slaughter man enough to pay some bills and provide meat for our own consumption. I had noticed behind the barn a strip of land that wasn't being used for anything except storing old broken down machinery. I asked Hans if I could use it to cultivate a small garden it was only twenty metres by fifty metres just lying there producing nothing. Hans said I could do whatever I wanted.

Later that evening I sauntered down into the village to the beirkeller, Dietre and Heinreiche greeted me and Heinreiche ordered a bier for me. They had been discussing the war but they subject changed to my activities. I told Heinreiche I was about to move further into the mountains. Dietre said I must be mad I should be setting myself up in business as a carpenter and making some money. He also said he had been looking at some old maps of the area but had found nothing of interest, not trails or anything. I asked if it was possible to send out letters to England and Spain. Dieter said it would not be easy due to the war but had received some books and things through the post. Heinreiche said he had received some brochures. He suggested I write my letter and give them to him and he would ask a friend to post them in Zurich.

I trundled my way back into the mountains with my supplies and made it to camp one. I planned to breakout early next morning and find camp two. I had ventured so far but had not made it as far as I wanted. After an early breakfast I set off leaving camp one tied down and secure. I travelled for about an hour over ground I had previously investigated but I wanted to push on further before I stopped for the day. I was on a sort of level plateau, high mountains to my left and a sheer drop into a valley on my right. I ventured a little higher to my left seeking an easy access along the plateau. After an hour of walking across easy accessible terrain I paused and decided to break for lunch. I sat on a rock and viewed the surrounding terrain. To my left I could see high mountains reaching up into the sky like a finger pointing upwards. The snow covered top glistened in the afternoon sunlight. I estimated it was a good couple of miles further inland. I sat there thinking I could get a good view from up there. On my right there was a wide gully running parallel to the cliff edge but about twenty-five metres away and there was a patch of the greenest grass I had seen for a long time. I decided to set up camp two and that patch of grass looked ideal. I clambered down into the gulley and tested the ground. It was very hard but the grass softened it a bit. My bivvy didn't take long to put up and soon my camp two was established.

The sun was still shining, I check my watch it was still early afternoon; I clambered back up the bank and stood looking at that high snow covered peak. I reckoned about an hour's walking would get me to the foot of it. With my binoculars around my neck I set off, my curiosity was overwhelming me I found it pretty easy going with just the occasional steep climb but it was a bit further away than I thought. I reached the foot of it and checked my watch it was three-thirty. I hadn't forgotten to mark my trail so I felt confident of finding my way back. The peak was also a lot higher than I thought. The snow line stopped practically halfway down leaving a steep but accessible climb halfway up. My curiosity had brought me this far so with renewed enthusiasm I began to climb. With a certain amount of effort combined with a couple of short breaks I emerged at the foot of the snow line, it was an impressive view. I clambered over a few rocks until I could see a suitable viewing platform jutting out over the cliff edge. I looked up to the snow covered peak which loomed menacingly about me. It made me feel so small and insignificant I felt as if I had come as far as I dared. With my binoculars I stood as close as I could and looked down the valley below. I could feel a cold breeze gently blowing on my back as I scoured the terrain. In the distance to my left a forest way down below the rocky terrain rising up at different levels. I could feel the wind on my back like someone's hand really pushing me towards the edge. The sun had disappeared behind a cloud and a peculiar feeling embraced me. As I looked over the edge in my mind a voice said one more step and you will be with Carmen. A cold chill ran through the whole of my body and then I began to sweat. Suddenly the sun burst from behind the cloud and a warm breeze came up from below embracing my whole body and gently pushing me back.

I could feel the warmth embracing my face and it felt very familiar it's what Carmen would do when we were alone. I opened my eyes, in the distance at the edge of the forest something was glistening amongst the trees. I raised my binoculars from which I could make out it looked like a part of a gable end of a building but there was nothing on the map to indicate any such thing maybe my eyes are playing tricks or these binoculars weren't that good. I put it out of my mind as I made my way back to base camp two. By the time I had scrambled down the bank and into the bivvy the sun was setting. I made myself a meal of beans and sausage and a hardboiled egg Ingerborg had put for me. I sipped hot coffee and sat looking through the flap at the distant mountains. What had brought me here I did not know and why was a mystery. That poster I had first looked at in the travel agency had attracted me like a moth to a flame and now I was hell-bent on making a trail through the mountains. I'm sure everybody was thinking I was mad, perhaps they were right but it was helping me in my mind with my loss. It had given me something to achieve. I had something to look for. I studied the map and read a little before turning in. Tomorrow I would return to the village and purchase another bivvy from Heinreiche for my base camp three. I would spend a couple of days around the farm helping Hans before I set off again.

I was asleep warm and snug when suddenly a bolt of thunder echoed through the mountains. Sheet lightening lit up the sky I listened as more thunder rumbled in the distance, I drifted back to sleep. At some time during the night I was awakened again by more thunder and lightning but this time it was closer. The ground started to vibrate violently. I sat up wondering what to do. Suddenly the vibrating got worse I thought perhaps an earthquake. A sudden roar erupted around me as a sudden gush of water ripped down the gully tearing at the bivvy and washing me away. I struggled as the canvas wrapped itself around me I was being pushed along by a huge torrent of water. It totally encased me dragging me under. I grabbed wildly at anything I could but I was being sucked down and the canvas had wrapped me up like a cocoon. My head was struck several times as rocks were hurled at me through the rushing water. I was now in a state of panic. I tried to unwrap myself from the canvas but it clung to me tightly. I had to try and free myself. Another rock hit my shoulder which I think caused it to break, my arm suddenly went numb. With my other arm I pushed at the canvas to try and give me a bit of space. I was under the water and all sorts of debris rained down on me. I clawed frantically at the canvas but it was impossible to grip never mind tear. I could feel myself being stripped of my clothing. I hadn't got my boots on so my socks were being ripped off. My trousers were all ripped to shreds and my shirt in tatters. I launched myself upwards in a vain attempt to get some air. A short burst and I was shoved under again. By now I was really panicking I was fighting for my life. I couldn't find the opening to the bivvy and more rocks were being hurled at me. I suddenly realised that at any moment I could be hurled over the edge of the cliff and crushed on the rocks below never to be seen again. I grasped frantically at anything and then suddenly remembered the jackknife I always kept on my belt. I fumbled around in the mucky water hoping that it was still there. Lucky for me my belt hadn't been torn off me and the knife was still hanging on it. My left hand was numb but fortunately I still had a good right hand I unhooked the knife but realised I couldn't open the blade without my left hand. I raised the knife to my mouth and felt for the blade with my tongue. All the time I was being hurled along by a giant wave being tossed about in a canvas bag. I grabbed the blade with my teeth and opened it up. I began slashing wildly at the canvas it was very tough. I managed to push the blade through and make a hole. Immediately more water entered my tomb and once again I was sucked under. I pushed the blade in again and pulled down hard. My feet were touching the bottom and my ankles were receiving some severe battering as I was being dragged along. I had managed to tear the canvas and pushed myself through. More rocks were being hurled at me and I was almost unconscious. I managed to shake off the canvas and started grabbing at anything as I was being hurled along. I realised my knife had been ripped from my grasp. My left shoulder and arm were completely numb. My left ankle I think was broken and the fingers on my right hand felt numb. It was pitch black I could see nothing. With my right arm I tried to hook onto something. I felt branches but had no power to grab them. I began fearing the worst at any time I could be crushed on the rocks below. A branch hit my arm as I was being hurled along in the torrent of water, I thought my arm was broken I made an almighty effort to shoot myself out of the water hoping I could latch onto something. I was met by a thorn bush which literally ripped my face to shreds. Ignoring the pain I tried again. I hit another bush and launched myself into it wrapping my good leg around the branches. I clawed with my right arm and managed to hook around a branch. I was lying there like a rag doll pegged out on a washing line. I hung onto those branches like grim death not daring to move in case they gave way under my weight.

Very slowly the grey of dawn began to peep through the clouds, below the water rushed by with a vengeance.

I could see very little but as it gradually got lighter my vision increased. I was nested in a thorn bush overhanging the gulley with the bank rising sharply on the other side. As I clung there the water seemed to slow down, it was not a raging torrent now but a fast-moving stream rushing past a foot below me. I waited with baited breath as it began to slow down more. For the first time I realised how cold I was. I had started shivering and my teeth chattered incessantly. I risked turning my head to see what was happening below me. The stream was now two feet below me and slowing down. I hung there a while longer watching the stream diminishing until it was no more than six inches deep and more mud than water. Carefully I released my good leg from around the branch carefully lowering it into the muddy stream. It sank up to my knee before I could feel solid ground I stood there on one leg watching the mudslide slowly move away. I started to get cramp in my toes and calf muscles so I had to try to reposition myself. My left shoulder was very painful and my left arm was useless. I think my collar bone was broken. I gently eased my right arm down but from the elbow down there was immense pain and my fingers were numb. I was a wreck but I thanked God for sparing me and suddenly realised I had prayed to God for the first time since Carmen died. I put all my weight on my right leg and with some pain and effort managed to free my other leg but my ankle would not take any weight. My left arm followed painfully as I stood on one leg in a foot of mud with nowhere to go. The flow of mud was now practically stationary; the far bank was almost six feet away rising sharply upwards to about twelve feet. With a weak sun struggling to make an appearance through the grey dawn I stood there practically stripped bare wondering what to do. A piece of branch was sticking up out of the mud about ten feet away. I thought if I could reach it I could use it to help me cross the river of mud. The problem was I couldn't move. After some thought I lowered myself down on my good leg with my bad leg moved sufficiently for my knees to touch the bottom. I was now in a kneeling position with my right knee able to move forward. With great effort and pain I inched myself towards the branch sticking up dragging myself. The almighty effort was causing me to sweat which I thought was a good thing. When I finally reached the branch I found it was firmly stuck in the mud. I put all my weight onto it but ended up slipping and falling full-length into the river of mud.

I cursed profusely and once again found myself asking God to give me strength. It took great pain and effort to get back onto my knees. I grabbed the stick and found that at least I had loosened it a bit. I muttered thanks to God, not knowing if I was getting through. With a bit of wiggling the stick finally released its grip of the mud and came free. It was about four feet long just about long enough for a walking stick. With renewed vigour I crawled on my knees to the opposite bank. I hauled myself out of the mud and just collapsed in a heap.

For an hour I just lay there soaking up the weak sunshine. I had hardly any clothes on: my shirt had gone, my shoes and socks had been lost and all I had left of my trousers looked like a pair of cut off shorts. I could feel the mud on my face and hair setting hard as the wind ripped through the gully. I had to move on as I would just rot here. The bank was steep only gradually sloping in a few places near the top. I was going to move crab like along it and try and pull myself along and up but I was feeling exhausted and now cold. Inch by inch I pushed myself up resting frequently to catch my breath.

I closed my eyes briefly and had a vision of Carlos with the pony and trap standing at the top telling me to hurry up. Adrenalin pumps around your body if your mind focuses on it. With a concerted effort I forced myself along, an inch at a time, forcing my mind to ignore the pain. I pushed on the piece of stick I held and pushed with my good leg. Gradually I was moving along the bank and climbing I began to sweat but if I stopped the wind would cut through me. It must have taken me over an hour but at last the top of the bank was only an arm's length away. I rested for five minutes to get my breath and then I launched myself on a painful last effort. I wished I had had one good arm to reach over the top but I hadn't – all I could do was to throw my good leg over and push up with my good elbow.

I lay on the top looking up at the blue sky. High above the eagles were soaring occasionally a couple of hawks would swoop down on then telling them to move off their territory. The sun came out and I lay there soaking it up. I was caked in mud from head to toe and probably looked like a gingerbread man, but what the hell. From the position of the sun I estimated the time to be mid-morning. I guessed roughly that my nightmare had started somewhere in the early hours say about two o'clock that would mean I had been tossed and battered about for six or seven hours. My body thought and felt it had been forever. I now had to focus on finding my way out of this mess. I managed to sit up and I looked around me. I couldn't see any familiar landmarks never mind my pile of three stones. With an almighty effort I managed to stand up and leaned against a rock. This gave me more visibility but still no familiar landmarks. I decided I had to move along the ridge keeping the sun on my back as it was facing me when I ventured into the mountains. The high peaks were on my right side I searched the horizon looking for the high snow-capped peak I had climbed the day before but it was not to be seen and some low clouds obscured some. I hobbled along taking frequent rests. The stick I had with me came in handy I managed to push it under my belt and to rest my useless left arm on it for support. My right leg and elbow were all that I could put weight on. It was a painful slow journey but I picked my way through the rocks looking for familiar signs. I rested and turned around to see where I had come from just then the low clouds lifted revealing the snow-capped peak in the distance pointing upwards like a finger – I knew I was on the right trail. I tried to find my way back to base 1 looking for the piles of three rocks placed along the trail but my eyes were so sore and my head hurt so much I staggered blindly hoping for a stroke of luck. My feet were cut and bleeding I had to find a place to rest. Suddenly I saw three stones placed on top of each other I staggered on regardless of pain. I saw my bivvy in the distance and made for it I clambered inside and almost fell into the sleeping bag. There just an apple I had left hanging on the ridge pole I grabbed it and ate it vigorously; its moisture lubricated my parched mouth. I lay on the sleeping bag and fell asleep it was the coldness that woke me up and I noticed that the sun was waning. I had to move on and try to make the farm before darkness fell. Ignoring the pain and the stiffness with the help of the stick I hobbled along a well-recognised trail, along the wood line into the field leading to the farm. It was still fairly light as I hobbled towards the farm. Lucky for me Hans was just leading the horse and cart from the barn. The dog started barking causing Hans to look up. He gazed in horror as I stumbled towards him. He whipped the horse into a gallop as he headed towards me that's the last thing I remember as my battered body collapsed in a heap.

I remained unconscious for several days. They had carried me into the farmhouse and laid me on the kitchen table where Ingerborg prepared lots of hot water. Hans had gone for the doctor and Ingerborg began gently removing all the caked mud that covered my whole body. When the doctor arrived she was just washing my hair. The doctor did a careful examination revealing a broken collar bone, a broken ankle, a broken wrist and several fingers. He said I would have to be taken to hospital but Ingerborg said "No" she would look after me herself. The doctor argued with her I was also suffering from exhaustion and hypothermia and would need to be put on a drip. Ingerborg was defiant, she said the nurses from the local clinic could come and put on the plaster casts and fit a drip she would not let them take me away. All bills would be paid privately. The doctor argued with Ingerborg that I needed hospital care but she stood her ground – she would look after me better than any hospital.

I kept drifting in and out of consciousness at times I could feel someone touching me or lifting me up. I felt encased like a mummy and sometimes I could hear voices I would wake up and call out as the torrent of water washed me down the gully. Carmen was reaching out for me as I stood on the ledge looking down into the valley, the warm wind brushing my face. I woke up suddenly to find my big friend Heinreiche holding me down and talking softly to me.

After about four days of torment I began to recognise voices and I could feel myself being washed. I opened my eyes to find Ingerborg gently washing my face as Hans stood near holding the bowl of warm water. They both gave a huge smile as I returned to full consciousness. The doctor called in during the day and gave me a full examination; he expressed how lucky I was to be alive.

I could hardly speak, my voice sounded like a circular saw biting into a thick trunk of an oak tree. Gently I was nursed back to good health I felt so lucky having such close people to look after me, even Olga from the travel agency had sat with me during the night to give Ingerborg a break and I had loads of well-wishers calling on me. In total I was bed bound for a month before I was allowed to get up. I felt like a medieval knight cased up in armour. I had to be helped up to walk or hobble around the farm house. Heinreiche had been a frequent visitor and had cared for me one night to relieve Ingerborg.

Six weeks later some of the plaster casts were removed, what a relief.

Nobody had questioned me as to what had happened up there in the mountains I think everyone assumed I had fallen over a cliff. One evening as Ingerborg sat by the fire and I was lying on the sofa, Hans had gone somewhere that evening. I thanked her for looking after me and for all the care she had given. She smiled and then said, "No more mountain climbing for you, Franz." I told her I'd not fallen. I told her how I had found a place to camp and how I had climbed that peak. I also told her of that feeling that had come over me as I stood on the edge. She put down her knitting and looked at me. "You had a calling, Franz, and someone is looking after you." I told her I didn't believe in God anymore or any of that religious stuff. She looked at me again. "But someone is looking after you, Franz."

As I grew stronger and my injuries began to heal I hobbled down to the village to see my friends. Dietre embraced me and said how good it was to see me. He made me comfortable and we had coffee. I asked him if there had ever been any buildings up in the mountains. He shook his head – nothing was marked on any maps as far as he was concerned. He said I must have seen some rocky outcrop penetrating through the trees. He also said I had had a lucky escape and should avoid further treks in the mountains. "Concentrate on being a carpenter and start your own business."

Part 5

It was June before I was free from the plaster casts. I walked around the farm and into the village getting my strength back. I called in on Heinreiche and asked if he had managed to get my letters posted. He said his contact had posted them in Zurich but that was weeks ago and had not heard from him since. He said the postal service was suffering because of the war and that there were German spies filtering into Switzerland watching everything. I then called in on Dietre and had coffee with him. He said he had been trying to get a copy of some aerial photos that the Swiss air force had taken years ago. He had a friend in the air force that was trying to get hold of some but so far had come up with nothing. I thanked him anyway and made my way down the street to the doctor's surgery. He said I had made a miraculous recovery and looked quite fit. I asked him if he would tell me how much Ingerborg had paid out for my care. He was a bit reluctant but I told him I wanted to repay her so he confided in me, it was quite a lot. My next call was to the bank to withdraw cash. I was determined to pay back what Ingerborg and Hans had paid out. I stood outside the farm looking up towards the mountains the yearning was still there, why I don't know but it was like a magnet drawing me. I had started cultivating the piece of land behind the barn. It was heavy work it hadn't been touched for years. Hans came and asked if I needed any help, I said I needed to build myself up again and I wanted to grow vegetables and such for the house. I also suggested that a lean to greenhouse at the back of the barn to grow some tomatoes and flowers. Hans nodded his approval adding that Ingerborg would like that.

Every now and then I would stop work and look up into the mountains. Ingerborg looked at me. "You are going back up there, I can see it in your eyes, Franz, and you are searching for something I know."

It was another month before I went to see Heinreiche and ordered a fresh supply of kit. He replied that he had it all prepared he was just waiting for me to ask for it. He knew I was going back up the mountains.

This was only my second year in Switzerland and I had settled into a new way of life. I thought often of Carmen and my family and still felt a longing for them. There were times when it became too emotional I would sink into a depressive state of mind and become tearful. Ingerborg was marvellous – a second mother to me and she would sit with me and we would talk. She would suggest at times that I accompany them to church and try and renew my faith in God. I told her I was not ready and my faith had gone. She said that someone had been looking after you.

It was the beginning of July the weather was lovely. I dressed in my new mountain gear and hoisted on my backpack complete with bivvy and sleeping bag and all the necessary requirements. I told Hans and Ingerborg I would be fine I had learnt a lot from my experience and would be very careful.

I reached camp one fairly quickly and was amazed to find it in good order except for the occasional loose peg everything was in order. I decided to make a coffee and consider my next move should I stay the night or move on and establish camp two. It was still early so I decided to move on checking if my three rock markers were still in position. My new map had to be marked up and new compass bearings checked. I took my time not wanting to make any mistakes. I came across what had been camp two. The gully was still there rock strewn but still covered in green grass. I gave it a wide berth heading for higher ground. The high peak still glistening in the midday sun I took a bearing using the peak as a guide and started off in a straight line to where I thought I had seen the forest. After two hours of trying to find an easy trail I decided to call it a day. I was getting tired and hungry. I looked for a suitable flat spot to put up my bivvy. I checked first as it was a secure spot not near any gullies or cliff edge. I cooked myself a hearty meal of hard boiled eggs and beans mopped up with Ingerborg's freshly baked bread. The eagles still flew high above on the thermals occasionally disappearing amongst the peaks. Apart from the occasional scream of a hawk it was very peaceful and I soon lapsed into a sleep.

Two hours later I awoke with a start. I don't know what had woken me up I crawled out of my bivvy and had a look around, all was quiet. I decided to walk a few paces to stretch my legs. The land seemed to climb a little obscuring my view as I climbed over some rocks to a higher plateau. I looked around I could make out some forestry over to my right but dipping down into a valley. I turned around and looked for the high peak. It was still there covered in snow way back in the distance. I began to wonder if this had been the forest I had seen from the peak. I decided that the next day I would move camp two nearer the forest. I realised that camp two was now about four or five hours away from the village – a good distance to travel if I got into any trouble. I decided to leave camp two where it was and just to go on an investigative walk towards the forest. I walked along the ridge marking my trail as I went and picking the easy way along. It's never easy when you are picking your way through and around rocks; sometimes you get so far and then you come to an impassable place and have to go back and try another way but perseverance is the name of the game. I eventually reached a part where the land to the right sloped right down to join up with the forest. I looked for an easy way down eventually finding a gentle slope which angled gently down to the forest. I followed the tree line for about an hour watching the ridge get steeper until it was almost a sheer face. Another half an hour brought me to the end of the forest. I looked around the landscape which had started to level out. As I peered back through the trees my attention was drawn to what looked like an old building. I walked through the edge of the forest and lo and behold I was confronted by what looked like some abandoned old brick building. I gazed up at the gable end just peeking through the trees. It was so overgrown I was walking through weeds and brambles that came up to my shoulder. This is what I had seen that day I climbed the high peak.

I made a path through the undergrowth making sure I didn't fall down any holes. The building looked as if it had been built hundreds of years ago. It was very derelict about sixty feet high to the gable end about thirty to forty feet wide and about a hundred and twenty feet long. I slowly edged my way around, the brickwork seemed in good order but the timbers had rotted. The roof looked the worst with old beams hanging down. I made my way around to what looked to have been the front. There was a sort of porch way entrance with what had been wooden doors hanging off. I looked closely on either side; there were extensions reaching from one end to the other approximately eight feet high with slits in the sides which must have been windows. I stood back staring at what I had imagined to be some sort of religious building looking at the shape of the openings reminded me of what I had seen in churches. I walked around the exterior of the building hacking my way through weeds and brambles. The brickwork looked solid enough. With difficulty I managed to get through the door into the building it smelt old and fusty. The roof slates had all come off and the framework looked very unstable. I had to step over lots of debris as I made my way inside. The floor was solid slabs but covered with leaves and all sorts of rubbish that had blown in over the years. It looked as if it had been deserted for many, many years. There was an inner building which by the look of it had been an inner chapel. As I made my way around it came to me this at one time hundreds of years ago had been a monastery or convent for some religious order. There was a huge fireplace at one end where it looked as if it was used for cooking purposes as well as heating. The row of small rooms leading off each side had probably been the cells or private rooms of the occupants, there were six rooms either side with a large area in front of the huge fire place. This would have been the dining area. I was amazed at how solid it all was after many years of being derelict. All it needed was a new roof. Many of the tiles lay scattered on the floor where they fell I examined some realising they were made of wood, they crumbled in my hands. I looked for any signs of occupation but there was nothing to indicate who they had been. No relics or anything it had been stripped bare.

I pulled out my pencil and drawing pad and made some rough sketches and measurements. I thought for a moment I would have felt a bit scared but I wasn't. I was completely at peace apart from the occasional creak of timbers it was very peaceful. I made my way back outside wondering why it had been abandoned and to what order it had belonged to. I decided I would do some research when I got back to the village. I looked at my watch it was getting on late afternoon and time for me to return to my bivvy and civilisation. I looked back the building had occupied a flat piece of land with ample spare ground around it. Within easy access to the forest both at the front and back I was going to come back here I thought as I made my way home.

I spent my night at camp two scouring my map for any sign of the building there was none. I broke camp early next morning and followed my trail back home where I was greeted warmly and sighs of relief. I spent two days working on the farm and developing the garden plot. I had made a rough plan of what I was going to plant and checked with Ingerborg to see if I had missed anything out. I had a pretty good supply of manure and dug it well in. Dad had taught me well: give something back, don't just take he always said.

Heinreiche made a surprise visit he had letters his contact had brought from Zurich. I had a letter from Mum and Dad and also Carmen's parents. Heinreiche apologised it had taken many weeks for them to reach us due to prevailing circumstances in France and Europe. I hastily scanned the papers of Mum and Dad's letter. England was suffering from Hitler's bombs and all the young men had been called up into the forces. Mum said she was glad I was out of it. Dad was still working but still wasn't very well; she was glad he didn't have to go down the pit anymore apart from that they were managing alright. Aunt Rosa and her husband sent their best wished hoping I was well and would return home sometime in the future.

The other letter from Momma and Pappa Martinez was warm and understanding. They were pleased I had written to them and wished me well. Carlos had married Rosita and were living in our casa and were very happy.

The wine business was doing very well and they were all hoping to see me again someday in the future.

Dietre had asked me to call and see him sometime so one day I sauntered down to the library for a visit and a coffee. He enquired what I had been doing and how far I had travelled into the mountains. I had a broad smile on my face as I laid out my drawings on the table. "But there's nothing on any maps I've looked at and certainly nothing recorded in any documents. I've researched it's probably some old cow shed built centuries ago by some extinct tribe," he joked.

I pointed out the key features I had drawn, the church-like windows, the inner chapel and the rows of cells. He argued that centuries ago some religious orders would break away and form their own sanctuary, perhaps, maybe that's what had happened but there was no evidence of this although these religious orders used to write everything down. "I can't find anything but still I will see what I can find," said Dietre. I asked Dietrie if he had any sort of camera. I had never owned one but I had seen the teachers at school using them. Dietre said he did have a Kodak box camera and he would try and find it before I left for the mountains again.

I gave my list of requirements to Heinreiche another bivvy and a list of other things. I intended going up to where I was going to establish camp three at that tumbled down building. I was very inquisitive and couldn't wait to get up there. Ingerborg and Hans asked me what I was going to do. I said I didn't know but that I I felt something was urging me on. I had intended trying to make a trail to the other side of the mountain but had been sidetracked by finding this ruin. Ingerborg told me that her sister and husband had a farm on the other side and if I managed to get through they would make me welcome.

I set off and told Ingerborg I would be back within a week. She hugged me and gave me her blessing. She also added that I should make my peace with God.

I only paused for a short break at base camp one just to check everything was secure. A drink of water and a biscuit and I was on my way to base two. I took photos with Dietre's camera as I went along and checked my compass bearings. The finger mountain, as I called it, loomed in the distance still adorned with a snow cap which glistened in the sunlight. Another short break and with renewed enthusiasm continued my journey. The little pile of rocks used as markers were a godsend. I didn't have to look for easy trails I had already done it. The building peeped through the trees as I descended down into the tree line. I was getting excited I had fears that I had imagined it all and it would disappear but no it was still there and as the sunlight reflected on the stone work it seemed to greet me.

I unpacked my gear outside the front door and stood looking at the building in front of me. I wandered around the outside cutting my way through the weeds with the small sickle Heinreiche had given me. First I thought I needed easy access all around the building, I cut and chopped my way through for about an hour and a half before deciding I had done enough for one day. It was getting hot in the July sunshine so I started to establish base there and take some photos. I sat outside my bivvy just looking at the building and drinking my coffee and just wondering why I was so fascinated by it all. It was a far cry from the vineyards in Spain – why had that poster in the travel agents attracted me so much. All I know was that calmness had come over me. I could think of my lovely wife Carmen and not burst into tears although the pain was still there and I was touched by sadness. All this talk about God left me cold.

It was obvious that whoever had built this place certainly knew what was what. The timbers alone would have been cut from the forest but I couldn't see where the stonework had come from, maybe there was a quarry somewhere at the moment all I could see was weeds and brambles. After I had rested I wandered through the building watching out for falling debris. I peeked into what I had imagined had been a chapel. Two rows of pews enough for about twenty people and a stone alter greeted me. The roof was still in good repair protected from the elements by the outer shell of the building. I walked into the main hall taking in as many details as I could. The camera came in handy as I made my way though each cell looking for any remnants of occupation. Each cell roof being of timber had collapsed leaving a lot of debris. In the main hall there were signs of animal occupation and the occasional fluttering of birds wings drew my attention. There were piles of what I took to be wooden roof tiles littering the floor. I picked one up but it disintegrated at the slightest touch. Beams which had been the mainstay of the roof hung down precariously. They would have come from the forest sawn and shaped to make 'A' frames and gable end supports.

There would have been quite a workforce here at the time of the building, carpenters, stone masons, and the lot. I knew from history lessons at school that these religious orders were craftsmen in their own right and very skilled hardworking people. Looking around I admired their labour of love it took to build this place. I took a look at the large fire place built into the end wall. It was built to last with a huge oven built into each side and large slabs for their cooking pots. I wished they had left some item for me to look at but there was nothing except debris. I picked up some dry grass and placed in the hearth and lit it to see if the chimney was clear but I wished I hadn't as a flurry of birds and such like emerged bringing down a hail of soot and feathers which covered me totally. I hurried outside to shake myself cussing at my stupidity.

That was it for the day. I cleaned myself as best as I could but still felt filthy and in need of a bath. I wondered around looking for water but found none. That surprised me there had to be some somewhere. There was still some daylight left so I wondered through the forest there had been a track there at some time, I could see where the trees had been cut down. I walked further for a few more minutes and found myself almost falling into a small lake which I assumed was their water supply. I found myself stripping off and having a complete wash down. The water was cool and refreshing but the lake needed some attention it was clogged up with leaves and weeds. It was a great relief to wash the soot out of my hair and nostrils. Walking back to the building the piece of land to my right looked as if it had been stripped of its trees at some time, probably as a fuel supply. The grass had grown long, almost hiding the stumps of trees dotted around. I took more snaps of the building using up all the film in Dietre's camera.

That night as I lay in my bivvy all sorts of things were running through my mind. Who did this belong to? Why had it been allowed to fall into such a state? It must have been abandoned many years ago. A lot of hard work had gone into this building, so why was it left to fall down. I don't suppose I was going to find out. My next thought was where I was going from here. I spent a further two nights looking around and enjoying the peace and quiet. The array of stars at night in the clear sky looked spectacular I made notes and inspected the woodwork. The tiles were all handmade from wood that in itself would have taken time to do. At college we had been shown some basic skills, which at the time I thought was a waste of time, but now it registered in my mind how things were made centuries ago. To say the least I was fascinated by this place but why? I had never been interested in old buildings before.

I decided to go back to the farm and do some research. I wandered around one more time but this time I was making notes of a different kind. I was making a list of tools that would be required to put this place in good repair. The roof was the biggest problem. New beams would have to be made with wood from the forest. That meant saws and an axe. Plus a tape measure plus many other tools I could list. Scaffolding made of wood had to be made. This would be a challenge for any construction firm but could one man on his own do it? This would be a challenge.

I left base three and made my way home. I couldn't just ignore that excited feeling running through my body. Six hours later I was walking across the field towards the farm.

Hans commented on how well I looked. As I sipped the coffee Ingerborg made for me I began telling them what I had discovered. When I met up with Dietre and Heinreiche that evening at the bier Keller Dietre said that he had already looked at maps of the area and found nothing but he was waiting for word from a colleague who was in the Swiss Air Force. Dietre said that many years ago the Air Force had flown the length and breadth of the mountains making photo maps. Dietre was trying to get a copy of our area but didn't hope too much, especially in these troubled times but also he had found a book on religious orders which he hadn't time to study. Heinreiche warned that there were spies in Switzerland both English and German and warned us to be careful.

The vegetable plot at the back of the barn was doing very well, Ingerborg had tended it with loving care. I suggested that she should sell some of the vegetables on her market stall, so we filled a large basket and I carried it into the village for her. At the end of the day she returned with her basket empty. She said she could have sold more. I suggested trying planting lettuce in a frame and perhaps when I had finished the lean to greenhouse tomatoes and flowers. Hans had his work cut out with the pigs, cows, sheep and goats there was always something to do and this had been going on for two hundred years since his ancestors had brought the farm. I asked if anybody had kept any kind of records, bills or such. He said that there were piles of stuff up in the loft that he sometimes thought he would get rid of.

I asked Hans about some panes of glass for the greenhouse, he shook his head, he didn't have any himself but he would ask around. I stayed around the farm for two weeks which seemed an eternity to me. Ingerborg would creep up behind me as I stood gazing up into the mountains. "There's something up there calling you," she said. I agreed but told her I didn't know what it was. "I know," she said but said no more.

Dietre called me into the library as I was passing. He held up a large map. He locked the door. "This is top secret," he said. He unrolled the map onto a table it was an Air Force aerial map. "You haven't seen this," he said. Tracing the mountain range with his finger he stopped at a place on the map. It looked dark green which he said was forest and then with a magnifying glass he zoomed in on a small rectangular shape just jutting out of the forest. "There, Franz, that is your building." I took the glass and peered at the shape. That's all I could see but Dietre was looking at some lettering underneath it "R.M" he murmured. I asked what it meant. He turned the map over and looked at all the symbols indicated. "Ruined monastery," he said out loud. "Franz, you have found a ruined monastery, congratulations. Now what are you going to do with that?" He laughed out loud. We looked at the photos I had taken and Dietre confirmed that's what it looked like. I asked him who it belonged to. He shrugged his shoulders. "Who knows," he replied, "more research needed and more questions to be asked."

That night as I lay on my bed I found myself walking through the forest visualising the monastery in the distance. What was it all about, why couldn't I forget and move on, why was I here?

I asked Dietre if he could find out who it belonged to. "Who do you ask?" I said. He said the land registry should know, he would make some enquiries.

"Do you want to buy it?" he laughed.

Heinreiche looked at the list I gave him and asked what I was going to do. I told him that I was going to build a log cabin in the grounds of the monastery and stay up there for longer periods and do more trail blazing. He suggested I buy a dog for company.

I was carrying quite a bit of extra gear which slowed me down a bit. I rested at both base camps realising that every bit of equipment had to be carried on my shoulders. I was going to have to limit what I could carry or else I would exhaust myself. I forced myself to go on and when I finally reached base there at the monastery I found that it had taken me nine hours to get back. I just crashed out and fell asleep. I was greeted by a starry sky when I woke up just time to cook myself a meal and retire for the night.

It was raining and a grey miserable day greeted me as I exited the bivvy; not a day for a walk in the forest but I could do something in the monastery. After a cereal breakfast I gathered up some tools and made my way inside. I began sweeping up the debris and lit a small fire in the fireplace making sure I stood well away from it. Believe me there was enough rubbish to keep the fire going all day. I sat and ate my sandwiches in front of the fire, listening and watching out for falling timbers from the roof and also anything coming down the chimney. The roof needed a complete replacement. The gable ends would have to be checked for stability before the roof construction could be done. The timber frame would have to be at least six inch timbers and stretching at least ninety feet with cross braces at least thirty feet. And then some means of lifting these timbers into place. If I had to do it I would construct the whole roof on the floor first then take it to pieces and hoist the beams up to roof level. I sat there dreaming away. Suddenly I had another thought. Instead of going back to the farm every two or three days why don't I build a log cabin inside the monastery and I could stay longer periods. I suddenly realised I was making plans that would never come to fruition. Somebody somewhere must own this place and they are not going to let some pit carpenter come along and develop it. Well dreams are dreams and we all have them. I walked out into the sunshine looking back into the great hall. It looked better after a good clean up. I noticed that the floor was covered in flat slabs very smooth and easy to walk on. How on earth did they do that? I took stock of my supplies and what few tools I had brought with me. I had enough for me to construct a lean-to inside the monastery or even to patch up one of the cells. I didn't have to use the bivvy all of the time.

Food for thought as I picked up my gear for my journey home.

At the farm everything was normal. I was greeted warmly and treated to evening meals, "With our own vegetables," Ingerborg added. Dietre had been asking if I had returned yet so that evening I made my way to the bier Keller where Dietre and Heinreiche were, probably discussing the war. Dietre said he had some good news for me but I had to buy the biers first. Heinreiche told me to keep a low profile and not to tell anybody I was English. Speak Spanish or Swiss he advised me. There had been strangers coming to the village and snooping around he feared they might be enemy spies or even Gestapo. Heinreiche says he locks his shop up and disappears when they are around, he just doesn't want to know them.

Dietre started telling me the good news. He had made enquiries through certain contacts and advised to ask the Land Registry Office about the building and its ownership. They said nothing had been registered with them and that their records only go so far back. Dietre had asked if the building could be purchased. The answer was no but if anyone wanted they could lease it on a long-term lease but would have to show plans and be able to give location details. Dietre said all this could be done from the aerial photos and map references.

I had planned one more visit into the mountains before winter set in. I asked Dietre if he would apply for the appropriate forms regarding leasehold on my behalf and if he knew anybody to ask about map references. He promised to look into it but only if I would put in some shelves for him in the library.

I stood looking at the finger mountain it amazed me how each time I came here it would be covered in snow with the sun gleaming on it. Was this some of indication for me to go forward that's how I felt myself thinking. My moments of sadness seemed to disappear when I was up here, although my memories and thoughts of my beloved Carmen always echoed through my mind and yet I felt so calm about it which I didn't understand.

I decided to make a lean-to shelter inside the monastery. It would be warmer and it would be somewhere to store my equipment. I was excited with what Dietre had found out. He was a good friend and nothing was too much for him. I would make him the finest shelves he could wish for when I got back.

I walked through the forest looking for suitable and manageable timbers for my lean-to. It was mostly mountain pine and easy to cut. By the time I had cut sufficient wood and carried it up to the monastery I was ready for a break. I lit a fire in the huge hearth made some coffee and relaxed.

The following morning I set to making my lean-to. It wasn't difficult and soon I was taking down the bivvy and moving everything inside. I had made the lean-to big enough to erect the bivvy under it so I had double protection and it was close enough to the hearth for the warmth of the fire also. I collected all my gear and tools and placed them inside the bivvy. With that done I made some coffee and ate the last of my bread. I checked that everything was secure. I don't know what the winter would do to camp three but I hoped it would survive. On my way back to the farm I dismantled camp two and packed everything into its bag and then stashed it into a crevice and piled rocks on top. The same with camp one I would not be returning until spring.

There was plenty of requests for my services as a carpenter. People in the village had been asking for me and I had quite a list of potential customers. Dietre had asked if I had returned yet so I went to see him first I had promised to put up his shelves but I found him anxious to show me something he had found out. Apparently there was a large monastery further along the mountain range who kept St. Bernard dogs and would help anyone trapped in the mountains. Dietre had found a book with all this information and apparently every so often a small group would break away and move further along the mountain range and start another order. Other monasteries had been located further away and had been mentioned in the book but the one I had found had not been mentioned, nevertheless, this is apparently what had happened. Dietre had also managed to get the required paperwork for me to lease this "stone building" as it was called on the paperwork. Everything was going to plan as I had wished it. Now all I was waiting for was spring.

For my twenty-fifth birthday Ingerborg had planned a party for me at the bier Keller. I was so surprised I hugged her and kissed her, she was more like a mother to me. My own mother had posted a birthday card to me and she must have posted it early for me to get it. I wrote to her letting her know I was well and in good spirits. I also wrote to Momma and Pappa Martinez and Carlos and Rosita wishing them well. I told them all that I was working on a project which was keeping me busy.

My party went with a swing friends and neighbours were invited and a good time was had by all. Olga danced with me and Christina managed to grab me. She began to question me about what I was doing in the mountains. I just told her I was exploring the terrain and sketching.

When the party was over Ingerborg Hans and myself walked up the lane to the farm. I thanked them for arranging it all. As winter crept towards us I turned over the farm garden and spread on some manure. Hans said he never used the manure for anything and it was just being stockpiled so I used quite a bit. Dad had always said we must put something back in the soil and not just take. It paid dividends. The crops yielded a good harvest.

Christmas came quickly and Dietre managed to get his shelves put up. Other work came in as word got around that I was a carpenter. The station master of the shuttle train asked me to renew his row of fencing along the track to protect people from stepping on the rails. Heinreiche wanted some cupboards making to keep things in. Ingerborg's kitchen also got some attention and Hans had a new door put on the stable. My days went by quickly. I asked Hans if I could look at the hoard of documents in the loft he gladly obliged and between the three of us we went through them a few at a time. Mostly they were bills of sale for sheep or pigs sold by Hans. Some went right back to the seventeenth century. Hans said his father and grandfather had always kept records and that as far as he knew the farm had been in his family for more than two hundred years. Ingerborg laughed and said, "I haven't been here that long but it feels like it." We would finish the evening off with a chocolate drink in front of the fire watching the snow fall. Things seemed quiet in the village during winter time. The markets stopped until spring and people just concentrated on preparing for Christmas. Heinreich and Dietre came for Christmas Day meals both men lived on their own. Dietre had lost his wife some years ago and Heinreiche never spoke about his private life. He had left all that behind when he left Germany.

After a slap-up dinner we all sat around a nice log fire and chatted. I was telling Dietre about the paperwork in the attic. He asked about people who came to the farm. I fetched some of the paperwork down whilst Hans enjoyed a snooze. Dietre tried to make out the names on the paperwork. He looked at one piece of paper from the seventeenth century very carefully scrutinising the names. "Look," he said holding up one piece of paper which had faded quite a bit. "It looks like Dr. Sharp sold to a brother Adrian and one dozen eggs and some other things which I can't make out." I looked at the paper it was signed at the bottom by Brother Adrian???? monastery. My hands shook as I studied the signature. Could this possibly be one of the monks from the monastery in the mountains? "Well, they did roam the countryside selling herbal medicines and holding private services in exchange for goods," exclaimed Dietre. "Well, so it says in the book I've been reading."

At the beginning of the New Year the paperwork for the lease on the building had been completed. I was now the new leaseholder of the property just listed as a stone building at map reference so and so. I had to pay a small payment each year for a period of ninety-nine years renewable after that time.

Hans asked what I was going to do with the building. I showed him my drawings and the photos. "There's a lot of work up there for one man," he commented.

I gave Heinreiche my list of requirements and he laughed out loud. "Who is going to carry all of this up there for you? I do not do deliveries." I had already planned it out. I would carry what I could up to thirty-six pounds per load and come down every other day for a fresh load. He said he would carefully pack each load and have it weighed and ready for me. He also asked what I was going to put on the roofs as he had several rolls of felt going cheap. I hadn't got that far in advance yet my first priority was to build a scaffold and then strip the roof off. I had collected some of the wooden roof tiles and had been using them as firewood. I would bring some more back with me and show Heinreiche. He said just to let him know when I was going to start.

It was still too early to begin as the mountains were covered in snow and freezing temperatures. It was mid-February I would be hanging around for at least another month if not longer. I did not want to rush. As the snow melted there would be torrents of water cascading down the mountain. I had not forgotten my bad experience, anyway what was the rush the monastery wasn't going anywhere. I asked Heinreiche if he had any weed killer I could take up with me. There would be other things but I would think of them as I went along.

The station master was pleased with his fencing and asked if I could renew the façade above the station office. That would keep me occupied for a while. I was getting familiar with the men at the timber yard and they willingly helped me with my timber requirements. Hans told me to use the horse and cart whenever I wished. There were little jobs I did for people in the village and I became quite popular. Their monetary donations were mounting up in my bank account and I had built up a nice little nest egg. Hans had managed to acquire some panes of glass from people who were doing property repairs and alterations so I had at least enough glass for the roof of our greenhouse. It was looking good. I had already turned the ground over and planted some early crops. Ingerborg was delighted.

It was the middle of March and we were getting some weak sunshine but it was enough to melt some of the snow so I decided to go for a stroll into the mountains assuring Ingerborg and Hans that I would be back for evening meal. I only took enough food for a quick lunch so I was travelling light. It was a relief to find myself in amongst the rocks again and peering up into the snow-capped peaks − I felt at home again. I wallowed in the fresh air and the silence. It was golden.

I reached base camp one; my bivvy was still tucked away in the orifice so out it came and I erected it. It was the start of a new venture. I made my way to base camp two and repeated the procedure. I gazed up at the finger peak still standing proud adorned in all its snow-capped glory with the sun enhancing its face. I ignored the urge to carry on to base camp three and began my journey home.

Heinreiche was a scheming old devil I made my way down to the shop to let him know I was ready to start carrying my supplies. As I approached the shop I noticed a huge white dog tethered up outside. He was huge I had only seen pictures of St. Bernard dogs in a book at school but this dog was equally as big. His tail began to wag as I approached which I took as a gesture of friendship. I entered the shop and waved to Heinreiche who was talking to man about something. They both waved and I started looking around the shop. Heinreiche came over and showed me my goods. I lifted the first pack and lifted it onto my shoulders. Heinreiche moved it around a bit until it felt comfortable. He then reached for the two-handed saw and the other saws and the other smaller tolls. He asked if I felt comfortable. I said I did but my hands were full with other tools. "You need some help," he said, a wicked smile crossed his face. The other man stood looking at me, he then went outside and brought in the dog.

"You need Romulus," said Heinreiche. I looked at them both slightly confused. "Franz," Heinreiche began, "Otto here has to take his dog to the vets to be put down, his wife will no longer let him keep it, too big she says." I looked at them amazed, what had they got in their minds. "He will be good company for you and he can carry some of your equipment for you. That's what these dogs do here in the mountains." The other man looked at me sadly; I could see tears in his eyes as he fondled the dog lovingly. I didn't know what to say I was shaking my head. I asked Heinreiche if he was playing a joke on me. I said the dog would be an extra burden on me and would need a mountain of food to feed him. Heinreiche said the man would pay for food for a year and the dog would carry more than his share on his back on a panier that they had fitted him with. He also said the dog was already a working dog and pulled a small cart around with milk from the farms. The other man stepped forward and said something which Heinreiche interpreted. "He says the dog is a lovely and loyal companion. It would be a shame for him to be put down, he will serve you well in the mountains, please take my dog with you."

Well, I stood there speechless, the dog was licking my hand and the man was holding the lead out to me.

As I walked through the village people stared as I led the dog by my side. When I reached the farm Ingerborg almost had a fit. She then burst out laughing. "So Otto has found a new home for Romulus," she said fondling the dog, "and now you have a companion, that is good, Franz."

Part 6

Heinreiche had loaded the panniers on the back of Romulus. He balanced the weight equally on each side. On the top he put four cans of dog food that Otto had bought. Romulus took it all in his stride and paced himself well as we began to climb. It was warming up the sun was shining brightly. I stopped after a while and sheltered in the shade for a while. Romulus sat and then lay down he seemed to know what he was doing. We reached base camp one before noon. I didn't know whether to stop for a break or carry on. I asked Romulus if he was okay to go on. He just carried on walking at a leisurely pace.

When we finally reached the monastery we were both a bit weary; I unloaded my backpack and then removed the panniers from my companions back. I looked around apart from loose debris everything looked as I had left it. The lean-to – still standing and the bivvy secure. I gathered up some fallen roof tiles and got a fire going. Romulus stretched out on the slabs and dozed off after I had put some water down for him. I put the bivvy and the lean-to in order and then set about preparing myself a meal. I unwrapped my sleeping bag and put it to air in front of the fire. I put a dish of food for Romulus and he scoffed the lot leaving the dish spotless. I took him outside and we walked around the grounds, he seemed quite happy just to sniff and cock his leg up several times marking his territory. With the bivvy being under the lean-to I could leave the flap open at the front. When I returned for the night Romulus seemed quite happy to stretch out half in and half out the bivvy. A proper guard dog I thought, nobody's going to creep up on me.

With a new dawn I awoke refreshed and anxious to get started. Romulus hadn't moved all night but now he got up, stretched and shook himself. A big tongue wiped over my face as I emerged from my sleeping bag. What a lovely way to say good morning.

My first task was to take a walk into the forest. I needed timber to build my scaffolding. At least a dozen four-inch saplings thirty foot long would get me started. I used a bow saw and soon I had felled half a dozen. With a hand saw I trimmed down each one. I then dragged them down to the path I had cleared leading up to the monastery. Romulus looked on wondering what was going on. I threw a stick for him and he quickly retrieved it dropping it at my feet. Well what had I let myself in for this dog liked to play.

I laboured through the day stopping only to quench my thirst. Romulus seemed content just to be close to me, occasionally I would throw the stick for him to fetch.

It was warm work and a thirty foot four inch piece of wood got a little heavy trying to drag it up to the monastery. By the end of the day I had cut twelve saplings and had managed to drag four into the monastery. I told myself that there wasn't any hurry I must pace myself and not to rush or I would tire myself out. The next day it rained so we just sat around the hearth all day. I was drawing my plans and Romulus occasionally got up and walked outside. I realised that I would also need to cut some smaller pieces of wood to use as struts on the scaffolding. These were more manageable and even Romulus carried one in his mouth.

As the days passed by the scaffolding was taking shape but it was time to go back to the farm. With nothing to carry back the journey was an easy one and both man and dog made it a fun journey. He was a good companion and would let you fuss him all day.

At the farm everything was ticking over, Ingerborg baking, Hans taking the horse and cart and fetching straw and hay from other farms in the area. He had acquired more glass panels which were now stacked up by the greenhouse. I repaired the sheep pen which had been knocked about a bit during the winter. I cleaned the pigs out and put fresh straw in the animal pens.

I started on the greenhouse next as it was getting near to planting time. Three days later I fetched Ingerborg to examine it. She was over the moon and produced some packets of seeds. Vegetables and flowers, she had also acquired several plant pots. The vegetable plot was looking healthy a quick turn over and I was sowing seeds. The early potatoes were beginning to show I started off the cabbage and cauliflower seeds in the greenhouse and within days the green shoots began to show. I had built a staging against the back of the barn inside the greenhouse and now Ingerborg and I started off with other seeds including the flowers Ingerborg had chosen. My dad had taught me well and during my day dreaming I would hear him say, "If it's worth doing, then do it well." I had prepared a compost heap during the year and now had a good supply ready to fill the plant pots. I was into my second week and was getting itchy feet. Ingerborg noticed and said it was time for me to get ready for my return to the mountains.

Heinreiche loaded me up with my supplies which included nails of various sizes. The weed killer was in a large can which he fitted into one of the panniers on Romulus's back the other side was balanced with cans of dog food that Otto had brought. He caressed his old friend and asked me how he had been. I said he was the next thing to being a donkey and was good fun to have around. He had also brought a leather harness that he used during the winter time for Romulus to pull a sledge. I asked if he was okay pulling things as I had a lot of timber to move. Otto patted the dogs head, Heinreiche interrupted, "He will pull anything you ask of him." So that was useful to know and when we had said our goodbyes we were on our way back to the monastery.

Once the timbers for the scaffolding were in the monastery I set to erecting it. As I fastened each upright securely and fitted the retaining struts I began to think. What if I built a log cabin against the wall I could key it into the wall enclosing the hearth. It would be better than the lean-to and more spacious. After all, I was going to be spending sometime on my project and could do with some extra comfort. It was food for thought and that evening I started measuring up and designing a log cabin. I was having such fun I hadn't even thought about my country being at war with Germany but I didn't look upon it as my war. I hadn't started it and if everybody left me alone I was not getting involved. I did worry about Mum and Dad though. I tried not to get upset about it. Dad was too old to be called up, besides, he wasn't very well. Mum had said in her letter that he was having a rough time with his breathing.

I turned my thoughts to building the cabin. Four inch logs would be thick enough considering it was going to be within the monastery walls. I measured lengths of twenty feet and Romulus coped very well dragging these from the forest. I had cut about fifty over a period of a week and Romulus and I felt very proud of ourselves. But it was time for another visit to the farm. Our supplies of food were getting low and we needed a break anyway. We made our way back down from the mountains feeling very pleased with what we had done. At a steady pace with the occasional rest it took six hours to reach the farm. I imagined it was about a thirty mile journey give or take a bit but to me it was pleasurable.

We were greeted warmly and Ingerborg was soon preparing hot food for us. Romulus received his fair share of fussing and soon stretched out for a well-earned rest. Hans had said that Heinreiche wanted to know if we had returned so that evening I sauntered down to the bier Keller to see my friends. Dietre had kept all the documentation regarding the leasehold in his library and was still researching its history. Heinreiche asked me to let him know when I was going back and what supplies I would need. I told them I had decided to build a small log cabin inside the monastery, Heinreiche asked if I had planned to spend the winter up in the mountains. I replied I had not thought about it. I asked about the war but Heinreiche put his finger to his lips. He looked around the bar which was pretty crowded. He said there were people staying in the village that they did not know so everybody was keeping hush and not getting involved with any strangers but it paid to keep a low profile.

I checked the plants in the greenhouse, they looked healthy. Ingerborg was quite happy pottering about and tendered the flowers with loving care. The cabbages and cauliflower plants were big enough to plant out so I set to it. The potatoes were hoed up and I made a cold frame for the lettuces. I had not heard from home and Spain for a while so I spent time in my room writing letters which Heinreiche would pass on to his contact for secure posting. I met up with Olga and Christina on my evenings at the bier Keller. We were all about the same age and got on very well. I did not want any romance and I made this very clear. The girls just laughed.

I had brought a couple of roof tiles with me from the monastery and I asked Heinreiche where the timber yard was. He said it was about three kilometres away. He said I could borrow his bicycle if I wanted to. I had never ridden one before – I never needed one. Heinreiche said it was simple and fetched his bicycle out and put it in front of the shop. He had to lower the saddle for me because he was a big man with long legs. I said I would push it up to the farm and practise a bit first. When I was clear of the village I got on the bicycle and put my foot on the pedal and pushed away only to end up in the hedge. I was glad nobody was watching as I made my second attempt, this time I managed a few feet before I fell off. Determined to master it I got back on a few more feet and I hit the hedge again. By this time I was near the farm gate and noticed Hans laughing his head off. He held the bicycle whilst I got back on. I pushed off with Hans holding onto the saddle, wobbling as I tried to pedal. After a few more attempts to get my balance I managed a few more yards. Hans told me to practise a few more times until I got the hang of it. As I rolled down the field Hans shouted for me to try the brakes. I did and the bicycle stopped dead throwing me over the handle bars. Hans couldn't stop laughing as he pointed out not to pull the front brake on first. Finally after a few more attempts I eventually got the hang of it. I decided to cycle to the timber yard very early next morning before anybody was about.

The foreman was a friendly man and when I showed him the roof tiles; he thought I wanted to order some. When I said I only wanted to know how they made them centuries ago he took me over to where another man was working and introduced me to Yan. He said he had made some a while ago to cover a shed roof. I asked him to show me how he made them. He took me into a large shed and showed me a special axe that he had come by. He then rolled out a large log about a foot and a half in diameter and two foot in length. Fortunately Yan could speak a little English he told me to choose the right wood and to saw it to length. He fetched a piece of log and put it onto the larger one and then reached for a large hammer. He held the axe onto the smaller log and gave it a sharp blow. The log split the whole length producing a rough-looking tile. He repeated it several times making rough tiles. He told me to make sure the axe was perfectly upright and to give it one sharp blow. I tried and after several attempts made my first roof tile.

I managed to return the bicycle to Heinreiche and thanked him. I showed him my roof tile and he smiled. "You will need to coat them with this," he said producing a gallon can of brown horrible smelling liquid. "It's called creosote and it makes wood waterproof." I informed him that I was not ready for it yet. He then asked when I was going back and what supplies I needed. I told him that I was thinking of building a log cabin first and again he laughed asking me if I intended to spend the winter up there. I told him I would collect my supplies in two days' time.

I was ready for lunch when I got back to the farm and Ingerborg had made a special for me, it was called apple strudel which I had never heard of and with a warm coating of what looked like custard it went down a treat. I told them I was going back into the mountains in two days' time and they both understood. My big friend Romulus never left my side he would stretch out by the side of my chair quite content.

I met up with my friends that evening before my departure. Heinreiche bought the beers and we chatted the evening away discussing many subjects including the war. My rendition of the Swiss language was getting quite good with the occasional correction from my friends. Heinreiche joked, "But you still sound like an English man."

The following morning I went to Heinreiche's shop for my supplies, Romulus wearing his panniers at my side. They were ideal for carrying the small packages of nails and also fuel for my lamps and not forgetting his own food supplies which Heinreiche placed on the counter paid for by Otto. "You will need more than this if you ever decide to winter up there," he added. I looked at him and smiled. I had described the axe that you had used to make tiles. "I will look for one," said Heinreiche. I turned around at the sound of the doorbell it was Otto he had come to see Romulus. He had another man with him who he introduced as Bernard. We shook hands and chatted away. I checked that I had everything and bid farewell. Heinreiche, Otto and Bernard followed me out of the shop. I was taken by surprise as another huge dog the same as Romulus stood there.

Otto said, "This is Remus the brother of Romulus, isn't he beautiful?" I said he was.

"It's just a pity he is going to be put down," said Heinreiche.

"Why?" I asked.

"Like Romulus he is too big for the house and Yan's wife has told him he must get rid of him, it's a pity he's so lovable." The dog came up to me and nudged my hand. The two dogs stood side by side looking up at me. I suddenly realised I had been set up by these cunning men.

"No, no I can't ones enough," I blurted out. I looked at Yan and saw the tears welling up in his eyes. As they helped me load Remus up with the dog food he paid for I emphasised that it was for a trial basis and that if things became a problem I would return the dog to you. It was agreed and Otto gave me a bear hug which was followed by Yan.

When Ingerborg saw the two dogs she had a fit of laughter. "They have been waiting for you," she cried. "Otto and Yan you are an answer to their prayers."

Well the dogs earned their keep never faltering in their stride. Romulus would lead and Remus followed. We rested for half an hour at the finger peak and both dogs just lay down and rested. When we moved on they just responded to my word.

By the second day we had cut and dragged enough timber to start building the cabin. I had made drawings and worked to them. Three days later all four walls were erected and we went down into the woods for more timber for the roof. We worked as a team and even found time to frolic. They both enjoyed fetching sticks I threw for them and played happily together. With water mud and moss from down by the pool I sealed all the gaps. I had left room for a small window which I would bring next time. I needed a piece of glass so I could look outside and see what the weather was doing. I had also calculated how much wood I had been burning each day. If I did decide to winter in the mountains I would need to start stock piling now. I also needed some small wheels to put under the lengths of timber − I would need to lift them up slightly making it easier for us to drag. At night I would be making my list of requirements. I calculated how much food would be required. What clothing and bedding I would need. Buckets and bowls were also on my list.

We made our way back down the mountain on the sixth day. We had stayed longer than we had planned and Hans and Ingerborg would be getting worried. They greeted me warmly and soon we were feasting on Ingerborg's good cooking. I had told them that I was building a log cabin and they asked how I was doing.

Ingerborg asked if I needed anything for it. I replied that if I decided to spend a winter in the monastery I would need lots of things like bedding and tinned food supplies. I asked Hans if he had any small window frames I could use. Ingerborg looked worried and asked if I was sure I knew what I was letting myself in for. Hans said he was concerned, not hearing from me for the length of the winter time they would be worried about me.

I shared their concerns with Heinreiche and Dietre that evening as we gossiped over our beers. "No means of contact," said Dietre shaking his head. Heinreiche said that if there had been no war going on he could have got his hands on a transmitter and receiver but that would not be possible now as the Germans could trace the signals and would soon be investigating.

He then came up with another idea. "Pigeons," he said excitingly, "they used them for carrying messages." Dietre and I looked at him. Heinreiche said that during the First World War they used them for messages. So now Heinreiche was telling me I needed to build a small pigeon loft and he would enquire from a friend of his about messenger pigeons. "Only for emergencies," he added and so it was another lesson was being learnt by me.

When it was time for us to return to the mountains Ingerborg had prepared some spare blankets and Hans had found a small window he had stashed away in the barn some years ago. Heinreiche had come up with a lightweight tarpaulin which he said would come in handy for the roof of my cabin. With my food supplies packed onto Romulus and Remus's panniers I was ready for setting off. I wrapped the window in a blanket and carried it on top of my backpack being careful not to break it. The dogs were anxious to get off and were halfway across the field by the time Ingerborg and Hans were saying their goodbyes. Despite the loads we were carrying we made good progress reaching the monastery seven hours later. I quickly unloaded our supplies and made a fire. Even with no roof on the log cabin was warmer. I realised I would have to put up some shelving for our supplies. I didn't want to leave anything on the floor. The next day we set off into the forest for roofing timber. The dogs ran anxiously on in front. Soon we were cutting and dragging. By the end of the day we had enough and it was afternoon by the time the timbers were lying inside the monastery walls. That was enough for one day, we sat around the fire enjoying our food. There were times of course when I would gaze into the fire and drift back into my past memories of life before I came to the mountains. I would hear Carmen's laughter echo through the monastery and feel her warm breath on the back of my neck. I would imagine the two of us chasing after our child. The tears were real, but then a couple of big tongues would lick my face and pull me around and we would go for a walk.

In two days I had used the tarpaulin and stretched it across the roof making it waterproof. I then gathered plenty of moss and covered it as an extra layer of insulation covering that with lighter wooden batons. The small window was fitted and served a good purpose. I could look out without going outside. The shelving was simply three-inch thick branches cut down the middle and secured to the walls with the smooth side upwards. I could place all my tins of food on them and also flour and sugar. I could also store the dogs' biscuits and blankets to keep them off the floor. All in all I was pleased with what we had achieved. I would now have to start on my fuel supply for the winter but that would be next time.

As we made our way back to the farm my thoughts were of what Heinreiche had talked about, communications, I watched as the wood pigeons flew through the forest, was it possible to send messages by pigeon, I would have to question my friend Heinreiche about that. He was the wise old owl who knew everything. I know he fought in the First World War but he never talked about it.

When we reached the tree line the dogs would run on ahead to let Ingerborg and Hans know we were back. Everything looked peaceful with the sheep grazing in the field. Hans was grooming the horse and Ingerborg was hanging out the washing. I was greeted warmly and soon we were all sitting down chatting. They were aware that I was contemplating spending winter in the mountains and asked how things were going. Ingerborg asked about bedding and Hans asked if I had finished the cabin. They both had heard of people who live in the mountains people who were native to Switzerland but weren't sure if an Englishman could survive the harsh winter. I said I would let them know in the spring.

Hans asked me to make the hen house larger as Ingerborg was doing well at the market and her eggs were in great demand and also early vegetables were going well. Ingerborg asked for more shelves in her kitchen for her baking. Their income had increased which was good news.

Heinreiche and Dietre welcomed me in the bier Keller. Heinreiche asked me to call in his shop the next day. I looked at him and said, "No more dogs, my friend, two is enough." He laughed out loud and shook his head. Dietre hadn't found out any more about the monastery but asked if I could show him the paperwork Hans kept in his loft maybe he could learn something from it. We quickly discussed the war and its effects. Heinreiche had heard bad things but would not discuss anything he said he was ashamed of his countrymen. The village was ticking over quietly still keeping a watchful eye on strangers who suddenly showed up for no particular reason.

A lot of things became scarce during the war and Heinreiche said that his supplies were not getting through but fortunately his contact in Zurich managed to get certain things which included mail from England. The following morning I made my way into the village to Heinreiche's shop, he led me into his living quarters where he produced two letters from England and Spain. I thanked him and couldn't wait to open them. Ma and Pa were still surviving the war but things were getting harder to get. Pa's garden produce was helping a lot but clothing and such were hard to get even sweets and fruit were a luxury. Pa was still having problems with his chest and sometimes he had to have time off from work. They didn't see much bombing where they were but Aunt Rosa had some near misses, the larger towns became targets.

In Spain they were ticking over, Carlos and Rosita were expecting their first child. Momma and Pappa had hoped I was alright and safe and hoped they would see me again in the future. The wine was still selling and they hoped to expand once the war in Europe was over.

I thanked Heinreiche again as he escorted me through the parlour to his piece of land at the rear of the premises. He had built himself a small pigeon coup and showed me his lovely birds. "I used to keep pigeons when I was young," he said proudly picking up one of the birds. "You should build yourself a pigeon loft next to your cabin," he said excitedly.

I looked at him and laughed, "What for, I've got enough to do as it is."

He looked at me strange like. "Because we need to keep in touch with you in case of emergencies." He took my arm and placed the bird in my hands. "We used to use these birds to carry messages during the war and that's what we could do here to keep in contact with each other." I said I would think about it. He produced four wheels and two axels something else I had asked for. I must admit there was nothing I couldn't get from Heinreiche. He told me to make sure I stockpiled enough wood for the winter and to get a good supply of blankets. He then produced the axe for making the tiles. I asked him where he managed to get that from. "The timber yard," he said with a huge laugh. A roll of chicken wire was strapped to my back and as I prepared myself for the journey back into the mountains. I asked what it was for and Heinreiche said, "The pigeon loft."

I bade farewell to them all saying I would return in a week. It was getting towards the end of summer and I needed to get cracking saving wood for the winter ahead. There were lots of things I wanted to do before I was hemmed in by the snow.

Once again Romulus and Remus proved to be the best thing that had happened to me. They were great companions and strong as horses when it came to dragging the timbers from the forest. The wheels I used to lift the heavy timbers up at the front had proved to be ideal making it easier for us to drag the heavier timbers up to the monastery. I had chosen several nine-inch diameter trees to fell and sawed them into manageable thirty foot lengths, these were going to be my roof supports which I hope to work on during the winter. The monastery smelled more like a timber yard than a place of prayer and meditation.

An occasional plane flew over the mountains I never knew whose they were but we would return into the shadows not wanting to be seen.

On occasional days we would break off from work and explore the mountains. I wanted to extend my trail further along and see what lay ahead. I marked the trail with the usual three stones and took compass readings. Ingerborg had said that she had a sister on the other side who with her husband also had a farm similar to their own but hardly saw them as it was a hundred and fifty kilometres by train. They spoke regularly on the phone and Ingerborg had said, "Don't be surprised if a man named Franz appeared at the farm." Well it was food for thought, but Ingerborg warned me it was near the German border and should not go there.

I knew now that I didn't have much more time before the winter would be here, so I had to make a journey back to the village to get more supplies. Food was the next important item, I had to get all that I could including the dogs' supplies and fuel for my lamps including candles as back up. The dogs' panniers would hold a gallon can on one side and could be balanced by tins of dog food on the other. I also wanted some sort of floor covering for them to lie on. The stone floor of the monastery was fine in the summer. Ingerborg had some pieces of carpeting and a couple of home-made rugs which she said I could have. We would load up and do a return journey to the monastery saw up some more logs which I stacked around each side of the cabin. Sleep overnight and return to the farm early next morning. I had given some thought to what Heinreiche had said about a pigeon pen and had come to the conclusion that my friendly cunning old fox was correct. I suspiciously thought that at some time in his life he had lived in the mountains, he was a wealth of information and I was glad to have him as a friend.

I wasn't surprised when Heinreiche said he had something for me. Two small pigeon baskets with two pigeons in each basket, he said they would travel in comfort on the dogs back with bags of corn to balance. We sat down outside his pigeon coup and he told me exactly what to do. I must keep them up for a few days. He showed me the small tube which fitted over the pigeon's leg and inside a piece of paper with a message on it. It read: Merry Christmas Heinreiche from Franz. I said I would make sure I posted it. "This is just a trial run," he explained.

Ingerborg had prepared some bags of flour and other ingredients for me. She showed me how to bake and make cakes. I was also given bags of vegetables and Hans showed me how to store them and keep them dry. I learnt a lot from them. They knew how to survive heavy snowfalls and blizzards. Ingerborg had also packed a bundle of spare blankets. Hans also suggested that on my final journey before I was locked into the mountains he would prepare a meat pack which would be already salted ready for storage if I could find somewhere cold. I told him that it wasn't far to the snowline I could store it very well. I still needed more lamp oil which Romulus could carry for me in his panniers. Remus carried tins of dog food and pigeon corn in his. They looked at me strangely as I fastened the pigeon baskets across their backs. We said our goodbyes and set off for the monastery.

The first job was to make a pigeon coup which I attached onto the back of the cabin. It was big enough to hold four pigeons and a sturdy pen outside for them to flutter about in. They would be sheltered by the walls of the monastery. I cut some long grass and dried it in front of the fire for winter bedding. Our side of the cabin was now stacked high with cut logs for the fire. I now set about cutting more to stock on the other side. This would also act as an extra lining against the cabin walls should the winter be really severe. I had saved piles of sawdust which I had planned to use on the floor of the cabin. The stone slabs would be cold to walk on. My food store was looking good – the shelves housed all my tins of food and even the dogs food had a shelf. The stash of blankets were neatly folded away and were dry. I planned on bringing in a day's supply of firewood each night and put it close to the hearth where it would dry out overnight. I also kept two buckets of water inside which I would have to fill from the well outside. Inside the monastery walls were my roofing materials which if the weather permitted I would work on during the winter months. My first aid kit sat on the shelf next to the bags of flour. It contained bandages and antiseptic creams plus aspirins and decongestants remedies which Ingerborg had provided. As I took stock of my supplies I figured I was ready for my lonely vacation in the mountains. My next journey to the farm would be my last for a while so I double-checked my supplies again and of course the dog food and pigeon corn. I went outside to check the pigeons they seemed happy enough cooing at each other. Heinreiche said to keep them penned up for a while before releasing them. I decided to try my hand at sending a message. I wrote "see you soon, Franz" and put it in the very small container that Heinreiche had attached to the pigeon's leg. I carried the pigeon out of the pen and let it go, it landed on the cabin roof and seemed happy to stay there. I guess my attempts at sending messages had failed.

As we made our way back to the farm, I couldn't help thinking if I was doing the right thing it was a bit late to have any doubts now. I quickly shrugged away these thoughts and soon we were being greeted by Ingerborg and Hans. I was shown around the greenhouse by an excited Ingerborg, the flowers were in full bloom, I checked the vegetable plot and everything looked ready for picking. After we had eaten, I set about digging up the potatoes and cutting cabbages and lettuces for Ingerborg to sell on her market stall on Friday. Hans had said he was having one of his pigs slaughtered. I declined his offer to assist him and decided to help Ingerborg take her produce to market instead. It took three trips to carry everything to her stall, flowers were cut, bread and cakes and all the vegetables and lettuce. Ingerborg soon had a crowd of people around her. I left her to it and visited Heinreiche. He greeted me with a big smile on his face. He held out the small piece of paper for me to see. "See you soon, Franz," he said he felt very pleased with our combined efforts. He said he had something else to show me. I followed him with interest into his private quarters. On the table was a rifle which he picked up and asked if I had ever shot anything.

I shook my head. "Never" I said.

He held the rifle out to me and showed me how to hold it up to my shoulder. "You must learn to shoot,

Franz." Confused I asked him why. He went on to say that sometimes in the mountains, wolves and even the occasional bear may stray down from the high peaks in search of food. I needed to be able to scare them off if this did happen. He offered to give me some lessons in shooting before I went back up to the monastery for the winter.

Two days later with the rifle and some bullets Heinreiche took me over the fields to where he had set up some targets. I suspected he used this place himself on occasions. After about four hours of tuition Heinreiche claimed I would be able to scare off any predator but told me to practise when I got back up in the mountains and to take good care of his rifle.

Ingerborg was over the moon with her takings on the market and said we need to expand the garden as demands had exceeded all expectations. Hans told her he would plough up another part of the field for her.

Dietre asked about the papers Hans kept in the loft. Hans said I could take them as he thought of them as rubbish. Dietre said he would spend the winter looking through all the old papers.

With another pigeon from Heinreiche and all my supplies loaded my dogs looked anxious to start the journey. We bade farewell to our friends in Carmen and set off on our journey into the mountains. This time it would be months before we saw them again. Ingerborg hugged me and with tears in her eyes told me to take care. I told everybody I was going to be very busy and the time would pass by quickly.

It was now late October and the weather was closing in. I cut as much timber as I could to make sure I would be warm during the cold spell. The cabin was surrounded by logs stocked right up to the eaves and even more against the monastery walls. The large roof timbers lay on the floor ready for me to start work on them. I measured the gable ends and the main central beam which were the load bearing structures. I had taken careful measurement of the olds ones still supporting the old roof. If I could construct the new beams I would be able to start replacing the roof come spring. I even had a go at making the tiles I got better at it gradually. What I would need is some means of lifting the old beams down and putting up the new ones. If I had still been working at the pit all I needed to do was go into the workshop and borrow some lifting gear but that wasn't happening here. I remembered my college days and the history we were taught about how the Romans coped but I didn't have any slaves and Romulus and Remus didn't look that interested.

I cut the timber for the first gable end a lot of sawing but at least it kept me warm, and I was enjoying it. I would take a break for a day or so and take the dogs for a walk along our new trail. So far the snow had kept away but not for long. I awoke one morning to find everywhere white over. It had now started to get cold and work outside came to a halt. I made sure the pigeons had enough straw for their boxes they seemed content enough.

The cabin was nice and warm and the dogs stretched out quite content with the occasional request to go outside. I busied myself drawings plans and stocking up with wood. I did try baking bread but it wasn't as good as Ingerborg's. I had put the fresh meat outside the cabin and when I last checked it the meat was frozen which was good. I would take what I wanted in the cabin and let it thaw out. Dietre had given me a small radio with some batteries so in an evening I would tune in and get some music also news of the war. The Germans were being very brutal and lots of civilians were being killed. Heinreiche despised his mother land and called them???? Being guided along by a maniac they called the Fuhrer.

I had survived the first month and was feeling quite proud of myself. I had cut a lot of the timber to shape and was now fitting it together, I only fitted them loosely. As I looked up to the roof I began to wonder how I would lift them into position once the old timbers had been taken out. It was food for thought and I would spend a lot of time thinking about it. I could feel the temperature dropping as we rolled into December. The peaks in the distance were now covered with snow making it a winter wonderland. I took the dogs out for a walk and they enjoyed it catching snowballs as I threw them. As Christmas Day was drawing near I decided to send Heinreiche a Christmas message, that's if the pigeon wanted to go. I wrote: Merry Christmas to you all from Franz. Everything is okay. I put the message in the container and attached it to its leg. Once more he hung about on the roof before taking off.

I cooked myself a chicken for Christmas Day and added a selection of vegetables. I also found a can of beer stashed in with the dog food. Heinreiche would have put that in. I ate my meal by candlelight and once again the memories came flooding back how Carmen and me would sit in the fire glow and drink our chocolate before going to bed. It was a sad Christmas for me but I told myself to pull myself together and put on the radio. The news wasn't good. The Germans had been accused of mass murder of the Jews in Poland and other countries. Troops were fighting in other parts of the worlds but Hitler was still rampaging all over France and even in the deserts of Africa. How would a person like him have been elected by the German people? Heinreiche was right − I remember the First World War was with the Germans. What a nation.

I had creosoted all the beams and gables and that made the monastery stink a bit but the weather soon took the smell away much to the pleasure of Romulus and Remus.

The New Year brought some wintery sunshine so we went out for a walk where it was possible. My meat store was still intact as the weather kept it nice and cold. The mountains looked as pretty as any Christmas card I had seen. Although it was still very cold we picked our way along the rocks for quite a while the ground seemed to level out a bit more here and made walking comfortable until we started to climb the ridge again. My piles of three bricks were still visible reminding me of my plan to find a route through the mountain. We walked back and followed the path down to the lake. It was frozen over but I could still hear flowing water trickling into it from source.

Soon the time had come for me to go back down the mountain to the farm; spring was getting near and the mountain almost clear in the low lying areas. Only in the high mountains and high peaks did the snow still hang about like a white blanket. I collected all my rubbish, empty cans and large bones and anything that wouldn't burn and put them in a bag to take back with me. I didn't want to create any little dumps in the mountains. I let go the remaining two pigeons with a message to Heinreiche to get the biers in.

The dogs became excited as we made our way up the ridge, they knew where we were going.

Ingerborg and Hans were looking for us as we broke the tree line above the farm. I was greeted with smiles, kisses and bear hug. They were very pleased to see that I had survived a harsh winter in the mountains. Heinreiche had called in to tell them I was on my way. As we sat down to a well cooked meal I told them everything I'd done and how much I had enjoyed myself with the two dogs as company. Hans asked if I had shot anything I shook my head. "Only a piece of wood," I replied. I looked around the farm garden and in the greenhouse Ingerborg had managed it well, Daffodils were almost in bloom and small pots of other bulbs adorned the shelves. Hans had ploughed up another piece of the field and it looked ready to sow. I said he could earn a decent living from just a small holding instead of pigs and sheep. I said goats would be more profitable from their milk. Heinreiche leapt for joy when I joined him in the bier Keller, my bier was already on the table. Dietre said he had some more information and Olga and Christina just popped over to wish me well. They were both good looking girls and would flirt with me. Saying two girls in the log cabin would have been cosier than two dogs. I fobbed them off telling them I was going to be a monk. I asked Heinreiche if he had any rope pulley blocks I would need at least two sets for lifting the main roof beams and gable ends into place. He said he would look if not he knew where he could get them. He asked how I was doing with the roof tiles. I told him it was boring work. He also asked if I had shot his rifle.

"Practice makes perfect," he said. I asked him what Germans looked like in case I saw any, "like me" he gave a loud belly laugh which echoed through his shop "but in uniform and carrying guns". He pointed out to two rolls of roof felt and asked if I needed them. They were heavy but he put one across my shoulders I found I could manage one at a time. I told him I also needed some bags of mortar but only in half-sized manageable bags. He said they would still be heavy he suggest he repack it in quarter-sized bags for when I next came. I told him I would buy the bier that evening as he had been a good friend.

After visiting Dietre who had found some old signatures on the paperwork from Han's loft and was trying to find out more information. I checked I had done everything I could at the farm and began getting stores together for another spell in the mountains. I told Ingerborg I was gradually making a trail over the mountains to the other side and asked what was the name of her sister's village to tell her sister to look out for me because one day I will make my way through to their farm.

There was a strong wind blowing around the monastery when I finally got there and a few more loose timbers and tiles littered the floor. My scaffolding was still secure so the next day I climbed up and started to remove the old beams and gable ends. It was dusty hard work. The timbers had been bedded in on a layer of mortar and fastened with brackets. The timbers were not in good condition the weather had eaten away at them and needed to be replaced. The floor of the monastery looked like a bomb site when I had finished and I had chipped away most of the old mortar causing a lot of dust much to the disproval of Romulus and Remus who disappeared outside as soon as I had begun. Late afternoon saw most of the heavy work done so I retired for the day to a lamb steak and vegetables courtesy of Hans and Ingerborg.

The next day we went for walks doing a bit more trail blazing. I still found myself following false trails and walked up a few blind alleys before finding an easier way through but that was ok part of the game and I was enjoying it that was the most important part. I took compass readings and marked positions on the map not forgetting the invaluable pile of three stones at strategic points. We had been travelling for about three hours when the land began to fall away from the high ridge. I followed what I hoped was a gradual slope for about two hundred metres and then the land opened up again into a sort of valley with its steep sides looking down on me. It was a natural valley with a stream running through it and bushes growing from its sides. I trod cautiously not wanting to be caught out ever again in a flash flood. The dogs lapped at the flowing water not a bit concerned. Slowly I made my way through the valley listening and watching the steep sides. It stretched out almost two hundred metres before gradually rising to the height of the ridge. I marked it on the map. Next I walked up the sloping sides of the ridge at about a hundred and twenty metres up the steep face I saw what I thought was a natural break stretching along the length of the valley. It looked as if the side section had broken away leaving a step in the side about a metre wide. I was curious to know if the other part of the ridge was ready to break away. I found the rest to be a solid wall of rock. It was obvious that at some time maybe due to weather conditions the loose shale had broken away and lay down in the valley. Anyway I thought that would be a readymade path should the valley be flooded. I marked it on the map with a question mark. Returning to the monastery we had a good supper in front of a lovely fire. It did get chilly of an evening as could be expected.

I worked slowly and I worked safely making sure that when I was working on the roof I always wore the safety harness. Heinreiche had supplied me with also two sets of rope pulleys which were invaluable. I had built two 'A' frames from which I hung a set of pulleys I could lift the larger timbers and manoeuvre them into position. Fixing them to the brickwork with metal brackets which Heinreiche had supplied the structure began to take shape. With the mortar I bedded them in and sealed any holes in the walls. The next job was to put some supporting four-inch cross struts down the whole length at two foot intervals this would then have the felt secured ready for fixing batons across to take the tiles. I know I had a lot more tiles to make and so cut the logs to size ready for when I came back from the farm.

Before I completely removed the roof tiles I noted carefully how they had been fitted. Like a slated roof they had to be fitted so that they didn't leak. It was a masterpiece of craftsmanship which had been carried out over two hundred years ago. Mine had to be laid exactly the same. The felt underneath helped to waterproof it but the felt alone wouldn't have been enough. I made more than enough roof tiles and I was glad when they were finished my wrists ached holding the axe and then the large hammer.

My journey back to the farm had been successful Heinreiche had bagged up the mortar mix in smaller bags more manageable so I was able to spend a couple of days sealing the gaps around the beams. I stood back and looked up at the finished roof from inside and out. Now I needed a good storm to try it out. That came shortly and as I sheltered under the roof I felt a sense of pride. I think my boss at the pit would have been pleased. I looked at the large expanse under the roof and new ideas would start to formulate in my brain. I would box it in and make a large loft of it. More timber more cutting but what else had I to do. I set about cleaning the place up and then went for walkies with my dogs. I noticed the stream along the valley floor had deepened a little after the storm but not too much it was disappearing underground at some point.

We walked for another hour past the valley. If we decided to go further the bivvys would have to be spaced out along the trail as before. A nights rest before we explored any further but I think the dogs would have to sleep outside. We made our way back but not before marking our trail in the usual way. I wondered how far we would have to travel before we reached another village. Oh well, that's what we had to look forward to this summer.

With the roof complete I looked around for other things I could do. I know that if I wanted I could still use the log cabin but I had only planned to use that as a temporary shelter. I was now looking for something else. The cells along each wall had always held my attention each one would have been living and sleeping quarters for each Monk. I checked each one in turn, all twelve of them were in a dire strait. Each one measured about three metres by three metres which would just about hold a small bed and a small table. I supposed that was enough for one monk. They had a small chapel communal working facilities and a large dining area in front of the hearth. The toilet facilities were basically a hole in the ground. I would have to improve things here.

When I next made the journey to the farm Ingerborg and Hans had really gone to work on the home produce and Ingerborg had plans to extend the fowl coup saying there was a demand for fresh eggs. People in the village even came to the farm for things. Hans was delighted and said he had reduced his herd of sheep and pigs and was now mainly occupied with growing vegetables. I told them how pleased I was at their success. Dietre had discovered more signatures more interesting signatures on the documents from the loft. There was brother Frederick and Brother Matthew as well as others which had faded over the years, but it seemed that the farm had supplied the monks with lots of things over the years and always paid in some form or other. Medicines played a big part and also religious services were held in the small community. The monks would be quite happy to sleep in the barn if they had nowhere to stay and would travel around the area offering their services.

Heinreiche and Dietre were already in the bier Keller when I arrived and my bier paid for on the bar. Christina made a great fuss of me as usual. I was questioned about the monastery of course and I quickly told my friends that the roof was now finished. I handed Dietre his camera back and showed him the latest snaps. I must admit the roof looked good and I felt really proud of what I had accomplished all on my own. My friends complimented me on my success never doubting my capabilities. Heinreiche said how hard I had worked on the project. "If only you had electricity and power tools, you would have been in your glory, Franz, but we salute you just the same." The glasses were raised, emptied and refilled at Dietre's expenses.

"How would it be possible to get electricity up there?" he asked.

Heinreiche gave a wicked grin. "I know how," he teased. I smiled back at him.

"The electricity company would never do it," I replied.

"Who needs the electricity company?" asked Heinreiche. I looked at him and smiled, he was winding me up again, typical Heinreiche. Deitre looked confused.

"Go on then, Heinreiche, tell us how," he mused.

"A generator," said Heinreiche softly.

"But they're massive, heavy things," I said.

Heinreiche smiled again, his huge frame rocked with laughter. "But I know a friend who knows someone who says that at a price a small mobile generator can be acquired from the German military that arc using them and are quite compact, enough to run small equipment for them."

I listened with interest what I would give to have a power saw and lighting. I asked Heinreiche to find out more and to see what he could do about acquiring one but it would have to be carried by me up into the mountains plus fuel to run it. I couldn't wait for a generator I had work to do. I did what I could around the farm plus a couple of other jobs in the village for recommended clients. I gave Heinreiche my list of requirements which included another roll of felt, more dog food and a few more requisites. I paid my bill and said I would be leaving the next day. As I made my way back up into the mountains I thought about working on the cells and making myself a nice cosy bedroom. I had already designed myself a double-sized bed. Well comfort begins at home.

I went down into the forest and searched around for roofing timber. There were six cells each side of the monastery, each almost three metres square. I tore off all the old timbers and tiles and redesigned the roofs. They were not a part of the integral structure but added on with access from inside the main building. I've seen a lot of churches with these added on type buildings. It was easy for me to cut lengths of planking. I could work from outside so that it enabled me to cut long lengths of timber, that's when I missed having the circular saw but I took my time what was the rush this was just like having a hobby. No deadlines, no foreman looking over your shoulder, stop when you want to, it was great. The roofing was the biggest problem around. The additions were just new doors and whatever bits of furniture were inside, it was all basic stuff really but I did improve on the originals. I felted the roofs, if need be I could make wooden tiles later. My double bed was going to be good and I took my time carving a nice headboard. I didn't have a spring base, it was slats on which I would place a good firm mattress which I would have to make myself. The doors were all plane pine boards which I would stain at a later date. I completed three of the cells before breaking off and going walkies again. It was late August and I had just started cutting logs for my winter months. We made it as far as the valley and I erected one of the bivvys in a nice sheltered spot above the valley.

The following morning after sharing my one-man bivvy with two Pyrenean mountain dogs I decided to walk a bit further before returning to the monastery. It was time-consuming trying to find an easy trail but eventually I climbed a slight rise and found myself looking out over a vast plateau. Far below I could see cattle grazing in lush green pastures. Further in the distance on the skyline thin whispers of smoke curling up towards the heavens. I took a reading with my compass and scrutinised the map I hoped I hadn't stumbled across a German village.

We were about five hours walk away from the monastery so I thought it time to start back. There was always another day. It was late afternoon when the front door creaked open the dogs ran inside and started sniffing around. I know they were hungry so my first task was to feed them. As I looked round I made the decision that the log cabin would have to go now as I had plans for the interior of the monastery. The following morning I began to dismantle it. The timber I had plans for, so I placed them in a pile. I worked on it all day. We sat in front of an open hearth that evening eating a hastily cooked meal. It was a surprise to see a large open space I had created now that the log cabin had gone. The roof space looked huge and soon my brain was full of creative ideas. The rear wall of the chapel was directly in line with the hearth but about fifteen metres away. I would build a dining area there with a healthy space in front of the hearth as a relaxing area from the rest of the monastery. There would be a hallway each side of the chapel leading to the cells and to the other end of the monastery where I had anticipated washrooms and toilets. I was planning this as I had imagined it had been built two hundred years ago. But of course this was going to take forever but there again what else had I got to do; I was where I wanted to be in the peace and quiet of the mountains with my beautiful four-legged companions. I had friends down below in Carmen. I didn't need people around me all of the time. I had spiritual company and I know now what brought me here. When I was ready I would refurbish the chapel to its former glory.

Part 7

Dietre called me into the library he had more maps to show me. All along the mountain ranges at some time during the sixteenth to seventeenth centuries monks had travelled and established small groups of different orders and in turn built monasteries the most famous of course the one in the St. Bernard pass, who with their St. Bernard dogs rescue people in the mountains.

I couldn't see St. Franz with his two Pyrenean Mountain dogs Romulus and Remus being as famous but it was interesting to find out about such things and Dietre was enjoying his researching.

As we talked over a pint of bier Heinreiche asked if I was going to spend another winter at the monastery. I told him I was and had knocked the log cabin down and was working on refurbishing the cells and toilets. "It will be like a hotel," he remarked. Dietre's eyes lit up. "Why not, Franz?"

"When this ridiculous war is over you could set yourself up in the guided tour business and allow hikers to stay at your monastery." We all laughed at the idea.

Heinreiche asked how I was going to keep warm in the cells during winter. The log cabin had proven to be alright but the cells are on an outside wall and could be cold. I said I would have to think about something.

Ingerborg asked if I had managed to find her sister's farm. I told her I was nearly there. She immediately went down into the village and made a phone call from the Post Office. She came hurrying back excited, "They will be looking out for you from now on. My sister's name is

Gerda and her husband is Rainer and they have cows in a field at the foot of the mountains."

It was time for me to start taking food supplies up to the monastery. I still had time to make a few more journeys so I started gathering things together. Heinreiche said he had already selected the pigeons for me to take and he also had something else I might be interested in. He lifted it up and put it on the counter in front of me. "What is it?" I asked.

"A wood burning stove," he said proudly. It stood eighteen inches high with a glass front.

"It looks heavy," I replied. He picked it up in his hands and lifted it off the counter.

"Not too heavy for a mountain man like you, here you try." I lifted it, guessing it weighed about twenty-five pounds I looked at my German friend who stood there hardly being able to contain himself from laughing.

"That will fit in your cell and keep you warm, my friend."

"How many cells did you say there was?"

Heinreiche was the nicest man I had ever known although he was always interested in other people's business — nobody knew anything about him not even Dietre. "Next time I will have the pigeons for you, Franz," he said as I left with the stove across my shoulders. I don't know anyone else who can be as persuasive as Heinreiche.

Ingerborg asked me what I lay on. I told her I had my sleeping bag which was padded. She showed me a mattress cover which when she opened it out was a full-sized one. "We used to fill this with straw and packed properly was very comfortable to lie on. You need something more than a sleeping bag now." She took me into the barn and told me to hold open the mattress. She gathered armfuls of straw and packed it into the cover when it was full she lay it on the ground and started to mould it into shape. "More straw" she would say and would pack it when she had finished, she rolled on it and punched and packed it into shape. "Try that, Franz." When I had given my approval she started to unpack the straw. Folding the mattress cover she handed it to me. "Take the cover, the straw will be packed for you to carry next time."

We set off fully loaded as usual with the dogs laden with their food which Otto was still paying for. I couldn't wait to get back. I wanted to do as many journeys as I could before the snows came. It was now early September, another month maybe and I would be snowed in for the winter.

I set about sawing logs for my fire and following Heinreiche instructions fitted the log burner in my bedroom up the corner on the outside wall. I had to chisel a hole in the wall for the metal pipe which was the chimney. I must admit Heinreiche was right as always it would have been cold without it. We worked for a few days and then on a nice September morning went for walkies. As I stood on the spot looking down at the cows in the field I had a burning desire to carry on. I checked my watch, it was lunchtime and the sun lit up a lovely blue sky.

I looked across the field at the man herding the cows as we entered the field he looked over at us. As soon as he saw the two dogs he waved and started to make his way towards us. "Are you Franz?" he called out. I acknowledged who I was and a broad grin crossed his face. "I am Rainer, I've been looking out for you." He shook my hand and made a great fuss of the dogs. "Please, Franz, come to the farm Gerda has prepared some food for us she is very excited."

I embraced them both. Gerda was a little younger than Ingerborg but very much like her. I was invited to sit down and soon I was eating a lovely cooked meal during which I answered a barrage of questions. They were very homely just like Ingerborg and Hans and I felt at ease with them immediately. I asked if they were bothered by Germans being as they were closer to Germany. Rainer said occasionally they were visited by sinister looking men who would walk around the village pretending to be tourists but everyone knew they were SS or Gestapo and kept very quiet. The villages had a system of notifying everyone when they had visitors. The church bell would suddenly be used for a training session by the bell ringers. Rainer asked if I was going to stay a while, I would be very welcome and Gerda had already made up a bed. He then asked if I would like a tour of the farm. He was very proud of his dairy herd and proudly showed off his milking shed. Gerda made cheese which was sold in the village; the milk was collected each day and taken to the local dairy. Gerda was asking about Ingerborg and her small holding saying what a brilliant idea it was and she would like to do something similar. I looked around the farm and behind the milk shed. There was a piece of ground that could be turned into vegetable plot quite easy. I told Gerda that next day I would plan it out for her and start her off. Rainer asked about the monastery and marvelled at how I had found it, no one else had ever ventured into the mountains like I had. Gerda kept hens and ducks and sold the eggs in the market. I said she could easily grow vegetables and do the same as Ingerborg. Rainer kept a few goats and two pigs which were fattened up for bacon. He also had a field that was solely for hay. I said that when the winter was over I would visit them again. I marked out the vegetable plot and also suggested building a lean-to greenhouse at the back of the cowshed. I suggested Rainer start collecting old panes of glass from anyone in the village. I started them off by digging a few rows and suggested they try to carry it on so as the winter could break the soil up. They were very pleased with my visit and said I was welcome anytime. Rainer suggested that we must arrange a signal to notify me if there were any Germans in the village. I suggested a flag but Rainer said it might look suspicious. He said if the cows weren't in the field there are suspicious characters around that would be the signal not to come.

I stayed another day and helped Rainer around the farm. There was always things that needed doing requiring another pair of hands and I was always eager to help. I said that maybe I would be able to get another visit in before the winter locked me in. I told them how Heinreiche and I had our method of communication during the winter and Rainer said what a good idea it was.

After a hearty breakfast we said our goodbyes and started our journey back to the monastery. I found that I could do the six-hour journey quite easily with the occasional fifteen minute break. The work I had been doing had toned me up nicely and my twenty-sixth birthday found me in peak condition. We sawed more logs for the winter and I made more wooden roof tiles to cover the roof of the cells. I checked my supplies before setting off for Carmen. I think if I stayed a few days this would probably be my last visit to the farm. I did want to visit Gerda and Rainer one more time before winter closed in.

It's always a pleasure coming down from the mountains and being welcomed by your friends they make you feel really important. Heinreiche had a broad smile on his face as I met up with him and Dietre in the bier Keller that evening and fired all sorts of questions at me. "Are you going to winter in the mountains again?" asked Dietre.

"Did you fit that wood burner?" asked Heinreiche. "Are you sure you don't want company?" asked Olga. We drank and laughed all evening it really felt good to relax and let yourself go once in a while and I enjoyed it. We discussed the war briefly.

Heinreiche became a bit uptight when we talked about the atrocities going on in Poland and other countries. "I condemn my countrymen," he said angrily. Dietre quickly changed the subject and struck up conversation on a lighter note.

Ingerborg and Hans had been busy in the farm garden and Ingerborg had made a killing with her flowers. Now the winter bulbs were being put in. Hans had harvested the root crops and had stored them ready for Ingerborg. The market stall was now so big and popular Hans had to take everything to her on the horse and cart and collect her at the end of the day with whatever was left over. Hans was thinking of having one of the pigs slaughtered for Christmas but hadn't yet made up his mind. I helped him extend the chicken coop and Ingerborg had thought about turkeys for the following year but hadn't decided for definite. She asked to give their blessings if I should see Gerda and Rainer again. She was thrilled to bits that I had made their acquaintance and said Gerda had phoned the Post Office right away with the good news.

Heinreiche lifted the wood burner onto the counter. "This is the last one I have, are you going to take it, Franz?"

I looked at my big friend. "What about the pigeons?" I asked.

He nodded to Romulus and Remus. "What about your assistants?" he asked with a raucous laugh. He then placed the rifle on the counter. "And this." The pigeon baskets were fitted onto the dogs' backs, two pigeons in each. Heinreiche reckoned I should let them breed and build a proper loft for them. It was a waste of time arguing with him.

Hans had cut up some joints of meat and put them in my pack. Ingerborg had baked bread and cakes. With the stove on my shoulders I was now carrying more than I normally did and the dogs too were well laden. With hugs and kisses we said our goodbyes and set off on our journey. It took almost eight hours of travelling to reach the monastery, we stopped for breaks and to rest our loads. I would not travel with such loads again − we were putting our lives at risk. By the time we reached the monastery we were well and truly fatigued. I lit a big fire in the hearth and we just crashed out in front of it.

The weather was getting colder now and I had to decide if I was going to visit Gerda and Rainer before it closed in on me. I had put the pigeons in the coup but one of the cocks began attacking the other cock so I had to separate them. After a week they were still as bad so I thought I would let one of them fly off and then I thought I wondered if Rainer would keep one. I decided to make him a present and start him off with his own coup.

Loaded up with things Ingerborg had asked me to pass on to Gerda and the pigeon basket on Romulus's back we set off. The journey took just over six hours of leisurely walking and resting. As we looked down at the farm I could see the cows in the field. Rainer hadn't forgotten our signal. We were greeted warmly and were soon enjoying a late afternoon lunch. The light began fading by the time we had eaten another sign of the approaching winter. Rainer said he would keep the pigeon in with the chickens in the henhouse. I asked him not to let it out for quite a while or it would fly back to me at the first chance it got. I stayed with them for two days enjoying their food and their company. I was told they had a son but he was too wrapped up in some business venture in Zurich to visit very often. Rainer had started to cultivate the land behind the henhouse and had planted potatoes as a first crop to break up the ground. He was gathering glass panels from wherever he could and already had some stashed away.

Gerda had folded two thick blankets for me to take to the monastery. I had measured up for the lean-to greenhouse and asked Rainer to start collecting odd pieces of timbers for the frame. We left at ten o'clock in the morning, saying our goodbyes with hugs and kisses and preparing more visits when spring came. As we made our journey through the mountains it started to snow, lightly at first but by the time we had reached the monastery it was getting heavy.

I awoke next morning to a blanket of snow and quite a blizzard blowing. As my bacon sizzled on the open hearth fire I looked around for things I would be doing during this winter. I had stored plenty of timber in and around the place so I wouldn't have to go outside. I looked upward at the open span of the roof, I had plans to make a huge loft and possibly put in another floor. I also wanted to enclose the dining area and the kitchen. If only I had a circular saw and a planer it would have been done in a flash. As it was I had a lot more sawing by hand to keep me busy. The dogs would stand in the vestibule with the outer door open longing to go romping in the snow but they wouldn't go far without me.

Mid-December found us completely snowed in. The snow covered peaks glistened in the morning sunlight as far as the eyes could see. I went outside to my meat store trying to decide if it was to be a pork joint or a chicken for my lunch. I scattered some pigeon corn in the coup. I suddenly noticed a pigeon flying around waiting to descent onto the coup. I stood back and allowed it in. To my amazement it flew in and started attacking the cock. I suddenly realised it was the one I had left with Rainer, I reached and grabbed hold of it and put it in a separate basket wondering how on earth it had escaped. I couldn't help notice the note sticking out of the tube fastened to its leg. I went back into the monastery and unrolled the piece of paper. I couldn't believe the message written on it. "Franz, please come, we need your help immediately, please come quickly" Rainer. I read the note again and again, was this a joke or was it a genuine cry for help from my friends? I walked around the monastery wondering what to do, I was completely snowed in, how could I help them? I walked outside and looked up into the mountains. I had never travelled them in conditions like this, how was I going to be able to travel now? It was a blue sky with a weak sunshine. The wind was bitingly cold. I made up the fire in the hearth with slow burning wood and placed the joint of pork in the slowest part of the oven surrounded by vegetables in water.

If I was going to make the journey I would need to start off at first light allowing for daylight hours to help me. I sorted out my warmest gear and snow boots. Not knowing what to expect I picked up the rifle. I also needed the short pair of snow shoes and a strong stave. The dogs were watching me intently wondering what was going on. It had stopped snowing by five in the morning so with my backpack carrying my necessities I walked out of the monastery closing the door behind me. Romulus started barking first and then Remus joined in. They didn't want to be left alone. I walked back and opened the door almost being knocked down by two anxious Pyrenean Mountain dogs. They were having a time of their lives charging through the snow and making tracks for me to follow. Eventually when they had got over their excitement they settled down and led the way very much to my surprise the seemed to know where we were heading even if I couldn't see the trail. I felt my way along trying to identify known passages through rocks. To my surprise they hesitated and had me wondering how they knew where we were heading. After a long hard slog I managed to identify the entrance to the valley but was shocked at how deep the snow was. It must have been ten to fifteen feet deep for the length of the valley. There was no easy way we could pass through here. We rested while I tried to figure what we were going to do. A misty grey dawn engulfed us and I had visions of abandonment. I looked up at the ledge a hundred and twenty feet above us. It looked impossible snow had fallen from above and blocked it off. In desperation I told the dogs to 'stay' whilst I clambered up the steep snow covered ramp to the ledge. I felt with my stave and began to scrape away the snow. On my hands and knees I felt my way along pushing away the snow watching it fall into the valley. I wondered frantically whether or not it was traversable. I cleared a path ten metres along and then called for my dogs. Slowly inching their way along they joined me on the ledge. I thought to myself *I must be mad, surely this must be a hoax.* I inched my way along and the dogs followed. After what seemed to be an eternity we finally cleared the ledge and were looking down towards the end of the valley. It was hard going, I never saw any of my markers but my dogs led the way and eventually we were looking down the slope towards the cow field only there were no cows to be seen. I pondered if this was because the snow was too deep for the cows or was that a warning signal.

We approached the farm, the grey mist giving it a sinister appearance there was no sound or any light. I approached the barn and opened the door.

Rainer appeared out of the gloom his sad face lit up when he saw me. He held out his arms to embrace me. I could see the tears welling up. "What's the matter Rainer?" I asked.

"Oh! Franz, something terrible has happened." He led me into the house where Gerda was trying to coordinate herself into getting breakfast. When she saw me she rushed to embrace me. "Oh, Franz, thank goodness you are here, can you help us please?" I sat her down and asked her what had happened.

"The French Resistance has brought two escaped prisoners here. They rescued them from the Gestapo in France and have been trying to get them across the border into England but they are being hunted by the Gestapo and have brought them to our village and left them here while they try and lead the Gestapo on a false trail. One of the resistance men is brother-in-law to our Mayor, that's what brought them here and now the mayor has asked us to ask you if you can take them out of the village into the mountains. The Gestapo are threatening to shoot anyone who is harbouring the prisoners. I'm sorry, Franz, we just don't know what else to do, you were our only hope."

Franz looked at Gerda and then at Rainer. "I don't want to get involved in this, this is not my war and it's impossible to travel the mountains in this weather. I have risked my life getting here, why doesn't the Mayor sort out his own problems without getting me involved?"

Rainer offered a package to Franz. "What's all this?" I asked.

Rainer looked at me clearly ashamed. "The Mayor has offered you a large sum of money to help us," said Rainer holding out the package. I took the package and slammed it hard down on the table.

"I don't want the Mayor's money, I have money, what I want is a generator and electric, not money."

Rainer picked up the package and left the house. Gerda was crying I followed her into another room where she opened the door into a bedroom. Two figures emerged covered in blankets. Gerda went up to them and beckoned them into the room. She removed the blanket from the first person revealing a mop of blonde hair. I gazed at the sad face of the woman, tears were streaming down her face. Gerda removed the blanket from the second person revealing a younger face but horribly blood-stained and disfigured, she was also crying. I gazed at them open-mouthed. "They're women," I said in amazement. "You're asking me to take two women up into the mountains in the middle of winter, it's impossible they will die in the mountains, we may all die in the mountains."

"We would rather die in the mountains than in the hands of the Gestapo," the first woman said putting her arms around the second woman who seemed to be a younger version. She unveiled the half-covered face revealing the broken face, the damaged eye socket, broken nose and broken jaw. The face looked horrific.

"Who did this to her?" I asked peering into the pale blue eyes of what had once been a beautiful-looking girl.

"The Gestapo raped and brutalised my daughter and smashed her face in with a rifle butt. Herr Gruber was his name."

I stepped back and took the older woman by the arm and led her to the window. The blizzard was still in full force. I wiped the window and pointed up into the mountains. "Can you see yourselves climbing up there for at least ten hours in this weather, you will die."

The woman looked at her daughter and then at me. "Better to die in the mountains than at the hands of Herr Gruber," she said defiantly.

"Okay," I said, "so let's get you ready for the worst journey of your life. For a start you need proper clothes and footwear."

Gerda said she had suitable clothing for them both. "We have two snowsuits made of bear skins, we don't use them ourselves."

Rainer appeared through the back door. "Franz, the Mayor has promised on his life that he will get you a generator." I asked Rainer if he had any long reins he could make harnesses for his two dogs. A long double lead for each dog and two staves one for each woman. He watched as Gerda dressed the two women in the bear skin suits. She also produced two pairs of bear skin boots.

"You can carry nothing with you only what you can carry in your pockets. Rainer, you must burn everything they have touched and spread black pepper everywhere. If the Gestapo bring tracker dogs they will soon follow us. Tell them you are overrun with rats and when we are gone let your cows into the field they will hide the tracks." I pulled the hoods of the suits well over their eyes.

"I can't see," the woman said.

"There's no need to see, let the dogs guide you, close your eyes and just let them lead you. Don't allow them to pull you only to guide you. Hold onto the lead in your left hand and feel your way with the stave and just take small steps one foot in front of the other. Just walk slowly and automatically, don't think about the journey think of something pleasant to occupy your mind."

Rainer gave Franz the bottle of rum. "Take a good drink it will keep your inside warm."

I then handed it to the two women, "Take a drink of this." I saw Gerda had prepared some food for the journey ahead she gave to each one. He picked up the womens shoes and put them in the large pockets of the bear skins. "You will need these if ever we make it over these mountains." I looked them over. "Are you ready maybe to die?" I asked.

We said goodbye to Rainer and Gerda. "Tell the mayor if he does not keep his promise I shall be after his blood."

"Okay, ladies, let's go and remember what I told you – my dogs are only to guide you, not to pull you."

The blizzard was still raging as they stepped out into the deep snow. Franz watched the women struggle to maintain their balance. "One small step at a time!" I yelled.

The going was slow and painful this was the worst weather I had been in. I had to keep looking back to see if they had fallen over. Slowly we crossed the first field, I looked back to see Rainer herding cows out into the snow. The women were struggling I could see but there was nothing I could do to make it easier. I and the dogs were treading down the snow to make it a bit easier for them. We crossed the second field and entered the tree line, the farm was now out of sight. I stopped to check as they were alright. The younger girl had been crying which I could well understand she must have been in great pain with her injuries I wondered what sort of person would be so brutal towards a young woman, he must be an animal this Herr Gruber.

I said we must push on, I checked the dogs' leads and asked if they were ready to carry on. We started to climb into the mountains I made slow manoeuvres hoping it would be easier for them. The wind was fiercely blowing the snow into my face. Was I glad I had grown my hair long and a long facial moustache and beard. I may have looked like a mountain man of the old west but that's what I was only in the mountains of Switzerland, anyway it kept my face warm.

We pushed on for another hour before I called a halt. We sheltered from the biting wind behind a rock. I pulled out the bottle of rum Rainer had stuck in my pocket and took a drink offering it also to the two women I said it was for medicinal purposes only to protect their inner organs. I asked if they wanted a bite to eat they declined. I waited fifteen more minutes before pushing on − I was feeling the strain so I don't know what these women felt, they must have been made of iron to endure this trip.

The weather was horrendous they couldn't have picked a worse day to escape from the Gestapo. My dogs ploughed through the snow but even they must be feeling the strain of two journeys the same day. I fondled their ears showing my appreciation I got wagging tails in response.

We were almost at the valley and I began to panic – would these weary women be able to cope with the ledge. I would go first and take the first woman with me crawling on all fours and using my small snow shoes to clear away the snow. I was finding it easy going so I halted at the widest part of the ledge and decided to go back for the other woman. Romulus lay down on my command and I told the lady just to rest where she was without moving. I managed to get past her and edged my way back along the ledge to where Remus lay with the other woman. I called him on and told the woman just to follow slowly on all fours. I kept looking back and giving words of encouragement. "Just feel the side of the ridge and move along it we are almost there." I worked my way past the first woman and checked as everybody was alright before edging myself along. The snow pretty deep this end of the ridge and so I had to crawl pretty slowly. We were just ten metres away from the end when I heard the low drone of the aeroplane. I looked back over my shoulder and could just see the spotter plane weaving left to right in a searching pattern. "Down!" I yelled. "Down flat as possible and don't move a muscle." I told the dogs to "stay put" and they obeyed. I tried to throw snow over our bodies as the plane zigzagged overhead. Not sure if we had been seen I unshouldered my rifle and checked it was loaded. From a peephole in the snow I watched as it drew nearer it was coming in very low but just above the ridge on the opposite side of the valley. He skimmed over and then zoomed upwards he turned around and came in for another look. I knew we had been spotted, I shouted for everyone to try and cover themselves in snow but I had a feeling we were in trouble. The plane rose high in the sky before diving down and entering the valley at a very low level. The pilot had seen us but what was he going to do. Rat-a-tat-tat the bullets screamed into the ridge above us causing a lot of snow and debris to come cascading down. I yelled for the dogs to "stay put" it must have been scaring them to death. The plane pulled up and rose high above us its engines screaming very loudly. I looked to see if he was going to do another run. He was but this time he was going to fly low into the valley. I propped myself up on one elbow and adjusted the sights for one hundred and twenty yards. If he was coming in very low he would be tilting his wing slightly so he could get a better look and to get his gun pointing over the side at us. I pushed my shoulder into the side of the ridge and lifted the rifle. Rat-a-tat-tat the pilot opened fire as he came in. Bullets spattered the side of the ridge. He was still a bit too far away from me although I felt the sting in my shoulder as one of the bullets ripped into me almost knocking me over. My left arm sagged useless as I adjusted my position. I brought my left knee up to support the rifle. Heinreiche was behind me telling me to take a deep breath and aim, hold your breath and squeeze the trigger is what he said as I aimed for the swede he had stuck on a pole when he was teaching me to shoot. The swede was the pilot's head as he drew closer still firing rat-a-tat-tat. I ignored the bullets ricocheting around me as I fired, reloaded, fired and reloaded, squeezing off the rounds in succession. I could almost see the colour in his eyes as he screamed past me. I watched as he eased the plane upwards and over the ridge on the far side of the valley. He was going to come in again. The plane screamed as it soared almost vertical and then the engine began to cough and splutter and then did a complete nosedive into the valley. Two minutes later there was an almighty explosion further along the valley. I watched as the black smoke blew towards us. "Thank you, Heinreiche," I murmured.

I called to the ladies that it seemed okay now to move further along. I called to the dogs who started to crawl towards me. I sat on a rock on a wide part and started to undo my coat. My left arm hung loosely by my side. "You're hurt," the woman said looking at the blood staining the snow.

"Yes, I took one in the shoulder. I have a wound dressing here, can you help me?" She quickly pulled aside my coat and began unbuttoning my shirt. I gave her the dressing and looked at the wound. The bullet had entered but had not gone straight through but it had broken my collarbone that's why my arm hung down useless. I gave her a wad of cloth for her to dab away the blood. I could see the hole, I looked up at the rock face to where I could see some icicles hanging. "Break one of those off and pass it to me," I said. She looked confused as I pressed the point of the icicle into the wound. "Now press on the wound dressing and strap my arm up to my chest using my scarf."

The first aid done, I suggested that a bite to eat before we moved any further. I asked if they were alright and I checked over my dogs. Another sip of rum and I was ready to push on we had reached almost the half way mark.

The blizzard had abated and it was now just a cold wind blowing against us. Once more I checked if the ladies were as well as could be expected. I myself felt exhausted my wound was still leaking I said to them, "At least you are out of reach of Herr Gruber." Whether it cheered them up I don't know, it was all I could think of to say. We travelled for another painful hour then rested for fifteen minutes. Apart from the sniffles from the younger woman nothing was said. I was amazed at how well they had coped. It must have been some ordeal they went through for them to want to suffer this journey to get away. I didn't want to get involved with the Germans and the war but now I had a German bullet in my shoulder so now I was involved.

The plane had crashed into the side of the valley the area was blackened by the explosion and had dislodged a vast amount of rocks and debris also causing huge amounts of overhanging snow to fall. I couldn't see any part of the plane it was completely buried. Maybe the spring thaw would reveal something.

At last the monastery loomed in sight I could see the shape of it through the murky mist that hung everywhere. As we made our approach the dogs got excited and started to bark. Both women threw back their hoods and gazed at the building. Within minutes we were standing in the vestibule. I turned up the oil lamp and guided them into the monastery apologising for it being more like a timber yard. The fire livened up as I undid the air vent and I could smell the pork joint and vegetables.

I removed their snowsuits and sat them in front of the fire. First of all I was going to feed my dogs. The kettle soon started to boil and the coffee cups filled. It was a welcome drink in front of a lovely warm fire. I pointed out where the toilets were and put two oil lamps for them to light their way. I also apologised for the very basic facilities. Hot water had to be carried from the kitchen, cold water already in there in buckets.

I laid out the table and started to layout the meal. The older woman who I had now fathomed out was the mother of the younger one asked where we were. I told her she was at my house in the middle of the Swiss Mountains and they would be spending the night here and commencing their journey early in the morning and that's all I could tell them. Who they were going to meet I didn't know, all I had been asked to do was get them through the mountains. Her daughter was having difficulty eating so I made a soup from the meat and vegetables and gave her a spoon, her mother helped her eat.

I had lit the wood stove in my bedroom and I checked that it was burning okay. The cell next to mine had not really been completed – there was only a single partly constructed bed in there and no bedding. This meant I was going to give them my room and bed and I would have to make-do with the bench in front of the hearth and my sleeping bag.

When the meal was finished and we had finished off another coffee. I suggested she take a look at her daughter's face we could clean her up a bit with some warm soapy water and try to make her comfortable. They agreed as long as we were very gentle. We sat her on the bench in front of the fire and either side of her gently trying to untangle her blooded blonde hair. It was matted and caked with dried blood and was difficult to do without hurting her. Her right eye socket was knocked out of shape and her eye was completely black. Her nose was broken and caked with blood and her jaw hung down horribly disfigured. We worked for a long time using the warm water to soften the dried blood. She cried out in pain at each touch. I warmed a cloth and kept dabbing her face. I had a jar of cream that I had found in one of the cells. Not knowing what it was I took it to the village chemist, who after close examination, said it was a soothing cream made from fresh herbs and was still useable despite being very old. I had used it on minor injuries myself so I decided to gently rub some on her face. It was warm and soothing and she did not complain. I then found some lengths of white cloth which I cut into longish lengths to use as bandages. Her mother gently wrapped them around her daughters face supporting her jaw and eye socket it was the best that could be done for her.

They slept in my bed I gave them all the blankets except one for myself. I stoked up the fire and began to prepare a saucepan of porridge for the breakfast. I had told them that we would be leaving at first light. As I stripped off my shirt the older woman came out and said she would put a fresh dressing on the wound which was now very inflamed. I needed urgent treatment to remove the bullet still in my shoulder. She bathed it gently and cleaned out the wound. From the way my arm was dangling useless at my side I assumed that the bullet had shattered my collarbone. I handed her a fresh wound dressing which she applied and then strapped up my arm.

She thanked me for all that I had done and if one day she could pay me back she would. I told her to go and get some rest as we still had a long journey ahead of us next morning. I told her that they had been very brave and had done extremely well. She said her name was

Margaret Anderson and her daughter's name was Joanna.

I slept until five in the morning waking suddenly as if out of a bad dream. My shoulder was throbbing so I took a couple of painkillers from my first aid kit. I suddenly thought I could have given the girl some last night. I placed the bottle on the table and went to see what the weather was doing. The dogs went out first and did their stuff before running up and down chasing snowflakes. It was still snowing but the wind chill had died down some.

The porridge was bubbling away on the hearth so I gently knocked on the cell door and called out "breakfast." It was a while before I heard the door open and the two bleary-eyed women made an appearance. First port of call was of course the toilets. I had placed a bucket of warm water in there for their disposal and a couple of towels. The oils lamps gave an eerie light but that was all there was, it wasn't the Ritz. We sat down and ate our breakfast. I asked if they had been able to sleep and they both nodded. The mother said the cream I had put on her daughter's face was very good. I said I wanted to set off as soon as we were ready; it was still a long arduous journey and we would need all the daylight hours we could get.

I made the fire up with slow burning logs hoping I would be able to make a quick return journey once I had delivered the two women to whoever was waiting for them.

I had a sudden thought I hoped they hadn't expected me to keep them at the monastery. I asked Margaret if anyone was meeting them, she said she didn't know what was happening perhaps the resistance men would be there. As a last thought I went to the pigeon coup and picked out a pigeon. I quickly scribbled a note. "Tell Ingerborg, two wounded fledglings coming in." I let the pigeon go hoping it didn't mind flying in the snow. We made decent progress I kept scanning the skies and listening for spotter planes but none came much to my relief.

We rested halfway and had a bite to eat and another sip from the rum bottle, which was almost empty now, I could see why the sailors were issued with it, it certainly warmed the cockles of your heart. My dogs were a godsend they sniffed their way through the snow guiding the two women safely and I was feeling more confident leading the way. The snow was easing off and a weak sun was trying to peep through the grey sky. In all it had been a nightmare of a journey and I would be glad when it ended, we were almost at the tree line when suddenly she screamed. I looked around to see the daughter slipping over the edge of the bank she lost her balance and began to roll down into the trees. It was a steep bank and she rolled over several times before she came to a sickening halt against a tree. I raced down the bank shouting to her mother to stay where she was. I reached Joanna but she wasn't moving but I could see that she was still breathing. Her leg was twisted beneath her and blood was seeping through her hair. I called to her mother to come down gently and to bring the dogs with her. I realised Joanna had broken her leg and had hit her head on the tree knocking her out. I told her mother that we would have to carry her the rest of the way. I felt in my boot for my sheath knife and fumbled in my pocket for whatever I could find. My mind raced as I looked around for saplings we needed to make a stretcher. I decided whilst she was unconscious to pull her leg straight and fasten a stick to hold it in position. I don't know whether it was the right procedure but I told

Margaret to hold onto Joanna whilst I did it. Fortunately, in amongst the rubbish in my pockets, I found some string with which I tied the stick to her leg and then bound them together. The next thing I had to do was cut saplings. I remembered from my boyhood days how the Indians in the films made a litter and let their horses pull it. I looked at my two dogs, yes they would do it. I searched for two long saplings and asked Margaret to find some shorter pieces. Within half an hour the litter was made, Joanne was still unconscious; gently we rolled her over and placed her on it. The long leather leads I made into harnesses for the dogs. I tied the litter to it and encouraged the dogs to pull. They were more than willing and soon we were back on the trail. Margaret held onto to Joanna to prevent her rolling off. As we left the tree line I fired two shots they would hear them at the farm and would recognise my distress signal. Hans appeared from the barn immediately entered the field he saw us at once and began ploughing through the snow towards us and Ingerborg followed. They could see at once that we were in trouble. Hans grabbed the dogs by their collars and lead them towards the barn. Ingerborg looked at the girl who was beginning to regain consciousness and then she looked at me. I was flagging weakened by the loss of blood I began to falter. Ingerborg put her arms around me and allowed me to lean on her. At the barn Hans unhitched the litter and between us we carried Joanna into the house and lay her on the couch. Ingerborg spoke to Hans who put on his coat and went out returning five minutes later with the doctor. Ingerborg led me into my bedroom where I collapsed on the bed completely exhausted. Margaret stayed with Joanna whilst the doctor examined her. I was drifting in and out of consciousness. After a while I could see the doctor probing for the bullet in my shoulder. He must have given me an injection and I passed out.

When I came around it was very quiet in my room. I could just hear the tick-tock of the clock on the wall. Everywhere was in darkness my shoulder felt very sore and I was all strapped up with my arm across my chest I lay there pondering where everybody was I was also very glad the nightmare journey was over.

Ingerborg came in and put the light on, I could see she had a tray with some steaming hot food. She put the tray down and sat on the bed. She leaned over and kissed my cheek. "Thank you, Franz, for all your help you have saved the lives of many people in Gerda's village. She has phoned and told me the Gestapo practically ransacked their homes and threatened them all. "You are a hero to them and they wish you well."

I tucked into the food with Ingerborg feeding me like a child. "Where are they?" I asked.

"They are gone, Franz, the doctor could do nothing for the girl's face, he has arranged for the resistance people to take them to a hospital somewhere in the mountains far from here. The woman called in to say thank you but you were unconscious."

I was allowed to get up and sat in front of the fire with Hans and Ingerborg recounting the hazardous journey to them. I told them I was anxious to get back to the monastery but Ingerborg told me that I had to go to the hospital in the next town for X-rays on my shoulder. She would take me the next day.

It wasn't far on the shuttle train and we were soon waiting in a queue for the X-ray machine. Within two hours I had been treated and my shoulder was now in a cast which I had to wear for six weeks.

Hans looked at me and said, "You will have to stay with us, Franz, you can't go into the mountains like that."

I looked at him and smiled, I nodded to the sun shining outside. "I will be gone tomorrow, my friend, and I'll see you in six weeks."

Heinreiche had popped up to see me, I thanked him for the use of his rifle. "Did you shoot anything, Franz?" he asked.

"Oh just some old noisy bird," I answered.

I was glad when I reached the monastery – the weather had abated and the sunshine illuminated the peaks my journey was slow but eventually I was entering the vestibule. The fire was almost out but quickly responded to some fresh fuel and soon I was resting in front of a lovely fire with my faithful companions at my feet.

Part 8

I rested well until I started to feel restless with only one arm I could use I was limited to what I could do. I read a lot and made drawings on how the loft would be when I got around to it. I had also thought about putting in another floor above the chapel, there was plenty of height. When I had finished all of the cells they would be fit to accommodate any of my friends who wanted to visit. I know Olga and Christina were anxious but I was concerned in case I couldn't get rid of them. I wanted Heinreiche to visit but he said he'd seen enough of the mountains in his lifetime. I wondered into the chapel I hadn't touched in here yet. As I opened the door my thoughts went straight to Carmen. I closed my eyes and stood in front of what had been the altar. This is where the previous owners would have held their prayer meetings. I don't know what I felt personally. I had abandoned God and my religious beliefs but I had thought that this place deserved to be refurbished and brought back to its former glory if only to the memory of those who had built it. I put it on my list of potentials. As I stood listening to the quietness of the chapel I felt goose bumps down my spine; I left the chapel and closed the door.

The toilets were the next place that needed refurbishing, I didn't like the hole in the floor with a footprint either side, something had to be done about that – our privy back home had been all boxed in with the cut up newspaper hanging on a piece of string comfortable reading included. The wash basins had been carved out of rock and mounted on a pedestal with a wooden plug in the plug hole and when you pulled out the plug your feet got washed. I took the dogs out for a short walk through the woods thinking of all the possible things I could do to improve the place. I also wondered if the mayor was going to honour his promise to get me a generator.

The six weeks dragged by but eventually it was time for me to visit the hospital. I travelled light with nothing but a list of supplies I needed. Ingerborg accompanied me to the orthopaedic hospital where my shoulder was X-rayed and then the plaster cast was removed. Everything was okay I just had to take things easy for six months and to avoid lifting heavy objects with my left arm. We left the hospital with smiles on our faces.

I went to see my friends in the bier Keller and celebrated my return to normality. Heinreiche said he had purchased four things with me in mind. When I asked him to tell me he burst out laughing "ten more wood burning stoves" he was hilarious and we all joined in with his raucous laughter. I had missed my friends and brought the beers all round even Olga and Christina joined in.

Dietre asked if I had found any relics or signs of the previous owners. He couldn't find any reference to any religious orders it could have been one of many without names or dates it was an impossible search. I said I still had plenty of work to do and would always be looking for clues.

It was still winter and the snow was still falling. I picked a sunny day to return to the monastery. I loaded my backpack with food and essentials. My dogs were loaded up with their own goodies. I told Heinreiche about the pigeon I had given to Rainer and the important part it played in the rescue of the Gestapo prisoners. He asked if I knew what had happened since. I told him I hadn't heard anything.

I opened the door of the vestibule and walked in. I felt at home again. The dogs too wagged their tails. The fire was just about still smouldering, I quickly opened the air vent and piled on the logs. As I looked around I wondered what it would be like to just flick a switch for all the lights to come on. I wondered if the mayor had got me a generator, I had to wait a few weeks more before the spring arrived and my first journey to see Rainer and Gerda and of course the mayor.

I kept busy cleaning up the place. I had neglected the cleaning due to my inability to get down on my knees and scrub floors. I looked at my bedroom and began stripping off the bedding. I shook the straw mattress and saw a shiny object on the floor and roll under the bed. Down on my knees I felt under the bed. The shiny object turned out to be a ladies earring. I held it in my hands and gazed at it. This was obviously Margaret's I never saw Joanna with any jewellery at all, probably torn off by the Gestapo. I looked at it and began to wonder if they escaped or had they been captured. I guess I would never know.

I finished my cleaning and had to admit it looked and smelt better for it. I went outside and checked on the pigeons. I decided to let them go but first I wrote Heinreiche a note. "Twelve wood burning stoves would be fine, can you deliver?" I could imagine the raucous laugh of his when he read it. The one pigeon didn't move I lifted it up to find three eggs in the nest. Well what did you expect that fighting cock had won.

When the time was right I got myself ready for the first trip of the New Year. I decided that Rainer and Gerda would be my first visit as I was curious to see if the Mayor had come up with anything. The trail was practically clear of snow and soon I was at the entrance to the valley. As I made my way through I came to a place that had completely changed. A huge pile of debris had broken away from the side and completely changed the landscape. I looked around for any sign of the plane. There was none, it had been swallowed up by tons of rocks brought down from the explosion. What remained was burnt out and charred. It would take years for any re growth to take place and I would have to find another way through.

Gerda was hanging out the washing when I broke the tree line and entered the field. I noticed that the cows were occupying the one corner – a good sign as all was well. She looked up when the dogs gave a welcoming bark and straight away started running towards me. She threw her arms around me and smothered me with hugs and kisses. What a lovely welcome Rainer had come out of the cowshed and was crossing the field. He grabbed my hand and was shaking it. "Franz, it is good to see you, my friend," he kept saying.

I sat down and Gerda immediately brought a steaming hot mug of coffee. Rainer was filling the dogs up with dog biscuits and making a great fuss of them much to their delight. When all the enthusiasm had cooled down I began to tell them what they were longing to hear. I told them how the spotter plane had caught us out on the ledge and how I caught a bullet in the shoulder. They too told me how the Gestapo had come to the village and made everyone parade in the main street. They threatened to kill everyone unless the prisoners were delivered to them. The mayor pleaded with them saying no one had come to the village. "We were all lined up," said Rainer, "and made to face the wall whilst his men searched every house in the village. They took over the village pub for almost a week before they suddenly disappeared early one morning. We never saw them again."

"And now, my friend, I think it's time to pay the mayor a visit." Rainer put on his coat and we walked into the village. The mayor's office was open and we walked in. A clerk asked if he could help us. I said I wanted to see the mayor. The Clark reached for his book.

"I will have to make you an appointment, the mayor isn't available at the moment, what name shall I say."

I looked him hard in the face. "Tell him it's the Gestapo," I said. He immediately crossed the office and entered another door, within seconds he returned and beckoned us into the other office. Rainer introduced me to the man sitting at the huge desk smoking a cigar.

His eyes opened wide when Rainer told him who I was. He got up from his chair and held out his hand to shake mine. I had a strong grip and felt him wince as I shook his hand vigorously. "Where's my generator?" I asked getting straight to the point.

The smile left his lips as his brain began to function. "Ah, Franz, I'm pleased to meet you at last," he spluttered. "Please take a seat, would you care for a coffee or something?"

Rainer looked hard at him, "Mr Mayor, we've just had coffee, Franz has come for his generator."

The mayor sat down in his big chair and smiled. "I have kept my promise, Franz, but first let me say a big thank you for doing what you did. We are all indebted to you. You may be interested to know I have heard over the grapevine that the people concerned are safe and sound. Please keep this information to yourselves, and now if you will follow me I will show you what I have managed to get at great risk to myself. Fortunately I have contacts on the railroads and have called in many favours to deliver what I promised you."

He led us into a room at the back of his office and removed a tarpaulin sheet. The large base measured eighteen inches by fifteen and was wrapped up in brown paper and tied up. I looked at it and tried to lift it. With some effort I managed to pick it up and place it on a table. "It is brand new," said the mayor, "straight from the warehouse in Zurich and also you will find under the sheet four jerry cans of diesel. I have kept my promise, Franz."

I grabbed the mayor and gave him a bear hug. I told him he was an honourable man and it was a pleasure doing business with him. He said he would have it all delivered to the farm by the afternoon.

I was over the moon and took Rainer for a drink of bier to celebrate.

"Will you be able to carry it?" he asked.

I nodded my head "definitely".

When the generator arrived at the farm I had already checked my backpack and had removed the pack itself leaving just the frame and harness. I adjusted the frame work to accommodate the generator. With help from Rainer I lifted the generator onto the frame and secured it. "Now see if you can lift it," said Rainer. With his help I hoisted it onto my back. We had to make some adjustments so that the weight was on my shoulders. I stood upright and checked myself for stability. It was heavy but we had balanced it well. We put an extra couple of straps on so that I could hold it firmly in position. I walked around the field to get the feel of it. "Well, what do you think?" said Rainer.

"Yes, I'm going to go for it," I replied. "If I rest frequently I'll manage it.

"What about the fuel?" he asked. I thought about it and asked if we could fill a couple of smaller cans to fit the panniers on the dogs' backs. Rainer thought for a moment then disappeared returning half an hour later with four empty cans he had brought from the painter's yard. "I'll fill these with diesel and see how they cope," said Rainer. I rested the backpack on a table and helped him fill the cans. "It will be more manageable," said Rainer. I agreed and we made the cans lighter. I said it would be enough for the dogs to carry and enough for me to get started once we reached the monastery.

We eventually set off and I told Rainer we would return as soon as possible. After an hour I rested against a rock just high enough to rest the back pack on without having to take it off. This was the way we did it and after a long slow day and many stops we were in sight of the monastery. As I took off my load, which was a great relief, I looked down at the generator and smiled. Yes it had been well worth it.

The next day I decided that I would take a steady walk down to see Ingerborg and Hans, I was greeted enthusiastically and pampered with hot coffee and freshly baked cakes. I told Ingerborg that her sister and village were well and all was quiet. I told them that I had been supplied with a generator and had carried it up to the monastery, I now wanted to go and see Heinreiche. "He will be pleased to see you, he has asked about you," said Ingerborg.

After a second cup of coffee I walked into Carmen to see Heinreiche. As I walked past the church I had a tingling feeling down my spine. I thought it was a reaction from carrying the generator and shrugged it off.

Heinreiche gave me a huge bear hug which felt like being run over by a steamroller. I was very excited as I told him about the generator. "And now you will be asking me about other things I can get for you," he laughed. "But first let's go and have a bier with Dietre." We sat around the table and exchanged conversation. They were good friends and I enjoyed being with them.

"So now what comes next?" asked Heinreiche, "electric lights and power tools." I nodded, of course that was my intention but I didn't know anything about electric. "But I know someone who does," said Heinreiche.

"Who?" I asked.

"Buy me another bier and I will tell you," he said. The biers were served.

"Who, Heinreiche?"

"Me of course," he burst out with his raucous laugh. "I'm also a trained electrician."

Well Heinreiche never fails to amaze me with his capabilities. After more biers we retreated to his shop. Dietre supplied us with sheets of plain paper and Heinreiche began drawing up a list of what was needed. Fuse box, cables, clips, sockets, light fittings etc. power drill. I asked Heinreiche about a small circular saw and maybe a planer. He produced his catalogue for me to browse through. He began to draw a circuit and wiring diagram. When he told me to look at it, I said it was confusing. He gave one of his raucous laughs. "Franz, now is a good time to learn another trade," followed by another laugh.

"In two weeks' time I will be closing my shop for one week, if you can get all of this equipment up to the monastery maybe if you promise a slow journey (remember I am sixty years old) maybe I may come and stay with you and help you but you must have some bier up there and I'm not carrying it."

I promised him I would and if he wanted to do some fishing all he would have to carry is his fishing rods. He looked at me wide-eyed. "Do you have a lake up there with fish in it?" he asked.

I nodded. "Just for you, Heinreiche."

He had most of the equipment in his shop so I asked him to get it ready and I would take it with me in a day or two. I chose a small circular saw and a small planer and asked if my generator would be powerful enough. He checked the details in the catalogue and said it would as long as I didn't overload it.

I was delighted and returned to the farm to tell Ingerborg and Hands the good news. They told me Heinreiche was in pretty good health and would probably be able to make it.

So with my supplies and electrical equipment fairly distributed we set off back to the monastery. I had managed to carry out some repairs for people in the village and also a quickie for the station master. All of this brought in sufficient income to pay Heinreich, although there was quite a bit outstanding but my friend said my credit was good. We offloaded our loads at the monastery and I set about stoking up the fire. Soon the evening meal was sizzling away. Whilst I had been walking plans and ideas ran through my mind.

I had decided re-erect the log cabin on the backside of the rear wall. I could erect it backing onto the hearth as this wall retained some heat so it would warm the log cabin somewhat. This was to be my workshop and where the generator would be. I worked on the construction for two days then decided to visit Gerda and Rainer.

When I got as far as the valley I looked at what had happened. The German spotter plan had nosedived into the side just above the floor level. The explosion had caused a massive slide of rocks and snow and had completely reformed what was a picturesque valley with a stream running through but now a big mound of fallen rocks and debris had caused a great mound covering the floor up to half the length of the valley. I had to find another way through. Even the ridge high on the other side had been swept away. I clambered over the giant mound trying to pick my way through. There were huge pieces of rock as big as a horse and cart blocking the way. I finally gave up and tried climbing up the ridge to see what was up there. As I walked along the top of the ridge I had a clear view of what had once been a small valley. The explosion had caused a huge rock fall from either side and had filled the valley for about fifty metres but not all the way up and once the mound of rocks had been cleared the valley opened up again. I would have to approach the valley from the other end and see if with a little groundwork I would be able to make it passable again. Meanwhile I had to skirt around and approach from the top. I decided this could be a challenge but not for today. Sometime I would bring a pick and shovel and a sledgehammer and have a go.

Gerda and Rainer greeted me enthusiastically and made a great fuss of the dogs. I could see that Rainer had collected timber and glass for the lean-to greenhouse so I suggested to Rainer that we made a start. The weather held out for us and within a couple of days we had erected the frame and secured it to the wall of the barn. We made each section so as what glass we had fitted in without having to be cut to size. We sat and had a welcome coffee. Rainer had filled more cans of diesel from the jerry cans so the dogs could carry them. I told him that my friend Heinreiche was coming to spend a week with me and we were going to start on the electrics.

"It will be like a hotel when you have finished," commented Gerda.

"But it will still be a monastery, I don't want to alter that," I said. Rainer said he would be able to fit the glass himself when he got some putty. I made a staging to fit the length of the greenhouse and Gerda to pick up some seed trays and some seeds and compost and start sowing.

She was delighted. "Next time you come you will see a difference," she said.

I said my goodbyes apologising for the short visit but I had to prepare for Heinreiche's visit. Loaded with meat joints and prepared chickens I bade farewell once again to my friends. The dogs were enthusiastic as ever and led the way.

We made good time and within the six hours I was opening the door into the vestibule. The fire was just smouldering ash in the grate so the first job was to bring it back to life and prepare our evening meal. I took a chicken and put it over the fire to cook it making sure I didn't forget to turn it. The dogs tucked into their tinned food and biscuits and lay down in front of the fire. I had to keep stepping over them but so what they're my faithful companions.

Next day I did a bit more work on the log cabin which was to be my workshop. The roof was ready to go on. I had assembled enough timber so I set to work on it. I kept looking at my generator. I hadn't even tried it out yet. I was going to wait for Heinreiche. I felted the roof and then fitted the logs on top. I took the dogs down to the lake for some moss and mud to fill in the cracks. By evening it was finished.

We rose early next morning and made our way down the mountain to Carmen. Once again we received an enthusiastic meeting. Ingerborg said that Heinreiche was very excited about his journey to the monastery and had prepared his fishing gear already. After a good meal and cups of tea I walked into the village where I bought some bottles of bier. I went into Heinreiche's shop and put them on his counter. A huge smile greeted me as Heinreiche produced his fishing rods. "When do we go, Franz?" he asked.

I said, "As soon as you close your shop we will be on our way."

"Come into my storeroom I have something to show you," he had a huge smile on his face. He opened his catalogue and showed me a picture of a circular saw mounted on a steel frame with an eight-inch blade. "Well, my English friend, what about one of these?" I looked at it and read what I could about it.

"How heavy is it?" I asked.

He led me into the store room and uncovered a box all wrapped up. "Try lifting this." His huge smile lit up the room, I was speechless, there was no end to this man's capabilities. I bent down and tested the weight and then lifted the box. It was about the same weight as the generator. "It comes to pieces you can divide the weight between the three of you. I'll carry the bier and I close the shop tomorrow so next day, Saturday that is, I shall be ready for my holiday in the mountains at your monastery and I hope there is fish in your lake." Again he broke into a raucous laugh and I joined in unable to stop myself. I regained my composure and asked how much it was going to cost me. With a glint in his eyes he said about three months wages and more shelves in his store room plus the fact that Dietre also wanted some work done in his private quarters. He went on to say that Dietre wanted to see me before we left so I told Heinreiche I would just pop round and see him now. He looked at the bier and said he may have to taste it to see if it was palatable to him.

Dietre was tending to customers when I entered the library he waved a welcome and I browsed around the book shelves. "Yes, Franz, that's what I want to see you about, writing a book, you must write about your achievements in the mountains and the monastery people will want to know about it you must write a book and I will help you. There's so much to tell, Franz."

I was taken by surprise that was the last thing on earth I had even thought about. I had expected him to produce a drawing of where he wanted the shelves. I told him that at the moment I was too busy even to think about such a thing but after some gentle encouragement from Dietre I promised to give it some thought.

The following day Heinreiche closed his shop for a week. He asked what time we would be setting off. I told him it would be six o'clock in the morning and to make his way up to the farm. Ingerborg said he would be welcome to an early breakfast with us and so it was with a good meal under our belts we set off. Hans and

Ingerborg waved us off telling me to look after Heinreiche.

We made it to the tree line as the sky began to brighten up, it was going to be a nice day. I asked Heinreiche if he was alright carrying the bier. "Yes, my friend, anyway I know how to lighten the load." Again the raucous laugh that seemed to echo around the mountains it was going to be a slow journey I had the weight of the circular saw on my shoulders. We had dismantled it to make my load lighter. Romulus had two blades in his panniers and Remus had the steel legs strapped onto his back plus a few cans of dog food. Heinreiche had stashed away some fresh lamb and chicken pieces in his fishing bag asking me if I knew how to cook. We rested about every hour, Heinreiche scanning the surrounding mountains commenting on their beauty. I pointed out the peak pointing up to the sky still clad in a white gown of snow and shimmering in the morning sunlight.

Heinreiche said he could understand why I had a yearning for the mountains and its serenity. We moved on for another hour, I asked Heinreiche if he felt alright to which he answered, "This is just a walk in the park for a fellow like me." The load on my back wasn't too bad and the dogs seemed to be coping alright. Heinreiche suggested we open a bottle of bier being it was a hot sunny day so at the next stop we did just that. My friend said that the load felt a bit better.

We eventually made the incline down to the tree line close to our destination. I told Heinreiche we were very close and to prepare himself for a surprise. "Shall I open another bottle ready?" he laughed. When we broke the tree line and the monastery stood before us I looked at Heinreiche who stood open-mouthed as he gazed at the building before him. "Franz, is this your monastery, it's absolutely fantastic, I am very proud of you and what you have accomplished," he walked around looking at everything and everywhere. He gazed in awe at the roof. "What a lovely job you have done, Franz, its perfect."

I opened the door and showed him into the vestibule. We shed our loads and walked inside. The light shining through the windows illuminated the corridors. While I offloaded the dogs' panniers Heinreiche wondered about inside peering into the chapel and toilets. He didn't say anything as he made his way into the living area. The fire had gone out but it didn't seem to bother him as he looked at the hearth and dining area. He also looked into a couple of the cells. He gazed up into the roof. "Franz, you have really amazed me, my friend, I imagined something more like a brick cowshed but this is like a mansion, you have exceeded all my vivid imaginations of what you had up here." He gave me a huge bear hug. "Well done, my English friend, I'm so proud of you."

I took him into my log cabin and showed him my generator. "Its German made so it will be a good one," he said adding, "I wonder which German lorry that fell off," followed by a loud laugh. He looked around and then we went back into the monastery for a further inspection I could see his mind working as he went into each room. I showed him which room I had allocated to him and left to light the fire and get a meal started. Heinreiche had a piece of plain paper in his hand and was drawing a rough plan on where he would start the wiring.

We sat down to a nice lamb chop and vegetables meal and a bottle of bier opened ready to pour. Heinreiche said we would need a fuse box somewhere handy inside the monastery with another one in the workshop for the generator and machinery but we would sort that out in the morning.

After the meal we wandered down to the lake. Heinreiche stared hard at the water looking for fish. "I don't like your toilet," he said as we walked back to the monastery. I agreed they were very primitive. "I shall order six porcelain ones when we get back, something else for you to carry up here." I told him I hadn't investigated the plumbing arrangements yet. That evening we sat in front of the fire talking and drinking. Heinreiche said we would start work tomorrow. He asked me if I had heard anything about the Gestapo prisoners. I told him what the mayor had told me. He looked at me suspiciously and said, "The Gestapo officer and four of his men had suddenly disappeared and never seen again."

I said I'd heard some rumour, "And there is a rumour going around that a one armed man had led them into the mountains on the pretence that he knew where those women were hiding, anyway they were never seen again nor the one armed man." He again looked at me smiling.

I changed the subject saying that no one could venture into the mountains during the winter.

The next morning we were both up bright and early. Heinreiche had already marked the walls with chalk indicating cables and sockets. The fuse box was on the wall close to my bedroom and then he drew lines where the cable would lead. We ate a hearty breakfast and began work.

Heinreiche tried the generator and said it was fine. He pointed out to me where to drill holes in the wall and he mounted the fuse boxes. By lunchtime there were lines of cables from the boxes along to places marked out on the walls. Heinreiche said to keep the cables as neat as possible so that at some stage I could box them in with wooden casings. He was so proficient he just fed cables through walls and along ceilings without even thinking about it using different cables for power and lighting. I asked him where he had learnt his trade only to receive a raucous laugh. It was my job to keep the cables pinned to the wall with cable clips and Heinreiche would inspect my work. He said that later it would probably be wise to get a smaller generator for the lighting circuit and keep the bigger one just for power in my workshop.

The next day was a day off, we were going fishing. We sat down by the lake and I let Heinreiche set up the rods. He didn't believe me when I told him I'd never been fishing. "My god, Franz, everybody's been fishing. How do you know there's any fish in here then?" I told him I didn't know for sure but it had got him up here so at least I'd caught something. It was my time to laugh out loud.

While we spent most of the day trying to catch fish many subjects were discussed. I asked Heinreiche what he did before he came to Switzerland. He turned serious. "Englishman, I keep my past secret as do you. What secrets do you hide, Franz?" I looked across at him, his face was serious, had I upset him by prying into his past.

"My past is so hurtful, Heinreiche, I don't like to be reminded of it but if you really want to know I'll tell you, I know it will remain a secret between us."

He looked back at me and nodded. "And I will take you into my confidence on the same terms, Franz."

I began at the beginning from when I was a child waiting at the garden gate for my Pa.

He listened to every word without interruption, his face reflecting sadness. When I had finished he leaned over and patted me on my back. "We have both experienced a sad past, Franz, and now I will tell you mine.

"When I left school I was lucky to win an opportunity with a large company. In Germany an apprentice learns everything there is to know within a company. I started off as an electrician but also I was taught building techniques and also plumbing, even decorating. I was doing very well until that idiot Kaiser?? decided to go to war. I was drafted into the army I had married and had a two-year-old daughter. I didn't want a war, I had everything I needed. When we invaded France the military general wanted to make sure the allies didn't creep up on us from Spain, so all along the border and along the Pyrenees snipers were placed covering all the mountain passes with orders to kill anybody who set foot in them. We were given small bivvys to lie in and supplied with food rations. We had to keep watch all day, only at night could we rest and then the night patrols took over. I killed many people who strayed into those passes − whether they were the enemy or just innocent hikers. We had two pigeons to each sniper and had to send in reports via pigeon post.

"After three years the armistice came and the war ended. We were dismissed and sent home. My wife and child had suffered terribly the Kaiser failed to look after my family's needs and they were suffering acute malnutrition. My daughter died within six months of my return and my wife suffered from deep depression. She was admitted to a hospital where she took her own life.

"Franz I know what you have been through, I've been there too and its hell."

I leaned over and put my arm around his shoulder. "Let's go and have a bier, my friend."

He suddenly stood up and started to reel in. "Hey, Franz, I've got one." Eagerly he handled the landing like a professional. "Look at that, Franz," he said, "here's our evening meal, that's a fair-sized fish."

He not only caught the fish, he gutted it and prepared it for cooking. I said he had done well and that it was a good time for a celebration and I had a bottle of wine stashed away for a special occasion. We never discussed our past again.

In the days that followed we worked together very well and soon it was time to test the wiring system. Heinreiche had a meter for testing and went round like a real professional.

"Okay, Franz, let's see if it works or blows up." I said he could start the generator and start the ball rolling. I would keep my fingers crossed. The generator struck up and sent power to the fuse boxes. One by one Heinreiche threw the switches, I cheered as one by one the lights illuminated the monastery. I gave my friend the biggest hug I could muster. I filled the glasses and we drank to our success. Heinreiche refilled the glasses and said, "Another days fishing tomorrow I think."

He would wander around the monastery and I could hear his mind working. "Franz, when you have finished here this could be a hotel. When we are in the bier Keller Dietre and Olga say you could run a business from here. Guiding hikers through the mountains and accommodating them overnight here in the monastery and then guiding them down the other side. It would be a good idea for you to think about. Olga says you could advertise through her agency and Dietre says you should write a book. I think they have some good ideas, Franz."

I looked at my giant friend. "No, Heinreiche, that's not what I planned, I want seclusion but if ever I do think about running a business I will know who to see."

We spent a few more days fishing and just messing about in the monastery. Heinreiche checked all the electrics before it was time for him to return to Carmen. "You know, Englishman, this war will be over one day and then we can return to a normal life. People will come flocking into Switzerland again and there will be smiling faces everywhere, it is a good place to settle down, I hope you will stay."

# Part 9

The war did end eventually after a surrender was signed and I began to get regular mail from England and Spain. Mum and Dad were just ticking over but Dad's health wasn't good; his bronchitis wasn't getting any better and he had to have long spells off work. Mum said she was fine but reading between the lines I knew she was struggling. I decided to send them a cheque to help out. I was financially stable I could always earn some money and Ingerborg and Hans wouldn't take anything from me.

In Spain all seemed well at the vineyard; Mamma and Pappa were doing well with the wine. Carlos and Rosita were expecting another child. More workers were employed to help so I guessed everything was going fine. With the war over everything seemed to be settling down everywhere.

Dietre called me into his shop one day and talked to me about writing a book. I agreed to try and started making notes. Once I got into it I started to enjoy recalling my activities, although when it came to our wedding and what happened I was thrown into a depressive state and would dwell on my lovely wife Carmen. I gazed at the photographs. Ingerborg knew and would come and sit with me in my room for long periods at a time, she was my second mother. When the depression lifted I would load my backpack and the dogs' panniers and back to the monastery we would go. The circular saw was now the main tool and Heinreiche had ordered a planing machine. There was no stopping me now I would be working all day in my workshop.

The floor of the loft had been completed I now wanted to put in another floor and make a room below, this was going to be my private living quarters. Olga had said she wanted to visit the monastery and see for herself I told her I did not trust her but she promised there would be no romantic ideas. I asked Heinreiche to order four ceramic toilets and four shower units for future installation. He said he would and asked me if I had any money as they would cost a packet. I gave him my assurance that I would be able to pay. He indicated that they might arrive during the fishing season. I had visited Gerda and Rainer and had started work on the valley floor trying to make it transversal. The huge rocks I had to go around but in time and a bit of zigzagging I found a way through. As always I was greeted with friendliness. Gerda as always sat me down and prepared lunch. They said the German visitors had been into the village asking about a one armed man, had anyone seen him. Of course there was no one around of that description in this village so after a brief walk around they moved on to the next village. I asked what they wanted him for, Rainer said it had been reported that a man with one arm had led the Gestapo into the mountains saying he knew where the English women were but they were never seen again despite a search by a group of soldiers.

"Well, the war will soon be over," said Gerda. Apparently a surrender has been signed and no one seems to be the winner. There have been huge losses on each side and mass destruction. The Jews have suffered atrocities at the hands of the Germans' and now the Russians are approaching Berlin, it won't be long now thank goodness. Gerda proudly showed me around her greenhouse blooming with flowers and lettuces and she had raised an orchid which was her pride and joy. Rainer had tended the outside garden and it was full to capacity.

I said I wanted to see the Mayor again and Rainer accompanied me to the offices. The mayor received us cordially, I asked if they could get me another generator a bit smaller one. "I will try, Franz, I will certainly try for you, give me a week or two, I have to call in a few favours."

I spent the rest of the day helping Rainer around the farm. We went for a bier and I was treated like a hero; my bier was free and everybody seemed to know who I was. I asked for the information to be kept secret in case the Gestapo ever came back. I was assured that the whole village was sworn to secrecy.

My next big job at the monastery was the toilets. I needed cement so I did a few journeys to Carmen and carried what we could. The toilets arrived and so I carried them up one at a time.

It was almost August and Heinreiche had hinted that he might close his shop for another week and come and some do fishing. I had carried all four toilets up to the monastery and a lot of piping. Heinreiche said he would need to get the cisterns also. By the time Heinreiche was ready to close the shop everything we needed was at the monastery. Olga hearing that Heinreiche was coming with me begged for her to accompany him also, adding, "You will be safe, Franz."

Well she had a backpack so we managed to fill it with extra food and told her she was going to be the cook for a week. We had just cleared the tree line when Olga slipped. Fortunately she didn't hurt herself but it was enough to keep her quiet for the rest of the journey. When we reached the monastery I showed Olga the lake and told her that's where we all bathed first thing in a morning. "Wow," she said, "roll on the morning."

Heinreiche always seemed to know what he was doing. First he wanted to know the water source so I showed him the well where I drew the water from. He looked down at the water level. A submersible pump will have to be used to bring the water up to a tank which we haven't got. He started measuring and asked if I could knock one toilet to pieces and mix cement and fit one of the ceramic toilets in its place. He searched around the grounds outside looking for another water source. There's lots of little river lets passing underground he said and they all seem to feed into the lake. It's a natural feed from the mountains but we do not want your toilets feeding into the lake, we will have to find where the monks drained away their waste. Heinreiche began probing and listening for the sound of running water. He would sink his probe and put his ear to it. I would never have thought of that.

Olga did her bit by cooking our food and keeping things tidy inside. She said men were the most untidy animals on the planet.

I managed to fit two of the ceramic toilets and then I fastened the cisterns to the wall as directed by Heinreiche. The existing toilet area had been built into two sections either side the vestibule, approximately ten feet square. Three toilets either side leaving a space for two showers to be fitted. There were holes in the floor where possibly the monks tipped away their water after washing. It was a pretty basic area and I could see more work ahead for me to make it more acceptable. We agreed that we needed a break so the next day we went fishing. Olga didn't fish so she took the dogs for a walk in the mountains with her camera. Heinreiche showed me a crevice in the rocks to the side of the monastery.

"Listen," he said. I could hear the water flowing rapidly. "That's our water source and a good pressure too."

We fished for most of the day. Olga joined us saying when we had finished she would like to bathe. I told her that we had been kidding her and the big sink by the hearth was more suitable and hot water was accessible. I received a clip around the ear and was accused of waiting for her to strip off. We allowed her another couple of hours whilst we struggled to increase our catch. The fish weren't biting today we had only caught two all day.

As the days passed by we had put the basics down. Heinreiche said we needed at least three submersible pumps to feed water into the monastery: Two for the toilet and showering area and one to feed into the kitchen area. He would have to find out what piping was needed. I had fitted four ceramic toilets and the cisterns all that was needed was the pipework. Heinreiche was still trying to trace where the monks had piped their waste into. We searched the area in front of the monastery and found a crevice twenty metres away. We couldn't see it because it was all overgrown with shrubbery which we began to clear away. Eventually we uncovered the crevice which disappeared into the rocks. Heinreiche climbed down and pushed his probe down as far as he could. He said he could hear water which meant it was a natural soak away which would save us a lot of digging. "Clever people these monks," said Heinreiche climbing out of the crevice. "We can install the showers as well now."

By the end of the week it had all been sorted. Heinreiche would order the submersible pumps and find out about the types of piping we would require. "I hope it isn't lead piping I don't like doing lead joints, copper would be best but industrial plastic would be better still."

We packed our gear and made ready for the journey down the mountains. "I've been thinking," said Olga. "You've got a readymade business here, Franz, it's a hiker's paradise, let me get something organised for you."

I laughed at her I had visions of her opening an office in my monastery. "Not so fast, Olga, this monastery is mine and for me alone." She pulled a face and gave a laugh but I know I hadn't heard the last of it.

We arrived safely and agreed to meet for a bier later. Ingerborg and Hans enquired how we had got on and asked if Olga had behaved herself. I said she wanted to turn my monastery into a hotel but I had turned down the idea. I said Heinreiche was a genius he seemed to know everything. Dietre was already in the bier Keller when I arrived later that evening. He had a pile of papers for me to look at. "I want you to read these when you have settled down. Don't rush, there is plenty of time."

Christina came over and gave me a strange look. "So you prefer Olga," she said.

I shook my head. "I've told you and Olga I'm not looking for romance of any kind nor ever will. We can be friends and that's all I want. You can come next time if you wish but you have to do the cooking." It seemed to do the trick and left with a big smile on her face.

"You must forgive them, Franz, you are a good catch for a female." Dietre smiled. "If I was thirty years younger."

There were people waiting for me to return, several jobs were lined up so I got down to business and started earning cash. This pleased Heinreiche immensely.

Ingerborg has a phone message from Gerda saying the mayor had acquired what I needed. My next journey to the monastery followed two days later. I was laden with two coils of copper piping and boxes of clips and joints. The pumps were not too heavy and the dogs coped easily and with their own food supplies. We dropped everything off at the monastery and continued on after a short break and some food. Rainer said he hadn't expected us so soon but I told him we still had lots of work to do before the winter shut us in. He came with me to see the mayor who was quite pleased to see us and immediately led us into the store room.

He uncovered a box which had generator stamped all over it. It was smaller and much lighter. "Can you please take it away now, Franz, there are certain people looking for it."

I nodded and gave him a hug. "I'll pay you soon," I said.

"Oh no, it's free," said the mayor with a grin on his face. We departed carrying the generator still wrapped up.

Rainer asked if I was okay for fuel as he still had some in the barn. I decided to take two more cans. I stayed overnight enjoying their hospitality. After a hearty breakfast we set off back into the mountains. We now had almost everything we needed to complete the plumbing installation. Heinreiche said I needed two hot water tanks before I could use the facilities to its full potential. The tanks were copper and not too heavy. I carried them both up in two days. Heinreiche said he would close his shop for a weekend and come up and complete the installation. I told Christina this would be an opportunity to visit and she was delighted. Heinreiche told me not to forget the bier. We set off at a leisurely pace and Christina enjoyed the views as we got higher into the mountains. It was the end of summer and I could feel the temperature dropping. The year seemed to fly by. It was a nice comforting thought that I would have lighting and hot water for the first time since I discovered the monastery. Christine walked around in a daze she couldn't believe what she was seeing. "You should not be here alone," she said.

"I have my dogs," I replied.

She gave me a long hard look. "It's not the same, Franz."

The hot water tanks were fitted – one in the toilet area and the other in the workshop fitted onto the wall and water piped through. The new generator supplied all the power needed and soon the hot water was flowing. I tested it by having my first hot water at the monastery. Christina too tried it out to her approval. I prepared a chicken and vegetables and Christina cooked on an open fire much to her delight. The bier flowed and we had a good weekend. We stood outside and gazed at the stars, Heinreiche smoked a cigar and I lit my pipe. Christina was happy with a large glass of wine.

We returned to Carmen and I went to see Dietre he was anxious to see me. "Franz, I have made a few notes for you I've talked about you writing a book. Whilst you are shut away in the mountains I want you to think about it and fill in the spaces. I had to smile who ever thought of me writing a book, I gave Dietre my word that I would think about it.

The winter was closing in and I had to make sure my food stocks were high so I did a few quick visits up and down the mountains. Fuel was something else to think about and logs for the fire. This was made easier now I had a power saw. Life was getting easier and I was still full of enthusiasm. I did a quick up and down journey to see Gerda and Rainer. I did a quick repair job in the kitchen for Gerda and helped Rainer in the cowshed. I said I would not be seeing them again until spring so as a favour to them I stayed overnight and Gerda did us a fine meal.

Now that the war in Europe was nearing an end with the Germans losing the battle and retreating I said I didn't think they would be bothered again by the Gestapo. I left next morning smothered with hugs and kisses and a load of fresh meat and vegetables.

The first snows of winter started to fall two weeks later. I was well stocked up with everything I needed I now looked forward to some quiet time on my own with my dogs. The corridors were both stocked with logs I didn't even have to go outside except to let the dogs out. I sat in front of the fire reading books supplied by Dietre and making drawings of what I was going to do upstairs. First I was going to have to build a staircase over the toilet area left of the vestibule and I still had the chapel to do. I had also to box the toilets in like the one back home in our cottage. I always felt comfortable there reading my comics. Some days during the winter we would get some extreme sunny days and that is when I would venture out down to the lake which would be frozen over and enjoying a walk throwing snowballs for the dogs. It was peaceful and often my thoughts were of my lovely Carmen. It had now been almost five years since I lost her and broke away from the family but my feelings for her had not waned, the tears would well up and the pangs of heartache were still as strong, but now I was at peace and would feel her presence around me and in that I sort comfort.

I did sit and read Dietre's notes and I began to fill in the spaces. The first was about my childhood which I will always remember meeting my dad at the gate and being in the garden. I had also looked in at the chapel and made a few sketches. It needed a new altar and the pews needed replacing. I would also put in a wooden floor and roof. Easy now I had my power saw and planer. I began stripping the chapel of all the old wood and burning it on the fire. Apart from the roof beams which were oak I stripped it bare. I spent a lot of time in my log cabin workshop sawing and planning. I would often be so enthralled I would forget my meal times. It was only when the dogs let me know they wanted to go out as I would stop.

Christmas Day I had off and cooked myself a grand meal and read books and magazines. I looked at Dietre's proposal and filled in a few more of the spaces covering my school years and when I left school to start work. I was enthusiastic about my love of wood and would describe the things I made in great detail. Also I described my apprenticeship years and of course my meeting Carmen. I stopped writing here as the memories would come flooding back. I did some work in the chapel, first I re roofed it I stained and varnished and then I did the same with the floor. I didn't like the coldness of the stone floor so I put a wooden one on top. I had unlimited access to a wood supply so the cost was nothing. I also copied the design of the old pews and made eight new ones. It was a pine roof and pine floor stained with an oak wood stain and varnished. The pews I made of oak and lightly varnished to compliment the wood grain. The altar was made of pine and stained and varnished a light pine as a contrast. I was enjoying myself and looked forward to my work every day with enthusiasm. How many people can say that? The arch-shaped door were in pretty good shape being made of oak they had stood up well over the years and only need a new coat of stain and varnish and new hinges. As I closed the doors at the end of the day I was feeling quite proud of myself. The fuel for the generators was getting low so I had to cut back on my work. Evening time I would sit in front of a log fire reading by lantern or candles. It sort of created a warm relaxing glow. I picked up where I had left off writing my story for Dietre describing the events that took place when I first met Carmen. I wondered why Dietre thought anybody would be interested in all of this but he was enthusiastic so I kept on writing it passed the dark winter evenings away and gave me a chance to reflect on what I had achieved. The most difficult part was when I described my wedding and what happened the following year. I put my pen down and left it for a while. Another two weeks passed before I took up the pen again.

I found writing about my rambling through the mountain most exuberating and the pen moved quite well with my mind recalling all the challenges. The most harrowing was when I was caught up in the flash flood that almost cost me my life and also the journey through the mountains during the winter with the two Gestapo prisoners. Looking back I suppose my life has been interesting to say the least but now I was living a contented life doing what I liked best with nobody to bother me, just me and my two Pyreneans.

Of course Heinreiche would insist on the pigeon during the winter in case of emergencies. March brought an end to winter and so loaded up with empty cans I made my way down to see Gerda and Rainer who greeted me as if I had been away for years. They had weathered the winter and was as glad as I was that it was over. Rainer had refilled the jerry cans with diesel which he got cheap being a farmer so he filled the cans and asked what I had been doing. We exchanged conversation as we sat around the dining table enjoying Gerda's cooking. "Home grown" she would point out as she served the potatoes and swede. She also told me that people in the village would ask "how is the Man in the Mountains" and "would he be able to do some woodwork for us when he comes again." So I had jobs in both villages when I was available. I didn't mind as long as it was only a day or two's work. I didn't want anything to keep me away from the monastery for more than a couple of days. They would ask how much for this or that and I just said "make a donation" which they did and more times than not they paid me more that I would have asked. The donations paid my bills and all was happy.

When I finally got down the other side and into Carmen I was again besieged by an excited group of friends who wanted to know how I was. Heinreiche and Dietre had already ordered my bier when I was finally able to tear myself away from Ingerborg and Hans. Heinreiche wanted to know about the electrics and plumbing and Dietre wanted to know if I had started writing. Olga made a brief appearance and asked if I would be interested in guided tours throughout the mountains now that the war was practically over and the Germans retreating as fast as they could people from neighbouring countries were anxious to visit Switzerland. I told her that I had not planned anything like that to which she said there was money to be made and her agency was looking into it, would I be interested. She had it all planned out. Visitors could travel to Zurich and catch the train to the next town where they could catch the shuttle to Carmen. Franz could meet them and take them through the mountains to the monastery where they could stay overnight and then he would guide them down to the other village where they could catch the shuttle back to Zurich. "It was simple," she insisted and asked me to think about it. Deitre thought it was a brilliant idea and so was writing my book, I gave him what I had written and he said he would go through it in case of spelling mistakes. I asked him what he was going to do with it and he laughed.

"Why make you famous of course," he said. I couldn't imagine anybody like me being famous, I was simply a kid from a mining family. I took it all in my stride and forgot about it. Heinreiche was asking what else I was doing. I told him I had been working on the chapel. I would spend all day with Ingerborg and Hans and then after a hearty meal I would wander down to the bier Keller. Christina always welcomed me like a long lost brother and even she mentioned Olga's idea about guided tours. I mulled it over in my mind. I didn't really want to be invaded by strangers I liked my own company and all the peace and quiet of the mountains that is what I had come for. I talked things over with Heinreiche and Dietre I still had things I wanted to do at the monastery. Dietre said it would bring in money and would make Carmen a famous little village. If I only did the tours during the summer and only during the weekdays I would make some money and also have time on my own at weekends.

Heinreiche said it sounded feasible but also recognised my need for privacy. "It would have to be your decision." I said I would give it some thought.

Whilst I was in Carmen I shopped around for a couple of candlesticks for the altar and I even bought a bible. That sort of put the finishing touches to the chapel but as I stood in the doorway and looked back I felt as if there was something missing. Suddenly it came to me I wanted a large wooden cross to hang on the wall behind the altar. I went down into the forest and looked around I eventually found what I was looking for a huge oak with thick branches. I cut off two of the lower ones each almost eight inches thick. Now I had found something else to occupy a rainy day. I cut the first log at least four feet long. I planed it and tried it against the wall. The cross piece was next two feet in length. I cut and joined them in the shape of a cross and then varnished them. They looked good and I hung them up on the wall but still I was not satisfied. Back into the forest for another piece of oak I remembered how when I carved those horses heads at the pit. I took my time and studied them well. In the bible was a picture of Christ on the cross. I studied it well and began carving.

After a month the rough shape had taken place now for the delicate work. I spent evenings in front of the fire whittling away remembering what Pa used to say. "If a job is worth doing, then do it well."

My journeys down both sides of the mountains were always pleasant, even on dull days I enjoyed the walk and there were always new things I hadn't noticed before. The spring and summer flowers always fascinated me and often I would gather a bunch for Ingerborg or Gerda. I wrote a few more notes for Dietre about the challenges of renovating the monastery and how important the friendliness of the villagers had been. I also thought a lot about Olga's idea. There was still a lot of work for me to do inside the monastery. I wanted to put another floor in below the loft, there was plenty of open space that could be utilised and I had visions of making it into my private living quarters. I had all the time in the world and all of the resources. I was never one for sitting around doing nothing, my brain was always active and looking for new ideas. I also wanted to build a larger workshop and to cultivate a garden. I could even raise chickens and have my own eggs perhaps a couple of goats for milk. But perhaps I did need something else in my life besides the monastery. I thought about Olga's idea and decided for one summer to give it a try. So my next task was to furnish more of the cells and obtain bedding and such items. The rest of this year would allow me to do that. I would be talking to Olga on my next visit to Carmen.

I finished the carving and mounted it onto the cross. It looked good to me I hope Jesus was pleased with it. For some unknown reason to me I visited the chapel more often whether it was to admire my work just to look at the cross I can't say but somehow I felt the peace within. One day as I stood looking at the cross I whispered a prayer asking for forgiveness for turning my back on him but I did add that it was his fault for taking away my lovely Carmen and child. As I sat there thinking I wondered if he had done it deliberately so as to bring me to the monastery.

My next visit to Carmen and I was handing more notes to Dietre and having conversations with Olga. She said she had already taken the liberty of mentioning it to her bosses in Zurich and they had asked if it was possible for them to visit the monastery. I told her to make sure they wore the right clothing. She was on the phone straight away and would see me later. Dietre said he would like my permission when he had finished writing my book to contact some business people he had been dealing with for years with the idea of getting it published. I gave him the go ahead just to please him.

Olga came running across to the library all excited. "Can they come next weekend?"

I told Ingerborg and Hans and they said it was a good idea if that's what I wanted. I said I would give it a try and I would be seeing them in a few days as usual. Ingerborg gave me some more blankets and mattress cases and she would prepare a meat and vegetable pack so as I could feed my important guests. Before I left I dropped in to see Olga. She had arranged for her bosses to arrive on Saturday morning if that was alright with me and could she join the party. I gave her a nod of approval and told her to put on some good boots and warm clothing.

As I made my way up into the mountains I suddenly realised I would have to visit Gerda and Rainer and to tell them what was happening. Rainer said he would fill me some bags of straw for the mattresses. I explained that I would probably be bringing some visitors with me next time I came down. I told them the visitors were from Olga's travel agency and carrying out some sort of survey but not to worry as it was all to do with me doing hiking tours. Gerda said she would prepare drinks and food for them. Rainer also filled more cans of diesel for me to take back and Gerda provided sheets and pillow cases. She showed me how to fill them with straw and pack them so as they were comfortable. She also suggested that if the idea was a success I would have to invest in proper bedding as not everybody liked straw mattresses to lie on. That of course presented another problem – how was I going to carry mattresses up into the mountains on my back. I asked Gerda where I could get such mattresses. She said there was a bedding company in the village and she would take me there before I returned to the monastery. Later that day whilst

Rainer kept his eye on the food cooking on the stove, Gerda took me into the village to a large store at the end of the street. It was filled with all sorts of furniture. She led me through the store into the bedding section there were lots of beds and mattresses on display. I said I could never carry a full-sized one into the mountains. She led me to where the single ones were on display. A sales man asked what we were looking for. "Single-sized and light enough to be carried," said Gerda.

The sales man led us around the department showing us a selection. "There's flock, spring or feather."

I remembered my mum making the beds and mauling the flock mattresses. Turning them over and shaking them into shape and then getting rid of the lumps. I walked past them and looked at the sprung ones. They weren't very flexible. "What about the feather ones, are they very light and flexible?" I asked. I picked one up and began to roll it up.

"There, sir, what about that?"

I picked it up it was very light so I ordered four and asked them to be delivered to the farm with four pillows. They arrived shortly after we returned to the farm all neatly rolled up and wrapped up. I decided to make my way back up the mountain. It was late afternoon but there was still plenty of light. I picked up one mattress and hoisted it onto my shoulders and rested it on my backpack. The dogs each had two pillows strapped across their backs. I told Rainer I would return tomorrow for another one I needed to get them sorted out for when the travel agency reps came visiting. I had to put on a good impression for them.

Next day we made an early start I had a quick look into the cell next to mine where I had put on the new mattress. It looked good with the sheets and blankets on in fact it looked posh.

Rainer greeted me and Gerda prepared lunch. I said I was going straight back and if I felt like it I would return the same day if the light was good and then I would stay the night with them. With another mattress on my back we set off into the mountains the dogs carrying cans of diesel.

We experienced some dark clouds on our way back but they passed over and once again we were blessed with sunshine. The last of the mattresses was laid out on the bed and we had a well-earned break. I had made up all four beds and was proudly viewing each cell. Suddenly it dawned on me that I didn't have enough clean linen for a change over. That was another item on my list. In two days' time I would be showing Olga and her bosses around my home that's if they turned up. I checked the meat store and decided I would put a lamb joint in the slow oven to cook while I went down to Carmen and the vegetables would all be prepared. I had cans of bier and a couple of bottles of wine all ready for them.

I thought I might have been nervous but I wasn't, why should I be, this is my place they are only visitors. We set off down the mountain to Carmen it was a bright sunny morning with the promise of a good day for hiking. The village was busy and Ingerborg has just done a load of washing and was hanging it out to dry. Hans was busy in the cowshed I said my hellos and made my way down to Olga's travel agency. She was all dressed up and was anxiously awaiting the arrival of her bosses on the next shuttle. Dietre came across and handed her a pile of papers.

When it was time for the shuttle Olga and I walked down to meet it. As the people got off she waved to two men all dressed up in hiking gear. I guessed these were her bosses. She introduced me to Anton and Bernard who happened to be brothers. After a friendly greeting I led the way through the village to the farm. They seemed quite impressed with our small village and said how pretty it was.

Ingerborg had laid a table and made coffee. We sat down and chatted away for a short while until I asked them if they were ready to move on. They made a great fuss of my dogs who happened to have had a good grooming and smelt better than they usually did.

We eventually set off for the mountains, they were suitably dressed and had good footwear. Apparently they both spent lots of time skiing at various ski slopes promoting their agency Olga of course was overjoyed she was promoting my businesses interests and had her bosses with her so she could have at first-hand their reaction. The weather held out for us and we chatted freely about the lovely scenery and how I managed to find my way through the mountains.

We made good time and six hours later we stood outside the monastery. They were very surprised at seeing such a building high in the mountains. I couldn't give them much information of its history just a rough idea on its age.

They wandered open-mouthed around the inside admiring the woodwork I had done. When they saw the inside of the chapel they knelt down and muttered their prayers. I showed them to their cells and started preparing the meal. I was bombarded with questions and Olga began jotting down notes. She also mentioned to me that Dietre had talked her into doing some typing for him. We feasted and talked until late evening before retiring for the night. The agency bosses wanted to go down to the other side in the morning so I suggested an early breakfast and an early start.

Gerda and Rainer were waiting for us when we arrived at their farm. It was midday and the table was laid with a light lunch. From what I could gather everything had gone well. Olga never said anything but was in a cheery mood. The agency bosses decided to catch the shuttle train from here and make their way back to Zurich where they would discuss their findings. Olga decided to go back with them rather than make the return journey through the mountains. We bid farewell at the station and I made my way back to the farm where I decided to stay the night.

Gerda started asking all sorts of questions but I could only say that I thought all had gone well.

My return journey went uneventful and arriving at the monastery in good time. I checked the visitor's cells and stripped off the bedding. I had to get it laundered somehow but didn't fancy having to do it myself. I put it all in a bag and made my way next day down to Carmen hoping Ingerborg might offer to do it.

I didn't hear from the agency for two weeks and then Olga delivered a letter to Dietre addressed to me. On my next arrival Ingerborg said Dietre wanted to see me urgently. I went down to the library where Dietre gave me my letter. I opened it and read it out loud.

"Dear Franz,

We would like to say thank you for our journey through the mountains and kind attention during our overnight stay at the monastery. We note that you yourself have to manage everything making it a very long day for you. This would cause concern from our point of view. We thought if you employed maybe two persons at your monastery this would lessen the burden on you. If you should decide that you would like us to get involved in promoting your business then we should require a substantial fee for all our work which would entail advertising, receiving bookings, arranging payment and in general a considerable amount of man hours and probably extra staff. We thought a fifty percent payment of all monies involved would be in order.

Please think over our proposition and let us know in due course."

Dietre hit the roof. "50% that's robbery." I looked at him and laughed and screwed up the letter. I told him I was going to send them a bill for their promotional two-day visit and to include 50% additional charge for operational purposes. Dietre gave a laugh and said he would write it for me.

Well that seemed to be the end of my business venture and I heaved a sigh of relief but Dietre said he had another idea. He produced a magazine called "The Hikers Guide to the Mountains."

"I contribute to this magazine and I am friendly with the editor and the publishers. Let me try something I will be your agent for a lot less than 50% maybe a couple of biers."

I wrote back to the agency declining their offer. I told Olga and she agreed that her company were too greedy and that Dietre could do as good a job. And so it was Dietre was my agent and through the magazine he supported my business took off. He also produced my life story all neatly type written by Olga. I returned to the mountains with all the bedding washed and ironed by Ingerborg. I asked her if she would like the job regular and I would pay her. She said she would but I should also ask Gerda if she wanted to help out.

Within a short time Dietre was receiving bookings and soon I was guiding groups of four people through the mountains providing food and accommodation. Dietre consulted Olga regarding what she thought was a fair price and they came up with something that seemed agreeable. No one ever complained but I did look forward to my weekends of solitude. Meanwhile Dietre had heard from his publishers and was very excited. He couldn't wait for me to visit him. "Franz, read this letter," he said pushing it into my hands. The publishers had agreed to publish my life story but there were reservations. The cost would have to partially be met by me and it wasn't cheap but they had agreed to let me pay for it by monthly instalments. Dietre was over the moon and suggested celebrations drinks in the bier Keller that evening.

Well within a year my business had taken off and so had my life story. Dietre told me he had received a request from the University of Paris asking if I would give a talk on my achievements. That did seem a bit daunting but with Dietre's gentle persuasion I could only say yes.

Part 10

"So, ladies and gentlemen, I had my hair cut, my beard shaved off and bought a new suit and now here I am in front of you telling you my life story." The room erupted in applause as Franz took a sip of water. He waited a while for it to die down and then held up his hands. "And now, ladies and gentlemen, there's something I can tell you that isn't in my book. When I took the two Gestapo prisoners through the mountains to safety I never saw them again that is until I went out this morning to look in the shop selling my book. I happened to glance down the street towards the coffee shop and that's when I saw her sitting at a table. I introduced myself but she didn't recognise this clean shaven, smart-looking man of the mountains. After a lot of explaining I managed to convince her of who I was. After a lot of gentle persuasion she agreed to come along this evening and relate what happened after she left with the resistance. Ladies and gentlemen, will you please welcome the wife of Professor Anderson? Mrs Margaret Anderson." The room erupted again into loud applause. Franz took Margaret's arm and led her to the microphone. He could feel her shaking and whispered gently to her. He stood by her side holding onto her arm.

"Ladies and gentlemen, first let me say in front of all of you that I and my daughter owe our lives to this man, if it hadn't been for Franz I wouldn't be here today. I want to say thank you Franz and to all the brave resistance men, especially Pierre Blerieve??"

Franz listened as she related her experiences to the crowded auditorium. Occasionally her voice wavered and a handkerchief would appear. "I was sitting at the table contemplating throwing myself in the river, I was homeless and jobless and with no money when I heard this man's voice I looked up but didn't recognise him. When he revealed who he was a wave of love and compassion came over me – here was the man who had saved my life and now like a guardian angel here he was again." She paused and gave Franz a warm embrace.

The audience stood up and the auditorium echoed to a thunderous applause. The professor came forward encouraging the applause. He addressed the audience saying it was one of the most intriguing stories he had ever heard. He added his thanks to Franz and Margaret for making this appearance. He added that they would be in the lobby shortly if anyone wanted their book signed by the author but first let's have a coffee break insisted the professor.

The professor said there were also two other people in the lobby who wanted to meet Margaret. They finished their coffee and made their way into the lobby where a table and two chairs had been arranged for them. The people were crowded around clutching their books and awaiting the appearance of the author. Some of the students fired brief questions but the majority just stood there holding their books. Franz shook hands with all of them. Many too wanted Margaret to sign their book which she did willingly after being prompted by Franz.

Gradually the satisfied crowd dispersed, the professor brought in two more well-dressed gentlemen and Margaret immediately recognised one of them as Pierre. She gave him a warm smile and a big hug before introducing him to Franz. After a brief conversation Pierre introduced the other gentleman. "This is Monsieur

Flavelle minister of patriots whom I work closely with," said Pierre. "He has something to say to you.

The man held out his hand to Margaret, "Madame Anderson, first of all I want to apologise for my department for they have treated you deplorably and so has your own government. You should have been entitled to a war pension from my government and also from the English Government. We are both guilty of dragging our feet in your case. I sincerely hope you will forgive our neglect. I now am taking charge of your affairs personally and I promise I will see that you get what you are entitled to plus any back pay we owe you. I can also tell you in case you didn't know your husband didn't get killed at the factory he was taken to Germany with some other of the scientists and put into a concentration camp. Unfortunately they all died of starvation and disposed of. We have not been able to find out any more than that, Madame Anderson, but a memorial will be erected somewhere in Paris where they will be remembered for their sacrifice."

She thanked him for all the information adding that now she could lay him to rest in her heart.

The minister asked her for a contact address, Franz told the minister his and gave her his personnel card asking her to write to him with her bank details as he would arrange for her pension to be paid directly into her bank account and he would also advise his counterpart in the British Government to do the same. Once more he shook her hand and so did Pierre giving her his contact number just in case.

Franz looked at his watch, the professor reminded them to use the restaurant if they had time. He shook hands with them both saying what a pleasure it had been.

They ate a good meal and then took a taxi to the station where the train to Zurich was waiting in the station. They chose a nice carriage but doubted if they would keep it to themselves for very long. However, when the train pulled out they were still the sole occupants it was to be a long journey and Franz noted that Margaret had dozed off. It had been a tiring experience for them both but Franz was over the moon with excitement he never thought for one moment that a book bearing his name would ever be on display in a book shop let alone be the subject of discussions at the University de Paris. He drifted off a while lulled by the sound of the train as it rattled along the tracks. Margaret admired the beauty of the mountains as they passed through small towns and villages perched high in the distance amidst the peaks.

The conductor told them it was another hour to Zurich and the train was on time and making good progress. Margaret excused herself as she made for the toilets. Franz looked up at her suitcase totally unsuitable for where we are heading. That's something else to be sorted.

She looked refreshed when she came back and Franz asked if she would be able to carry a backpack instead of a suitcase. Also when we get to Zurich a spot more shopping for boots and mountain clothes, heeled shoes don't go in the mountains he said.

They all fitted into the backpack and Franz hoisted it up on his back. Whilst they waited for the train connection they ate a good meal in the café. Margaret asked how long it would be before they reached Carmen. Franz pointed to the train pulling into the station. Half an hour on that one to the next town and then ten minutes on the shuttle to the villages, Carmen is the second village so it won't be long now.

Zurich looked a nice town and there were plenty of people around in their lightweight clothes. Margaret thought how nice it would have been for her and daughter Joanna to spend a day shopping, that's if they had any money of course. The shuttle jugged along stopping to let people off at the first village. Margaret commented how pretty these farming villages looked nestled away in the hillsides. Franz picked up his backpack. "Let's go and look at our own village shall we?" People in the street didn't recognise him without his long hair and flowing beard so they managed to pass through and up to the farm without any interruption. Ingerborg was hanging out the washing when they entered the farm gate and walked up to the house. She gave joyous welcome when she laid eyes on them, although she only recognised Franz. He gave her a big hug and then asked if she recognised his companion.

Ingerborg shook hands with Margaret and looked at her carefully. She shook her head and told Franz she didn't know who the stranger was. Franz roared with laughter as he revealed Margaret's identity. Ingerborg was taken aback, she cupped her hands to her face in amazement and then reached out to give Margaret a welcome hug apologising profusely for not recognising her.

Hans came out of the cowshed when he heard all the commotion he too was flabbergasted at the revelation. He too admitted no recollection adding that she looked better this time around. With the greetings over and Franz making fuss of Romulus and Remus Ingerborg led them into the house still with her arm around Margaret.

Over warm cups of coffee Franz told then of the University and how he had met Margaret that morning and how she had joined him on stage. The air was electrified with excitement as Franz said it had been the most exciting day of his life and said he was now famous but wanted to keep a low profile.

After the evening meal Franz said he needed to go and see Dietre, he would not stay very long but it was important. Ingerborg said she would show Margaret to her room and make her comfortable.

Heinreiche and Dietre looked up and welcomed Franz as he stepped into the bier Keller drinks were ordered and Franz was invited to sit down and tell all. He quickly ran through the visit to Paris and all that had taken place. He thanked Dietre for his involvement in getting his book published and then revealed what had happened in Paris his meeting with the woman the Gestapo had chased all over the mountains. Of course everyone wanted to meet her right away but Franz put a hold on it temporarily. "Let her rest before you start asking her all the questions. She will be here for a while and you will all get a chance. Now I must go back to my guest, I'll see you all soon."

Dietre informed him that there were bookings already and his first was in one week's time starting from Carmen. Franz said he would make sure he was here to greet them. At Ingerborg's invitation they decided to spend the night at the farm and then make an early start in the morning.

When Franz took the dogs out before he retired Hans decided to join him. "She must have had a terrible time," said Hans.

"Yes, she did," replied Franz, "and now I want her to relax and have a long rest before she returns to England. I intend to see that she is home for her daughter's wedding later this year."

Hans asked if she will be alright at the monastery whilst he is looking after his guests. "She may not like being left alone at the monastery."

Franz hadn't thought of that. "Perhaps she might want to travel with me or she could come down and stay with Ingerborg and you for a couple of days it won't be long."

Hans nodded. "Yes, she would be more than welcome and Ingerborg would make a fuss of her."

Early next morning with their backpacks sorted and loaded they said their goodbyes and set off. It was a lovely spring morning as they made their way into the mountains. "That's where Joanna fell," said Franz pointing to the slope.

"It seems so long ago," Margaret replied, "it's hard to imagine that took place just because I went to France to find my husband."

Franz carried on at a steady pace pointing out different features in the mountains. The spring flowers were in full bloom decorating the rocky escarpment. He pointed out the place where he was swept away in the flash flood almost to his death. He also pointed out the peak in the distance still covered in snow and glistening in the sunlight. They sat on a rock and rested and enjoyed Ingerborg's fresh baking. "They're such lovely people," said Margaret, "no wonder you like it here so much."

Franz offered her a drink of water. "Yes, they are the best people I've ever met and everybody in the village are the same, so friendly."

Taking it easy down the incline to the tree line Franz held onto her arm in case she slipped. She thanked him remarking, "I bet you are as agile as a mountain goat." As they walked up to the monastery Margaret gazed around in wonder. "It's so beautiful here in the spring, isn't it?"

Franz replied that every season had its own beauty he loved all seasons and found walking in the mountains so exhilarating he never wanted to live anywhere else on the planet. "I'm so at home here, so relaxed, so happy."

She entered the vestibule and slipped off her backpack. "Now I remember this," she whispered.

Franz immediately reset the fire and soon the log fire was illuminating the dark shadows. Franz started the generator and the whole place came to life.

Margaret walked around. "I can remember some of it but you have done a lot more to it since then you have been busy, Franz."

He carried her backpack into the next cell to his and showed her the new mattresses. "No more straw," he added.

"It certainly makes a difference with the electric," she said. Franz looked at her and smiled. "Yes, that's thanks to you."

He set about feeding the dogs and then put a chicken on the spit with some hastily prepared vegetables. He opened a bottle of wine asking her if she preferred red or white. "I don't mind," came the reply.

There was still some daylight hours left so Franz asked if she would like to take a steady walk down to the lake. Saying that she didn't know there was a lake she eagerly agreed.

"It's so beautiful here, Franz, you have everything."

He looked out across the lake. "No, not everything, Margaret."

Silence took over as they walked back to the monastery both wrapped up in their own thoughts. Her words echoed through his mind "you have everything, Franz" she didn't know the heartache and the loneliness that would often take over. She didn't know of the nights he would walk in the mountains calling out to Carmen and she never saw the tears he shed.

He told her she had done very well at the university and had put the icing on the cake. He went on to say that if they hadn't met that day no one would have been any wiser as to what had become of her and her daughter. He also renewed his promise to get her back to England in time for Joanna's wedding. He joked that if ever she wanted to come back to the monastery he would find her a job housekeeping.

"That's the only way I could hope to repay you, Franz."

He explained to her that in three days' time he would be going back down to Carmen to meet four hikers who he would be bringing back to the monastery for an overnight stay before he took them down the other side to catch a train and how he would be picking up four more hikers and bringing them back to the monastery. He told her that this is what he did. Would she want to accompany him or would she prefer to stay at the monastery which would mean she would be all alone for approximately twelve hours. He noticed that she looked a bit insecure.

"I didn't know you did that," she murmured.

"Or you can come with me and stay with Ingerborg until I bring the other party down or with Gerda and Rainer down the other side. The whole weekend I spend here."

She looked away looking a bit embarrassed. "I seem to have created a problem for you, Franz. I don't really feel like staying here on my own for twelve hours, I would be a bit scared." Franz looked at her and smiled knowing it was a lot to ask.

He knew she would be alright on the journey down the mountain but to turn around in one hour and make the journey back was asking a bit much of her. It would be better for her to stay with Ingerborg until the next journey. They would enjoy being together and Ingerborg would take her out to places. Franz let her think about it answering any questions she put to him. She, on the other hand, didn't fancy being left alone in the monastery, maybe in a while when she got used to it but not at the moment.

"I'll come with you to Carmen and stay with Ingerborg until you come next time. She is a lovely person and I will enjoy her company. Even if we just spend the weekends together will be fine with me, Franz, yes, that will be fine."

Ingerborg clapped her hands and hugged Margaret. "We will have some fun together," she promised.

Franz was happy with that. He gave Ingerborg a wad of notes. "Can you make sure she opens a bank account in her name."

The hiking party had arrived and were waiting at the library for Franz. He was introduced to the group of French people, two husbands and their wives on their first outing since the war had ended they were excited and made every effort to converse with Franz speaking French and partially English. Ingerborg had prepared a light meal for them to eat before they set off into the mountains. They all made a fuss of the dogs because they were their local breed. Margaret and Ingerborg waved them off. Franz watched his guests as they followed him assessing their capabilities. They were in their early forties so he assumed they were reasonably fit. He paced the journey stopping every hour for them to rest for ten minutes. When they reached the finger peak he pointed out that he had been looking at that for at least five years and it never altered. Always clad in a white robe with brilliant sunshine on it. The two men were engineers and their wives were both secretaries all lived in or around Paris. They told Franz of their experiences at the hands of the Germans' and how bad it had been. Several camera shots were taken of them as a group and of Franz with his dogs. Fortunately the weather had held out for them and as they made their final approach to the monastery the whole area was swathed in a ray of sunshine. The sunlight filtered through the windows illuminating the inside. The visitors looked around open-mouthed and made complimentary remarks. They seemed content with the accommodation and had soon settled themselves in. Whilst the visitors wandered around their new surroundings Franz had stoked up the fire and began preparing the evening meal. The joint in the oven was cooking well and the vegetables on the hob were almost ready. As Franz prepared the table the guests were exploring the grounds outside with lots of photographs being taken. They were an amiable group and chatted away freely. The dogs followed them around and received a lot of attention. Franz had put out a selection of wines and biers for them to choose from and the conversation flowed throughout the evening. The sky at night was very prolific and time was spent pointing out the many constellations. Franz said that an early breakfast was planned as they would be continuing their journey at first light. Copies of his book were displayed throughout the monastery and his visitors seemed eager to purchase their souvenir copies duly signed by Franz of course.

Another group would be waiting for them when they reached Gerda and Rainer's farm. It would be an hour's rest for Franz before he would return to the monastery with his second lot of visitors. Rainer had prepared a large lamb joint for him to take back although before they had left Franz had prepared a large chicken which was in the oven ready for when the next group arrived. Vegetables had been prepared before Franz retired for the night and would be on the hob boiling slowly. Sheets had to be stripped off ready to take down to Ingerborg and fresh ones had been put on the beds. This what Franz called a quick changeover before they left the monastery.

The group leaving shook hands and gave Franz the thumbs-up. They had enjoyed their trip through the mountains with him and said it was highly recommended. The second group were all men not much older than himself and very keen to get started. Bidding farewell to Rainer, Gerda and the leaving party, Franz set the pace for the return journey. Two of the group were photographers for some newspaper and two were student artists. They all seemed to know each other and chatted away vigorously leaving Franz in front with the two dogs leading. They would call out to Franz if they wanted a photoshoot or if the artists wanted to do quick sketches. During the first ten minute break they asked Franz all kinds of questions which he was glad to answer. When they reached the valley one of the group asked if there had been a landslide pointing out the variation of the landscape. Franz replied there had been a couple of years before when a huge avalanche had swept down the mountain almost covering the whole valley.

When the party reached the monastery again the oohs and aaahs were voiced which made Franz proud of his achievements. Many photos and sketches were made and taken by the man and questions like who helped you do this or that. Surprise showed in their faces when Franz said he had done it all himself. It seemed very unlikely that these men were capable of knocking a nail in a piece of wood.

The meal was appreciated by them and soon they were supping at the biers which seemed more appropriate than a cup of tea or coffee. An after tea walk down to the lake with the dogs and then back inside to a couple of more biers and joviality amongst themselves before an early night. They voiced their opinions and in all it would seem that none of them could live the existence that Franz lived but they enjoyed getting away from things for a short while and would recommend it.

Early next morning as the sun rose the party left for the descent down the mountains into Carmen arriving just after midday. They were welcomed enthusiastically by Ingerborg and Margaret who had lunch ready for them. Franz relaxed on the porch talking to Hans. Margaret came over and asked Franz if he was alright. Smiling at her he said he was fine and asked how she had been. "I've had a wonderful time." Ingerborg had taken her shopping and shown her around another village. Franz asked her if she would like to stay another couple of days with Ingerborg or come with him and the next group up to the monastery. She thought for a while. "You will be back in two days I'll stay with Ingerborg until you return and then I think you are free for a few days.

"I'll come back with you then, that's if you don't mind?"

Franz said he didn't as long as she was alright, he reached in his coat and pulled out a wad of notes. "I want Ingerborg to take you to the bank and open a bank account in your name. Don't forget you have to let the Minister of Patriots know your address and bank account number. Take this money and open your account, Ingerborg will go with you, Margaret, will you do that while I am gone and if you could write to your daughter let her know where you are she will be worried about you."

Franz said goodbye to the departing visitors and greeted the new group who had been engaging in conversation with them. He had a quick chat to Ingerborg and Hans whilst the French group had a quick lunch which Ingerborg had prepared. Waving goodbye they began their journey; two men and their wives were following Franz and the dogs. They were a friendly group from the north of Switzerland who loved hiking in the mountains.

One man was an electrical engineer and his wife a school teacher the other was a draughtsman and his wife also a school teacher. They were amicable and spoke English and Swiss. Everybody seems to be able to speak our language thought Franz but we English don't know other languages unless studying at university. The Swiss were taught our language at school. Again Franz was generally asked how he became a guide and how long he had been doing it. He answered the simple questions with simple answers. This group travelled to different parts of the mountains every year but were now stretching their legs towards France now that the war was over.

When they reached the finger peak Franz pointed down below to where you could just see the corner of the monastery peeking out through the trees. The travellers looked in amazement. They were expecting a small village amongst the peaks. Franz said there were no villages for many miles. He had one idea the women folk were a bit disappointed with no shops being around. When they eventually descended the ridge and made their way along the tree line there seemed to be mumbles of disillusion which changed to gasps of disbelief when Franz led them to the monastery. He opened the vestibule door and welcomed them in. He went and started the small generator and threw on the lights.

"It's a medieval castle," said one of the women.

"No," said Franz, "it is a monastery."

The group wandered around open-mouthed shooting questions to Franz. "We thought we were coming to a medieval castle come hotel," said one of the women. Another one of the group said they didn't know what to expect.

Franz showed them to their cells and said the evening meal would be ready shortly. He hoped the chicken portions and vegetables were to their liking and the wine he had chosen. They eventually made an appearance after several visits to the toilets which Franz imagined would be brought up as a subject. Both men asked for coffee and the women requested tea with their meal. This took Franz by surprise but he quickly produced both removing the wine from the table. "Not, now please we will take the wine later," said the school teacher.

The engineer asked if his only source of power was the generator. Franz said it was. The engineer went on to say he worked for a company who developed wind generators and this would be an ideal spot for one. Franz said he hadn't heard of electricity from the wind. The engineer who said his name was Sven said he would explain. It sounded interesting and Franz listened intently. It would be nice if the diesel could be stopped but the whole idea sounded expensive.

"Come," said Sven, "let us look outside while it is light. A steel tower would have to be built and fastened to the side of the monastery to house the turbine and the propellers this in turn turned a shaft which in turn turned the generator.

"I will do a drawing for you," said Sven casually holding up his hand. "Which way do you get the wind from?"

Franz said nearly always coming over the mountains.

"Do you get some wind most days?" asked Sven. Franz said most days but during the summer not so strong. Sven thought for a while. "They are not cheap, Franz, but I have an idea. We are developing a new model and this would be an ideal location to try it out. If it only produced enough power for your lighting system it would help, wouldn't it?"

Franz agreed it would. Sven began roughly taking measurements and making site locations on his drawing.

Franz replenished the empty wine bottles and sat down to join the group. They were laughing and joking now and seemed to be in a good mood. "You have done a remarkable job here, Franz, and you say it is all your own work, then you are to be congratulated on your achievements." Sven also said he had done extremely well for a young man. He added that when he got back to work he would approach his management team with a proposition and he would write to Franz and let him know if any decision had been made but he didn't promise anything.

The following morning after a cereal and sliced toast breakfast everybody was in the vestibule with their backpacks on waiting for Franz.

It was a fine morning the sun just rising and very few light clouds. Photos were taken as they looked back at the monastery settled in its own little valley with the morning sunlight blessing a new day. They chatted freely as they made their way along the ridge. Sven fell in besides Franz. "I shall be writing to you within a few weeks and let you know of any developments, I cannot guarantee anything, Franz, but I will try."

Rainer greeted them when they reached the farm the table was laid and a light lunch was offered to the group. Franz sat on the porch with Rainer and asked how everything was. He said the garden produce was selling well and Gerda was making money. The soil was good and another dressing of manure planned for the autumn turnover. The greenhouse yielded tomatoes and the seedling for lettuce and cabbage were doing well. He said it was the best thing that could have happened, although he still kept a few cows for the milk which was also bringing in money. He pointed to a pile of freshly laundered sheets. "Don't forget to take them," he said.

The departing group came over and said their goodbyes as a new group entered the farm gate. Franz welcomed them and Gerda provided refreshments; this time the group consisted of three middle-aged women and a younger-looking male who looked more like a butler than anything. Their English wasn't so good so Rainer interpreted a lot of the conversation.

Franz checked their backpacks and watched as they loaded them on their backs. Some adjustment had to be made to two of them or else the woman would have been suffering from sore shoulders.

With a smile and a wave they began the journey into the mountains with Franz keeping a close watch on the party. The dogs' panniers had been packed with tins of dog food and Rainer had put a bundle of clean sheets across each ones back. Franz had put some fresh baked bread and other delicacies in his pack, also eggs, butter and fresh milk. Gerda always made sure of the food requisites.

An hour into the journey Franz noticed that one of the women was favouring her left foot. He halted the party for a fifteen minute break and approached the woman. She had purchased new boots for the hike and it was the first time she had worn them. Franz sat her down on a flat rock and told her to remove her boot. She winced as the boot was gently prized off. Franz removed her thick sock, it was soaked with blood where the blisters had formed. Franz told her she should have worn the boots in before taking a hiking holiday in the mountains. He gently cut away the hanging skin and began to apply a thick cream. He let it melt into the flesh before applying another thick coat. When that had melted into her foot he applied a jelly compound which he covered with a gauze. She produced a fresh sock from her backpack and Franz put it on for her. The boot was applied and the party carried on. The man had offered to carry the woman's backpack as well as his own but Franz said not to. "We all carry our own," he said. The party chatted amongst themselves taking photos of each other and of the majestic scenery opening up in front of them. The man caught up with Franz and started conversation. Apparently he was a nephew to the three aunts and had offered to chaperone them on this trip before they packed him off to university for a paid for education. Franz said he would certainly remember his short vacation in the mountains with his aunties and their generosity with his education.

The women faired pretty well on the journey once they had got into a regular stride even the one with the blisters. Franz was thinking to himself once they reached Carmen the next day he would have a few days off. Deitre said he wanted to keep all the weekends free.

They all faired pretty well on the hike. The other women were pretty robust and the young man held his own amongst the rocks. By the time they were a short distance from the monastery Franz reckoned they were ready for a meal and a nights rest. Casual remarks were made as they made the final approach. Franz thought he caught the words penal servitude? But shrugged it off. He escorted the group into the vestibule and helped them off with their backpacks. Generator started and the whole place lit up. He showed them to their individual cells and left them to make themselves at home. The young man was first to make an appearance he said it was very quaint and asked what it had been used for before. Franz told him he thought it was a 12th century monastery. He marvelled at the work Franz had done and said he was interested in ancient history.

Franz presented the evening meal a nice lamb roast with all the trimmings. Wine was served to the satisfaction of the ladies, the young man joined Franz in a bier. The conversation around the table changed from one topic to another to the next until the woman with the blisters said she was going to retire. Gradually the others followed leaving the young man and Franz. They discussed everything from the war to what he was going to study at university. Finally Franz started to clear away and prepare for an early breakfast bidding him goodnight the young man retreated to his cell. Franz had told them an early start would be required but when he knocked on the cell doors announcing it was five o'clock there was a chorus of abuse from the females. Franz guessed they would be dragging their heels and it would be a delayed start. However, once on their way Franz pushed the pace a little saying they would miss the shuttle.

A quick lunch saw them on their way but there were no promises of a return visit. Franz called in to see Heinreiche and Dietre. When Franz mentioned wind turbines Heinreiche said he had been reading up on them. Deitre confirmed he had no bookings until Monday morning at Gerda's and Rainer's farm. Franz hurried back to the farm and asked Margaret if she wanted to go for a hike up to the monastery. She was more than ready. Offering her thanks to Ingerborg and Hans she gathered her belongings saying she would be back in a few days. The rain clouds had started to form and there was a chance of some rain but this didn't dampen the enthusiasm to get moving. Margaret asked Franz how he had got on with the groups of hikers. He replied that woman are worse than men and tend to mess about more than men. This received a curt reply that not all women are the same followed by a loud laugh from Franz. Margaret told Franz that she had opened her bank account and sent the details to the French Minister giving Ingerborg's address. She had also written a long and personnel letter to Joanna telling her she will be at her wedding. This all seemed to raise her spirits and Margaret seemed very happy in herself. They walked leisurely through the mountains. Franz was glad to be back in the company of someone he knew. Margaret rambled on about what Ingerborg had told her and about the shuttle's journeys to other villages. He said she was a proper mother figure and loved them both to bits.

Franz had things to do when they reached the monastery – there was always wood to be cut for the fire and always trees to be felled for future use. First he had to clean up after the visitors. Margaret immediately took charge of the domestic stuff and sent Franz out into his workshop, the dogs followed also being given their marching orders. He decided to go into the woods and cut timber stopping only for a quick sandwich and coffee he cut down three pine trees each eight inches in diameter. These were the start of the new floor. He eyed the trees that would provide the main beams and in the winter they would be outside his workshop waiting. He called his dogs and together they hauled the first three lengths up to the monastery. Margaret had come out and said she was preparing the evening meal and it would soon be ready. Franz patted the dogs and decided to call it a day.

Sunday was a nice sunny day. Franz cut a few logs and then asked Margaret if she would like to go for a walk in the mountains. He took her along a trail he didn't use very often, it didn't lead anywhere but it was a nice change and had spectacular views. Margaret commented on the peace and quiet of the mountains comparing them with the hustle and bustle of Paris. She had been glad to leave the city and said she could appreciate what Franz saw in it all. They walked casually making odd comments about a varied array of topics. Margaret asked Franz if he could live forever in the mountains alone. He said he would not have a problem with that.

There's always people down below if ever I need to socialise with anyone; I like my own company I like being left alone with my thoughts and I'm always planning things in my head, I never get bored.

"So you wouldn't like anyone permanently living with you?" asked Margaret.

Franz gave her a sideward glance. "Why are you offering?" he laughed.

She blushed and turned away. "No, I'm just wondering what uncertainties await me when I go home."

A few minutes silence and then, "Well, I'll tell you what, Margaret, you can always come back to the monastery, I can see you like it here as much as I do."

She cast a sideways glance in his direction. *There, she thought to herself, what an offer.*

They circled around and started their way back. "It's been a nice relaxing day today, I like it when it's like this," said Franz.

"Well, it's certainly been nice and peaceful, I think I'm getting around to your way of thinking but it was nice staying with Ingerborg she really is a lovely person."

He glanced at her. "Wait until you meet Gerda, she's Ingerborg's sister and they're like two peas in a pod."

Early next morning brought them on their way down to Gerda's and Rainer's farm. Franz had packed four empty fuel cans into the dogs' panniers. He hadn't heard from Sven and the weeks had been ticking by, perhaps it was a nonstarter and it would be best to forget the idea of a wind generator but the idea had stirred his imagination and Heinreiche had shown an interest.

Gerda looked hard as the couple broke the tree line and crossed the field. She knew it was Franz but who was the other person. As they drew near she saw the blonde hair poking out from under the hat. Franz had a broad smile on his face when he saw the frown on Gerda's face. "Brought someone to see you," smirked Franz.

Margaret held out her hand and smiled at the perplexed look on Gerda's face. "You don't remember me, do you, Gerda?"

The look turned into a huge smile as the memories flooded her brain. Gerda gripped her hand and then gave her a huge hug. "After all these years," she whispered. "How are you?"

Rainer came out and greeted Franz and the dogs but was also perplexed by the stranger who Gerda was hugging. When introduced he too gave Margaret a hug simultaneously they asked about Joanna.

Franz said Margaret would fill in all the details later as she was about to stay with them for a few days if it was alright. Gerda at once put her arm around Margaret and led her into the farmhouse. The new party of hikers arrived at the farm within the hour. Gerda provided the light lunch and Margaret made herself comfortable in the bedroom Gerda had allocated to her.

The new party of two men and two women chatted away in perfect English as they introduced themselves. Two fashion designers and a doctor and an industrial chemist. The two women designers were dressed the part. Franz guessed their gear came straight out of the front window of their shop in Stuttgart. They spoke German amongst themselves but were polite enough to speak English or Swiss when in company. Margaret made an excuse to stay in the bedroom. It was obvious the sound of German voices upset her. They donned on their backpacks which Franz checked and were soon entering the tree line. Their ages ranged from forty to forty-five, quite fit and talkative. Photos and group photos were taken even the women cuddled Romulus and Remus and said it would be a good photo for their clothes catalogue if they did a winter section. Of course they offered to pay for the photo of the dogs but Franz waved it aside. The two men chatted to Franz asking all the familiar questions adding that they too liked to get away from the mad rushing crowds of the cities. The doctor's wife was very chatty and would slip in with Franz as he walked. She asked about his wife and was very surprised to find such a good-looking man unattached. What does he do when he's all alone in the mountains and he should find himself a female to share the long winter months with. He said he had other plans which produced a wicked smile from the women. The men were always engaged in conversation and Franz wondered why they had come hiking. As they made their final approach to the monastery the two women seemed to be bickering over something.

He opened the vestibule door and invited the hikers to remove their backpacks and enter. He started the generator and unloaded the cans of diesel from the dogs' panniers.

He led the way down the corridor and allocated the cells to the party. The women at once enquired why they were all single cells. Franz explained that it was a two hundred-year-old monastery and that's how it had been built. The men didn't seem to mind, it was just the women who said they didn't have anyone to talk to in bed, the men smiled.

Franz invited them to wander around freely while he prepared the meal. He had put a pork joint in the oven and it was almost done. Wine was put on the table but the men preferred a lager. The women took wine but were soon enquiring as to what else was available. Franz produced a bottle of schnapps which was promptly opened and sampled. He informed the group of an early morning start and advised not to drink too much schnapps. He began cleaning away and preparing the morning breakfast. The party broke up at about eleven o'clock and departed for their cells. Franz sat down by the fire and began making notes of supplies he would need to bring back. One of the cell doors opened and a female made for the toilets. It wasn't until he felt an arm around his neck as he realised the woman had returned. She smiled as she embraced him from behind. It was the one who had asked him what he did all alone through the winter. She was obviously making advances but Franz didn't want any of that. He stood up and faced her. The flimsy dressing gown had parted revealing a pair of lily white breasts. It was all Franz could do to push her away from him. She pushed herself into him and reached up to kiss him.

"No, please I do not want that," gasped Franz trying to break free.

"All I can say is you must be a faggot," she hissed pulling her dressing gown around her and storming off to her cell. *Well*, thought Franz, *it's certainly not gone out of fashion*.

Early morning call brought disgruntlement comment from the visitors. It was plain to see that the empty bottle of schnapps had gone to their heads. The two women weren't speaking to each other and the men could just about tie their laces. Porridge and toast were just picked at by all four. Franz wondered if he should have put out the caviar. Six hours later as they broke the tree line hardly anyone had spoken. As they were invited to sit down to a light luncheon Gerda cheerily asked if they had enjoyed the hike. She was greeted with low grumblings and one man cheerily said it was wander bar but it wasn't seconded by anyone.

Franz caught Gerda's eye and smiled as he shook his head.

The next group were four university students on a short break. They were very vibrant and enthusiastic. They played with the dogs and helped each other with their backpacks. Franz put fresh meat cans of bier and bottles of wine in his pack. The dogs carried their own food plus two piles of freshly laundered sheets and pillow cases Gerda had prepared. Rainer chatted away asking him if everything was working out alright. Franz commented on how different people were – some were okay whilst others could be a bit trying.

The journey started off well with a sky filled with sunshine but as they proceeded dark clouds filled the horizon. By the time they were two hours into the mountain's trail the heavens had opened and torrents of rain poured down on them. They sheltered in a small cave and put on their wet weather gear. It was a great relief when Franz noticed that the sky was getting brighter as the dark clouds passed over. A huge rainbow shone over the mountains giving off beautiful display of colour. The students took many photos saying they would not have missed it for all the world. As the torrents of water gushed down the gullies below them Franz told of his experience and warned that the mountains could also be dangerous. They broke the tree line surrounding the monastery the students gasped at the sight of the impressive piece of architecture standing before them. They all thought it was going to be a log cabin. Franz pointed to his workshop and said, "That's a log cabin," the first one he had built inside the walls of the monastery.

The rain had freshened the area surrounding and now the sunshine was breaking through causing steam to rise from the ground. It gave off an eerie effect making the path down to the lake look spooky. The boys entered the vestibule and gaped in wonder at the high wooden roof and surrounding panels that greeted them inside. They entered the chapel and all stood silently in prayer in front of the altar. Franz had the feeling he was going to get on well with this group. He showed them to the cells and asked if they were suitable. While they unpacked their gear he set about preparing the meal. Oddly enough the boys preferred tea or coffee to drink. The students all attended the University de Paris and knew the professor. One of the students had read my book but had not attended my talk while the other three had been climbing in the Pyrenees. They laughed and joked throughout the evening and eventually cans of bier were requested. After a while they loosened up and become more jovial and engaging. A visit outside to look at the starry night before retiring to their cells Franz wished all his hikers were as amiable.

Early next morning found the group climbing up the slope towards the ridge. More photos were taken and rough sketches made of the surrounding peaks they would certainly have their memories.

Margaret comments on how happy everyone seemed to be and guessed Franz was well pleased with this group. It was a free long weekend with no more hikers until next week. Franz said he would stay the night and then he and Margaret could start out early in the morning for their weekend in the mountains. Margaret enjoyed being with Ingerborg and Gerda she said they were a laugh and encouraging her to speak Swiss. She had met Heinreiche and Dietre but she wasn't sure about the big German. He told her that if all Germans were like Heinreiche the world would be a better place. She told him she was settling in fine and was resting in-between going out with Ingerborg and helping around the house. She was definitely a happier woman.

The weeks passed by quickly and Franz decided to ask Margaret if she was happy going up and down the mountains or would she want to stay at the monastery while he did the hiking. She thought for a while and then asked, "Would I be safe here on my own?"

Franz assured her that it was safe. "Nobody comes here without me, nobody can find the way."

She gave a little laugh. "Maybe I'll try it sometime but not yet, give me a little more time," and so it was.

A month later she developed a cold that knocked her off her feet. Gerda said she should stay with them and be looked after but Margaret wanted to spend the weekend with Franz at the monastery. She followed Franz into the mountains against everyone's advice. Franz could see she wasn't well and watched over her all the way. He lit a fire in her cell and made her go to her bed. He made use of what medicines Gerda had put and also mixed honey with lemon drinks which he kept for his own use. She slept a lot of the time which Franz reckoned would help her. The dogs realised she wasn't well and they both slept outside her cell. The night before Franz had to pick up his next party of visitors he looked in on Margaret she was awake but still looked peaky. "I shall leave in the morning but I'll leave the dogs to keep you company, you will be safe, Margaret, I promise." She agreed that with Romulus and Remus outside the door she felt safer.

Ingerborg was alarmed when he arrived at the farm house and told Franz he shouldn't have left her. It was a quick turn around and Franz with the new party were soon cutting the tree line into the mountains. The new group were well into their thirties, four young building contractors from Paris who wanted a break from the hectic building programme that was going on through France. A couple of ten-minute breaks for drinks of water and they were soon negotiating the incline from the top of the ridge to the tree line heading to the monastery. They asked Franz a variety of questions in their pigeon English. "How old is the building, Monsieur?" and "How did you discover it?" Franz managed to answer most of them to their satisfaction. He thought it would be a good idea to get some informative leaflets printed to hand out to the hikers. Inside the monastery the builders started examining the construction scrutinising the stonework and the timberwork. They were very impressed. Franz showed them to their cells. This time he used the ones on the opposite side. He wanted to keep his and Margaret's private. The dogs greeted him with their big tongues and wagging tails. The door was open to Margaret's cell he could see that she was still in bed so he closed the door and closed the partition across keeping the kitchen and dining room closed off.

He then set about stoking up the fire and checking the meat in the slow oven. It was a pork joint and a variety of vegetables from Rainer's and Gerda's farm. Bier was served with the meat to everybody's satisfaction. The hikers would then wander outside for a smoke and a look around. Franz knocked on Margaret's door, she called out for him to enter. He had prepared a light meal for her and placed it on her table. She greeted him with a smile and said she was feeling better having slept soundly most of the day.

The hikers had found their way down to the lake and first thing they asked Franz was, "Are there any fish in there, Monsieur?" When Franz told them there were they babbled excitedly about coming again soon on a fishing trip Franz indicated a four-day trip would have to be arranged. The evening went well with several cans of bier being consumed. Nevertheless the hikers were up early next morning ready for the next part of their journey.

Gerda greeted them as they reached the farmhouse. Her first question was of course, "How's Margaret?" Franz assured her that Margaret was getting better, staying in bed with medicine to help her recover and with Romulus and Remus for company.

The next group of hikers were two Swiss couples on a short break from their floral business and garden centre. They said that the summer had been hectic and they wanted a getaway break before they started to prepare for the autumn and winter planting. They all spoke fluent English so Franz had no problem with communication.

Margaret grew stronger as the days went by and was soon joining Franz up and down the mountain. She said that at times she would stay at the monastery with the dogs as company and let Franz lead the hikers. She said she could find enough to do, cleaning and changing the bed linen. She even hinted that if Franz could buy a sewing machine she would even make some curtains. Franz said next time Margaret accompanied him down into Carmen he would take her shopping and she could choose a sewing machine. He would not trust himself to buy one. They shopped around and found a shop in one of the other villages that had a selection. Ingerborg said she would like to help. Margaret asked Franz if Ingerborg would be capable of making the journey into the mountains. "If she wanted to we could make the journey easy for her," was his reply. Hans said Ingerborg was quite fit for a sixty-year-old who had lived in the area all her life he said she would be alright as long as it was a steady climb. Franz lifted the machine onto his backpack. Yards of material were rolled up and put into the dogs' panniers and the women carried the poles.

They set off early after a hearty breakfast. Ingerborg dressed in her mountain gear and quite excited. Franz took it steady with plenty of rests but Ingerborg kept up well and said she was enjoying it. Her eyes almost popped out when they reached their destination. She marvelled at what Franz had achieved and walked around inside admiring all the roof work and panelling. Whilst Franz prepared the meal Margaret showed Ingerborg around making her comfortable in one of the cells. The sewing machine stood well on the dining table and after a hearty meal the women unrolled the fabric and started measuring. Franz whispered something to Margaret, she smiled and nodded her head.

It was early morning when Franz took the trail down to Gerda's and Rainer's farm. They were surprised to see him. There were no hikers scheduled until the following week. Franz watched Gerda's face as he asked her to come up to the monastery to visit her sister. She was ecstatic as she talked it over with Rainer. Franz said it would be a short visit, only a day or two. When he mentioned the sewing machine and making curtains Gerda was over the moon she collected cotton and curtain hooks and rings from her work basket. She insisted Franz should carry the eggs and bacon and a freshly made cake. Waving farewell to Rainer she was halfway across the field before Franz could catch up with her. Rainer had put a bottle of wine into Franz's backpack. Franz had to tell her to slow down before she wore herself out. "Franz, I have longed to do this, I haven't seen Ingerborg for two years."

Margaret had told Ingerborg that Franz had gone into the forest to cut down some trees and wouldn't be back for quite a while. "Why didn't he take the dogs with him?" she enquired.

"Oh, they won't leave me alone when I'm here," said Margaret casually.

Gerda admired the views of the mountains. It had been many years since she had left the farm, there never seemed to be time for leisurely walks. *I'm really enjoying this, Franz.*

When Franz opened the door to the monastery he could hear the sounds of the sewing machine and women chatting away. He let Gerda go in first and laughed as the two women saw each other and screamed out loud. They embraced each other and the tears fell. Margaret could hardly contain herself as the sisters rattled away in Swiss. "They are good company to be with," she said.

Franz started the meal and Margaret came over to lend a hand. "I'll let them chat away, they've so much to talk about." Franz eventually told the ladies it was time to clear away the sewing machine and let him lay the table for the evening meal. They both thanked Margaret and Franz for a lovely surprise. The following day out came the sewing machine again and more curtains made. It had been agreed amongst the women that all the cells would be fitted with brightly coloured ones they were only small ones so they were made quite quickly. Franz had to drill the walls and fit the curtain rods. Next would be the windows along each corridor and they were bigger and a lot higher so Franz had to use his ladder to measure and drill for the rods. That took up most of his time that day but when they broke for lunch he took them for a walk down to the lake. Ingerborg said straight away that Hans and Rainer like to fish so maybe at some time they too should visit. It was a wonderful happy break for them all but soon it was time to take the women back home. Gerda was the first to make the journey home, of course there were tears of emotion as she said her goodbyes promising to do it again.

She told Franz that it was better than any birthday gift and how much she had appreciated it. A quick turn around and Franz was on his way back to the monastery. Ingerborg expressed her thanks and said it had been a wonderful surprise to her.

Early next morning they set off to take Ingerborg home. Margaret said she felt well enough to join them. They had changed the bedding and the dogs had light loads of sheets and pillow cases in their panniers. Franz expected to be busy the next few weeks, it was the end of July and holiday time. Dietre had said there were plenty of hikers booked in right up until September.

Ingerborg posed the question: "How long will Margaret be staying in Switzerland?" Margaret said she would decide when she heard from her daughter about her wedding. Franz said nothing, he wished Margaret would stay forever, he liked having her around.

Hans greeted them and handed them a pile of letters Heinreiche had delivered. Margaret retreated to her room to read hers Franz took a quick look at his and saw his mother's handwriting, also Momma Martinez had written also another who's handwriting he didn't recognise. He pushed them all in his pocket and decided to read them later. He had to have a quick lunch and fill up with supplies before the new party arrived.

Margaret was very excited when she read her letter, it was from Joanna and it was telling her that the wedding was all arranged for the end of September. She had also received a letter from the French Minister of Partition telling her she had been awarded a pension from the company her husband had worked for and the French Government had also awarded her a war widow's pension. He informed her that he was still in negotiations with the British Government.

Margaret was delighted with the news and Ingerborg began asking about making arrangements for her to return to England for the wedding and to resettle herself. Margaret said she was going to be very busy, she would very much like to in England before the wedding so that she could help out with the arrangements. Ingerborg said it was the most natural thing in the world.

Franz did a quick turn around with the new party. Two married couples from Northern Switzerland celebrating their twenty-five years of married bliss. It was a happy trip both couples fluent in English and very light-hearted. They laughed and joked on their journey through the mountains, playing with Romulus and Remus and taking lots of photos. They were delighted with their accommodation and said it was most unusual. Franz put on a good spread and the wine flowed throughout the evening. Before going to bed Franz read his letter. It was from Sven the engineer he had put forward a suggestion to his company regarding the siting of a wind turbine at the monastery and the boss of the company had given Sven the go ahead for siting one of the experimental models if Franz could record the data. He said it wouldn't be too big and would fit on the side of the building. They would send it by rail to Carmen and wondered if Franz could manage to carry it up to the monastery. It would be in kit form and easily transportable. The actual turbine itself weighed approximately thirty-five pounds and none of the parts measured more than four feet in length. Franz was thrilled to bits, Sven had asked Franz to telephone him at the earliest convenience. That was something else for Franz to think about. He began to feel a bit sad at the thought of Margaret leaving – he had become very fond of her and enjoyed having her around but he had known all along that it was a temporary arrangement and he had made her a promise to help her return to England when she was well enough.

The Swiss group enjoyed their stay and amused themselves with walks up into the mountains and playing cards during the evening. They remarked on the good work Franz had done and wished him well. A quick change of bedding and preparation of a lamb joint in the oven and Franz was ready to join his guests for an early start. The two couples had been friends all their lives and lived in the same town. Franz thought how good it was and wondered if he would ever experience such luck.

Rainer and Gerda greeted the party and prepared a light lunch. The next group had arrived but were looking around the village for souvenirs. When they did show up he was surprised to find four women in their late twenties all students from a German university. They were fit-looking women and Franz guessed they were athletes of some description. Their arms were very muscular. Probably discus throwers he thought. They were very friendly, hard to believe they had been the enemy a few years ago. He hoped Margaret wasn't around when they arrived at Ingerborg's and Hans's farm.

They had no problem with the journey up to the monastery. They were in fact more agile than Franz himself. Lots of photos were taken of the girls themselves and only one of Franz and his dogs. On reaching their destination Franz pointed to the path leading to the lake. The girls became very excited and when Franz had shown them their accommodation the girls grabbed their towels and headed for the lake.

It had been a hot day so Franz had prepared a large bowl of salad with cold meat for a change. The freshly made bread from Gerda laden with butter followed by a fruit cocktail and of course a freshly made cake. There were no signs of the girls so Franz decided to take a stroll down to the lake. The girls were frolicking in the water naked as the day they were born. He immediately turned around and headed back. These girls weren't ordinary girls. They did eventually present themselves for the evening meal giggling amongst themselves.

Well one happy party thought Franz as the wine was served. When they arrived at the farm Margaret was inside with Ingerborg. Hans served the girls with a light lunch before they departed. They called out their Auf wiederseins as they departed for the station.

Margaret asked Franz if she could leave mid-September and he agreed; next time he came to the farm they would be free to make arrangements. He suggested she should check her bank account to see if all the pensions had been paid in he would also arrange for Dietre to work out her share of the profits. She said she didn't want any payment as she had done very little. Franz reminded her of his promise to pay a percentage.

Picking up the new parts they waved as they made their way up to the tree line. A group of active retirees enjoying their freedom from the throws of work, two school teachers and two shop keepers. Friends for years taking a short break.

They were jovial and although not fluent in English between them the conversations flowed freely. Franz would sometimes speak in Swiss to the best of his ability but as Heinreiche would say "you still sound like an Englishman".

Rainer had planted some bushes around the allotment and they were in flower adding colour which made the area very attractive and brought comment from the hikers. Gerda gave Franz a roll of material to make more curtains with when Margaret had time. Breaking the news that Margaret would be leaving soon brought out disappointed looks from Rainer and Gerda they had become close friends. Gerda asked if they would see her before she left.

The new group were middle-aged and lived not so far away in a small town and had heard about the monastery they were filled with curiosity never ever knowing about it. Franz told them that he had found it by accident and knew nothing of its existence. One of the men produced a photo of a blackened white sketch he had purchased in a secondhand shop and showed it to Franz. It looked so much like the monastery except for small details that Franz said it could be it. There were no names or anything to substantiate the identity so they would scrutinise the monastery and compare when they arrived. The foursome said that they had walked other parts of the mountains but had not ventured this way. Franz enquired as to whether they had discovered any other monasteries in the area but they hadn't but one of the men had an uncle who owned a farm several kilometres away who like Hans had found paperwork in the loft dating back to the 1700s. Receipt for sales to a religious order. The man with the picture gave it to Franz it was a copy and he could keep it. When they reached the monastery they walked all around the perimeter looking at it and comparing with the photo. The mountains in the background were identified and the doors of the vestibule. There were many similarities and it was decided that it must be an old sketch one of the monks must have done. The man said he would send Franz the original sketch so he could hang it in its rightful place.

Margaret came and sat with Franz whilst Ingerborg fussed around the guests she knew the village they came from and had visited it some years ago.

"Did you check your bank accounts, Margaret?"

She said she had and had been surprised at how much money she had. "I don't know where it's all come from," she remarked. "Surely there's been a mistake, I've never had so much money in my life."

Franz said that all the years of back pay by Governments benefit department would account for most of it plus what she had earned working at the monastery. Dietre always paid it directly into her bank account every three months. "It was the same for everyone – even Olga received a small percentage and don't forget the English government owe you a widow's pension plus what your husband was paid by the company it all mounts up, Margaret. Let's go and see Olga and see what she knows about travel arrangements."

"Are you travelling by train or flying?" asked Olga.

Margaret looked at her surprised. "I've never been on an aeroplane," she said in a surprise voice.

Olga said that it was now possible to fly to many destinations now that the war was over. "You can fly direct from Zurich to London if you wish."

Margaret looked at her in amazement. "How much would that cost?" asked an excited Margaret. Olga picked up the telephone, "I'll tell you in a minute."

Franz looked around at the brochures advertising holidays. "You can go in style, Margaret." Olga wrote something on a piece of paper and passed it to Margaret. She passed it on to Franz, he looked at it. "It's cheaper if you go by train but it's quicker by plane, why don't you treat yourself. You could be in London two or three hours."

Margaret gave Olga the okay to book her a ticket on a flight leaving Zurich at 12 o'clock on Wednesday of next week. Franz would keep that day clear as he would like to accompany Margaret to the airport.

"I shall have to go to the bank and withdraw some cash," said Margaret checking her purse.

Franz pulled out his wallet. "I said I would make sure you got home for Joanna's wedding, allow me to keep my promise." He paid for the ticket and gave it to Margaret. "There you are I've kept my promise, all I've got to do now is deliver you to the airport."

Margaret seemed embarrassed. "I can never thank you enough, Franz."

Olga presented the necessary documents telling Margaret to make sure she has her passport. "Will we see you again?" she asked Margaret.

The question caused an embarrassing look. "Who knows," she replied quickly avoiding the look from Franz.

Ingerborg posed the same question when she was alone with Margaret. "I love it here I really do but Joanna is my only family, I shall have to see what happens."

"Franz won't be the same without you around," said Ingerborg, "you have kindled a flame in him I haven't seen before."

Franz and Margaret decided to go back up to the monastery to pick up a few things to take back to England. Margaret was very excited but Franz took on a solemn mood. He was going to miss having Margaret around. They decided to visit Gerda and Rainer Margaret wanted to say farewell to them both.

Gerda put her arms around her and asked the same question, "Will you be coming back?"

Rainer hugged her. "You will always be welcome here, Margaret."

As they made their way back to the monastery Margaret made a comment: "It's so hard to leave, Franz, they're such good friends almost like family, we've become so close."

Franz reached out for her and put his arms around her. "I'm going to miss you most of all, please come back to us, there will always be a home for you here."

Margaret felt the tears running down her face. "If things don't turn out right in England I will return, Franz, I promise."

As they said goodbye Ingerborg and Hans were deeply upset. "Please come back," Ingerborg whispered in her ear.

Franz checked as they had the ticket and passport for the airport. "Have you enough money with you?" he asked.

"I have changed my cash for the right currency and I have my cheque book with me," said Margaret showing Franz her documents also a letter from Joanna arranging to meet her in London.

They took a taxi from the railway station to the airport and Franz carried her luggage to the desk. Everything was in order, she looked at Franz and the tears started to well up. He reached out and put his arms around her. He wanted to kiss her but wasn't sure what her reaction would be. She pulled closer to him and offered her lips. "Thank you for everything, Franz, I owe you my life and much more." She kissed him passionately and he responded.

"Please come back, Margaret," he whispered.

The train journey back to the farm seemed to take ages and Franz lapsed into a sad mood. He gathered his backpack and what supplies he needed and set off into the mountains. Ingerborg knew how he was feeling and said they would see him soon.

There were only two weeks left to the hiking season and Franz was looking forward to building the staircase to the new floor but first he had to fit the supporting timbers all around the interior walls. It was a big job and he had to erect the scaffolding first. The timber supports he had made during the winter and were in his workshop coated with creosote ready. He had got to drill through the brickwork, one inch holes to fit the supporting bolts through. Franz hoped Heinreiche had got the masonry drills for him. Forty-one inch bolts and the back plates were heavy to carry. He shared the load between himself and the dogs.

The new party were from Sweden and spoke very good English. Two married couples seeking a late adventure in the mountains. Slightly older than himself but looking quite fit and capable. After a quick lunch they began a steady walk up to the tree line. The one lady began questioning Franz straight away. "How long does it take to get to the monastery and how long had he been doing it?" and other fact-like questions. Her name was Brigitte she informed him and wanted to draw sketches. Her husband was a botanist and studied plant life. The other two were writers and wrote articles for Swedish magazines. Her husband Sven would often go scrambling over rocks to reach a plant or flower and would suddenly disappear. Franz had to tell him not to wander off without telling him. They reached the monastery after a seven-hour hike. Franz had to keep stopping for the group to catch up.

"My husband is a pain in the butt," said Brigitte closing up to Franz. "Sometimes I wish he would wonder off and get lost." Franz was surprised at her remark, *obviously they had been married for too long*, he thought. As soon as they reached the monastery he watched the botanist wonder off into the forest. He unpacked and sent Remus after the botanist.

He led the group down the corridor to their cells. "Ah, separate beds that's good," said Brigitte she smiled at Franz and gave him a look.

The joint of beef in the oven smelled delicious. Franz stirred the vegetables and enquired if it would be wine or tea or coffee. A chorus of wine answered the question.

The botanist appeared with several plants in his hand, obviously very pleased. Brigitte ignored him as she appeared in the dining area wearing a smart dress. The other couple just dressed casual. After the meal they went outside to sketch while it was still light. The botanist retired to his cell to label his plants. Brigitte asked Franz to show her around outside and followed him as he led her down to the lake. "Where is your wife?" she asked. Franz replied that he did not have a wife and that he enjoyed the quiet life living alone. Brigitte gave a sigh. "What a waste," she said.

It was almost dark when they reached the doors to the vestibule. The others were seated around the table sampling the wine. Franz looked at the sketches they were good. "Maybe I should get some copies and put them on sale for other guests."

"We will send you some," said the other woman.

"Okay that will be fine, I'll let you know how they go," said Franz. The botanist said there were some very special plants growing around and most of them were not associated with mountainous regions. Franz told him that the monks who had built the monastery must have brought them they also specialised with herbs for medicines. The wine had been drunk so Franz fetched more and put it on the table. Brigitte immediately filled her glass and filled her husband's making sure he drank it. Franz also refilled his glass. The writers declined as it was almost their bedtime. Brigitte emptied and refilled it she encouraged her husband to drink it up as it would help him to sleep. She also filled Franz's glass. Franz began clearing the table preparing food for breakfast announcing that it would be an early call. This encouraged the group to drink up and retire for the night. Brigitte encouraged her husband to empty his glass before she led him to their cell. Franz made up the fire and put the porridge on a slow cooker. He then laid the table for the morning. Brigitte came out of her cell dressed in a bathrobe and went to the toilets. Franz walked along the opposite corridor to the men's toilet. When he came out he looked at the staircase he had built leading up to the new floor. He walked up the stairs examining its structure. "Where does that lead to?" asked Brigitte standing on the bottom step. Franz told her that it was a new floor he had put in and was going to be his private quarters. She walked up the stairs and asked him to show her around. He didn't have chance to refuse she was already entering what was to be the lounge and was walking around peering through the windows. "This is good, Franz, did you do all this yourself?" She walked across the dimly lit room to the door in the corner. "And where does this door lead to?" She pushed it open and walked into the corridor that led the whole length of the building.

"That will lead to bedrooms, I've only finished one so far."

She ventured in and opened up the door. "Oh my goodness, look at this," she said feeling for the light switch. It was oak panelled with pine flooring. The shower unit fitted along one side and the toilet in a separate cubicle alongside it. The other side was completely taken up with a huge wardrobe. The window was huge and housed a dressing table to beat all. She wondered open-mouthed around the room until her eyes caught site of the four-poster bed. She screamed with delight as she flopped onto it. The huge waterbed was something new even to the Swedes.

She bounced on it unaware that her dressing gown was almost hanging off her exposing her naked body. "Oh, Franz," she cried ecstatically, "I could fuck on this forever, come on, what are you waiting for."

Franz stood rooted to the spot. She reared up and grabbed his arm and pulled with all of her might. In less time that it took to bat an eyelid Franz felt his clothes being torn off him. He could only lie there as she stripped him naked. He could feel his body being explored as she wriggled into all kinds of positions. Finally she was underneath him with her hands manipulating into an operative position her legs wrapped around his back humping him like mad. His head was swirling like a mill pond his mind taking on all shapes. First it was Olga then Christina and then Margaret all taking on the shape of this over powering Swedish express train. He could feel the sweat running down his back and into every crevice exposed. He could feel her sweat mingling with his own as she tried to pump the life out him. Finally with a scream like that of a banshee she collapsed on top of him. "Jesus," wept Franz.

"That was some fuck," she whispered.

Porridge was served with toast as an extra. Franz gulped down his third cup of coffee as the group sat down at the table. Brigitte arrived last looking radiant and well refreshed. "Comfortable beds, Franz," did you make these as well?" she asked.

They gathered in the vestibule with their backpacks whilst Franz bundled up the bedding and strapped them onto the panniers of Romulus and Remus. He read the short note he picked up from under her pillow. "Thanks, Franz, if ever you come to Sweden." They indulged in polite conversation as they made their way down the mountains. Franz was hoping for a more sedate group when they reached the farm.

Saying their goodbyes Brigitte whispered, "10 out of 10."

His new group were another four men from a golfing club. Franz made them welcome. He looked back as Brigitte waved he was hoping they hadn't burst the seams on the water bed.

Now that the season had ended Franz looked forward to what he liked best woodwork. Sven the engineer had wrote to him saying his boss had agreed to put a wind turbine up at the monastery next season and it would be arriving at Carmen Railway station early January. It would be up to Franz to get it up to the site as soon as possible. The steel structure had been reduced to pieces not more than four feet in length and of light material. Franz said he would make sure it was there ready for the spring. When it was erected all Franz had to do was take regular readings and phone them through to the firm every week or so. The turbine itself weighed thirty pounds in weight and the turbine blades were all separate and manageable but for the moment Franz had to concentrate on the new floor only part of it had been started. He had erected the scaffolding and lifted the beams up into position. The holes had to be drilled every ten feet and the retaining bolt inserted and then the beam had to be lifted and bolted securely to the wall. When that was done the cross members to support the floor boards had to be fixed across everyone a foot apart and each four-inch by two inches thick stretching from wall to wall. This took two whole weeks to complete. Next the floor boards stained and varnished on both sides, another three weeks. When it was completed Franz stood back and admired his work. It would have taken months and months without the generator and power tools. He opened a can of bier to celebrate and took the dogs out for a walk.

His thoughts were often of Margaret – he wondered if ever she would come back, he missed her. He thought of Brigitte also, which brought a smile to his lips, what an experience he pitied her husband.

He dug out a foundation hole for the wind turbine and laid a concrete base, it wouldn't be long now before he would be humping it up to the monastery. He looked in on the pigeons cooing away in their pen. One had been sent to Heinreiche Christmas Day with seasonal greetings to them all.

The evenings would be spent drawing and designing the new bedrooms and also furniture for the new lounge. He had left the stone wall for the chimney breast blank he wanted to sculptor a fancy fireplace and he planned on visiting a renowned stone museum and learning how to do it. His mind was so full of ideas he would be pre occupied for years to come. Each morning he would visit the chapel and stand in front of the altar. He never said anything out loud but all kind of things ran through his mind. A brisk walk through the snow down to the lake and then back to work.

Spring arrived early this year practically all the snow had melted so he decided on an early visit to Carmen and to see his friends. Ingerborg rushed out to greet him and Hans came running in from the cowshed to say hello.

Ingerborg gave Franz a pile of letters that had come for him. He scanned the writing looking for one from England. He opened the envelope and looked at the photos of Margaret and Joanna taken at the wedding. Margaret looked beautiful, he couldn't take his eyes off her. Ingerborg noticed this and smiled. "You hadn't forgotten her, have you, Franz?" He shook his head. Letters from Ma and Pa and from Momma and Pappa Martinez and also from Sven telling him that the turbine had been sent and for him to look out for it and confirm its arrival.

After a good meal and a chat Franz retired to his room, he poured over the letter from Margaret reading how well the wedding had gone and how she was renting a flat not far away from where Joanna and her husband were renting an apartment. They had been very busy decorating and furnishing their new abodes and generally making up for lost time. Both had jobs which left Margaret at a loose end at times but she could always find things to do and was settling in to the way of things. She didn't mention returning to Switzerland which disappointed Franz, he was hoping she would say "miss you all and looking forward to coming back" but she didn't. Ingerborg also had a letter from Margaret but did not disclose the contents.

Franz visited the bier Keller of the evening and was warmly greeted by Heinreiche, Dietre and Christina. Olga also popped into welcome him back. He was given a list of people who wanted work doing and said he would do what he could but didn't want to leave the monastery for long periods of time, especially at this time of year.

Ingerborg's kitchen was the first priority and then Dietre's new office. Heinreiche said he could wait but the station master wanted important work carried out as soon as possible and also for Franz to collect his stuff from the station. He managed a full two days' work before setting off into the mountains with his first full load. The turbine itself was the heaviest so that became the priority and then the rotor blades. Within a week most of it was on site, the rest was nuts and bolts and small stuff. It was all there ready for Sven and his team.

The next project was finishing the flooring he worked at a steady pace and saw the job completed within the week. Now the hiking season had begun and Franz made his way down to Carmen to meet his first group. They were retirees with a zest to explore the mountains. They were amiable and Franz got on well with them. Rainer and Gerda made then welcome. It was a good start to the season. When he got the chance he caught the shuttle to a village further on where he had heard about a stone mason. Franz had made a decision and asked if he could have a go at making it himself under the supervision of the stone mason. It was a challenge and he looked forward to it. There was no rush so he agreed to spend an odd day here and there chipping away at the stone. He made sure that each piece was capable of being carried on his backpack.

Sven arrived with his team at a pre-arranged date and Franz welcomed them at the station. Sven and two of his colleagues with their tools, working steadily the turbine took a week to complete. Sven explained how it worked and showed Franz what readings he would have to take. They started it up and watched as the blades began to rotate. The team were pleased with the results. Sven explained that the sail on the back would turn the propeller shaft in the direction of the wind and the propellers would catch most of the wind. Readings were taken and the wiring completed. The turbine was monitored throughout the day and Sven said it was doing a good job of lighting up the monastery and heating the water for the toilets and showers. Heinreiche had supplied them with two copper tanks which Sven suggested should be lagged up. Franz said that if it was successful he would have another for the other end of the monastery. Sven told him not to rush things as other methods were being developed to harvest the sun's rays. Solar power he called it.

It was well into March when Franz received another letter from Margaret. She had found herself a job as a courier for a bank. It paid good money but she wasn't all that keen. She sent her regards to everyone and said she missed them all.

Franz had started on a second bedroom in the new room below the loft; he anticipated that at least another six rooms could be added, that's if he wanted to start a hotel business.

Ingerborg had indicated that next time he had a free couple of days she wanted something special but would not say what it was. Two more weeks passed by before he told her that a free spell was coming up and that he would be available for whatever she wanted him to do. She still wouldn't let on to what it she was had in mind.

He handed over the hikers to Hans who had prepared the lunch. Franz said his goodbyes and walked into the farmhouse where Ingerborg was making coffee for him. "Sit down in there," she said "I'll bring it into you."

He sat on the settee and began browsing through a magazine. "Who does that fancy car belong to?" he asked, glimpsing through the window at the vehicle parked alongside the barn. Ingerborg didn't answer Franz felt a pair of arms embracing him from behind.

"It's mine," said a soft voice he had heard many times before.

He leapt to his feet spinning round to face Margaret. "Have you come to take me home, Franz?"

He wrapped his arms around her drawing her to him, their lips met as they passionately embraced. Ingerborg wept with delight as she gently closed the door.